NOOSE

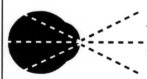

This Large Print Book carries the
Seal of Approval of N.A.V.H.

A JOE NOOSE WESTERN

Noose

Eric Red

WHEELER PUBLISHING
A part of Gale, a Cengage Company

Farmington Hills, Mich • San Francisco • New York • Waterville, Maine
Meriden, Conn • Mason, Ohio • Chicago

Copyright © 2018 by Smash Cut Productions, Ltd.
Wheeler Publishing, a part of Gale, a Cengage Company.

ALL RIGHTS RESERVED
Wheeler Publishing Large Print Western.
The text of this Large Print edition is unabridged.
Other aspects of the book may vary from the original edition.
Set in 16 pt. Plantin.

LIBRARY OF CONGRESS CIP DATA ON FILE.
CATALOGUING IN PUBLICATION FOR THIS BOOK
IS AVAILABLE FROM THE LIBRARY OF CONGRESS

ISBN-13: 978-1-4328-6067-7 (softcover)

Published in 2019 by arrangement with Pinnacle Books, an imprint of Kensington Publishing Corp.

Printed in the United States of America
2 3 4 5 6   23 22 21 20 19

To Dallas

CHAPTER 1

A lone wolf is an easy target.

Joe Noose considered this as he raised his Winchester rifle to his shoulder, settling the crosshairs of his gunsight on the distant figure standing by a horse near the Hoback River two hundred yards away.

Adjusting his aim an inch up and to the right of the figure's shoulder for trajectory in the northwesterly wind, he calculated for windage, elevation, and bullet drop as he felt the cold metal of the trigger resistance against his forefinger.

No mistaking his target even from this distance — nor the missing nose on his face from the wanted posters for Jim Henry Barrow that offered a thousand dollars reward for his capture, dead or alive.

Noose's gloved finger was tight on the trigger and his quarry in his rifle crosshairs had not spotted him yet.

The bounty hunter would try to take him

in peacefully, picking his moment to call out the man's name and order him to put his hands behind his head.

If he resisted, Noose would put one in his shoulder, which usually subdued even the most uncooperative type.

He meant to take his target in alive like he always did.

Noose heard something. His finger loosened infinitesimally on the trigger, senses alert.

There it was again — a near-imperceptible disturbance in the distant woods like horses' hooves stepping on fallen leaves and twigs, but slow and quiet like the horses were being ridden with stealth.

It wasn't the first time the bounty hunter had heard the horses; he had heard them on and off all day throughout the full twelve miles he had ridden chasing down his latest meal ticket.

A twig snapped to the east a few hundred feet out.

Who they were and why they were following him, Noose didn't know, not yet at least, but he was aware of their presence. Being alert and ready was the most important part of avoiding an ambush. He doubted the unseen riders were part of any gang Barrow belonged to because Barrow, as far as he knew, rode alone. The thug was too stupid, drunk, and violent for even the most low-life gangs to claim as a member. Yet anything was possible.

These riders moved like ghosts. They were good. He had to give them that.

It had taken Joe Noose less than a week to catch up with Jim Henry Barrow.

While pulling a stickup, the bank robber had shot a guard in the Victor bank and fled across the Wyoming landscape up into the rugged and treacherous Hoback Canyon. He'd gotten away with a hundred and twenty three dollars and in the escape lost the handkerchief on his face so several customers had been able to identify him by his distinctive bullet scar that had taken his nose years before. Barrow had an hour head start on the local Victor lawmen who had been forced to turn back when one of their horses broke a leg. Noose happened to be dropping off a prisoner to the jail when he heard about the robbery and the killing. The sheriff had wired the U.S. Marshal's office in Jackson Hole and gotten the reward authorized and Noose had gone after it.

It had been a long hard ride across twelve miles of sheer forest and steep mountain range that was as hard going down as up. The trek had nearly killed his horse and he had to walk the animal half the time, but the outlaw's trail had been fresh. Noose expected, rightly so, that once Barrow made Jackson Hole, the big valley on the other side of the pass, he would get a boat and make off down the Snake River. Which was exactly what the man Noose was aiming at was doing this very second.

It was the tracks of the other horses that unnerved Noose. He made them out to number twelve, riding together.

In the last two days, he had crossed the fresh hoofprints twice while doubling back after a wrong turn. The bounty hunter figured it must be a gang. Who they were Noose didn't know but he wondered why all those men and horses had fetched up in the remote wilderness with him and Barrow. What worried him was whether Barrow had a gang Noose didn't know about and planned to meet up with them. It could be the presence of these others was sheer happenstance: a group of settlers or hunters passing through. But Noose didn't believe in coincidence; his belly tightened because he knew if it was a gang and they were with Barrow, it was going to get bloody, very bloody, very fast.

Another broken twig on a pine tree. A little piece of torn duster. More tracks. The riders' sign had caught his attention repeatedly during his pursuit of Barrow. Noose hadn't seen them because he had been staying out of sight, keeping downwind, not wanting to get made if whoever this gang was, was with the man with the thousand-dollar reward on his head. As far as Noose could tell, they had not noticed him, either. But who were they? he kept wondering.

Now, here, by the river, his man was alone and Noose had him in his gunsights — it was time to make his move.

"Barrow!" he shouted from his safe cover.

The outlaw suddenly straightened and made a quick break for his saddle and the rifle stock that jutted out. Quickly adjusting aim, Noose squeezed the trigger — the gun bucked, and an explosion of stones flew up at Barrow's feet, stopping him dead in his tracks. He winced, put his hands behind his head, and shouted up onto the ridge where Noose was dug in. "Don't shoot! I'm unarmed, dammit!"

"Throw down!" yelled the bounty hunter, leaping out of his cover and side-skidding his boots down the ridge, scattering pebbles and rocks, keeping his rifle leveled with one arm as he kept balance on the hill with the other. "Kiss the ground!"

The criminal lowered to his knees. "You

the law?"

"Close enough," replied Noose, who had crossed the bank of the river in three long strides and produced a set of steel cuffs.

"Bounty hunter?"

"That's right."

"You son of a bitch." The man flattened.

"Shut up." Noose patted him for weapons, confiscated a Colt Peacemaker, and cuffed him. In one swift move, the bounty hunter pulled the rifle from the man's saddle and quickly rummaged through the saddlebags for firearms or knives but found nothing but a ratty bedroll and some week-old jerky. Tossing the other rifle back toward the ridge, Noose grabbed the glum man by the scruff of the neck, heaving him to his feet and shoving him up into his saddle on his horse. The bounty hunter moved with practiced professionalism, like a well-oiled machine. "I'm taking you back to Idaho," he said. "We can do it the easy way or the hard way."

Boom!

A big red flower bloomed in Jim Henry Barrow's chest, blossoming out his back, and he was catapulted clean out of the saddle, landing flat on his back on the ground, stone dead with his torso blown out. Blood pooled in a huge lake beneath the blasted corpse and ran into the river, in a spreading red discoloration.

Noose whirled, clenching his rifle with both hands, looking wildly around him for whoever shot the man.

Then the riders appeared. There were twelve. They rode down the ridge, across the river, and out of the trees.

Twelve rifles. Twelve Stetsons. Twelve dusters. Twelve killers blocking out the sun.

"He's ours," said the leader.

Noose gazed up at a tall, skeletal man with gaunt features and a handlebar mustache. He was looking down the barrel of a smoking Sharps rifle at him. The killer had black bullet eyes. "I would drop the gun," he advised.

So Noose did. Slow.

"You murdered him," Noose said coldly, keeping his empty hands in the open.

"Reward's the same either way." The leader smirked. "We just put paid to it."

"I was taking this man in alive," Noose said, unblinkingly holding the mounted man's mean gaze. "I had him disarmed and restrained. He was mine and that reward is mine."

The gaunt scarecrow of a bounty killer smiled. "We say it's *us* got him and we say the reward belongs to us. It's your word against ours, mister, twelve to one." He indicated his gang, a few of whom chuckled. "You can count, can't ya?"

"What's your name?" Noose snarled.

"I'm Frank Butler."

"I'll remember it."

"You do that. Now shut the hell up, you're sucking my air. You just lost money, you could lose a lot more," Butler said coldly. "Don't be stupid. Walk away. Our business is done here."

Noose just stood and looked on as one of the big feral bounty killers Butler addressed as Sharpless dismounted and heaved the bleeding corpse face-first over the dead man's empty saddle.

"Let's get back to town before this crud starts to stink," said Butler as he and his riders spurred their horses and rode off with the dead man's horse in tow.

Noose stood by the creek. He whistled to call his horse. It trotted out of the trees to him.

Five minutes passed before he swung into his saddle and followed the gang's tracks.

He figured he'd given them enough head start.

CHAPTER 2

Times were tough for killers, Noose reckoned.

A thousand dollars wasn't much divvied up twelve ways.

The corpse was slumped sideways over the saddle, festering in the sun and buzzing with flies. The horse was tethered to the rail outside the bar, alongside the twelve other horses, who kept their distance from the other animal, tails swishing at the swarming insects. Noose could see why. Barrow was already starting to stink.

The men must be inside the bar.

There was nowhere else they could be, because other than the saloon there were few other buildings in Hoback, Wyoming. It was barely a town. Noose trotted slowly on his horse, eyeballing the feed store, the corral, and the U.S. Marshal's office. There were two horses in front of that.

The bounty hunter tethered his horse

outside the corral. He swung out of his saddle onto the hard earth, checking to be sure both his Colt pistols were fully loaded before he entered the bar. He could use the drink, if not the company, but it was the company he was here to deal with. Shooting a glance to the hot sun overhead, he tipped his hat brim to shade his face.

Today was going to be a hot one.

So he entered the bar, and sure enough, there they all were.

As Noose pushed through the swinging doors, the twelve hulking figures of the big men assembled around the saloon became visible in the gloom, bent like a row of malignant vultures over the long wooden bar, just big shadows until Noose's eyes adjusted to the dim light and he could make out the faces. It was them, all right. Stink eyes slid buzzardlike to regard him over their hunched shoulders over their shot glasses of whiskey as he entered, spurs jingling, in the quiet room. Nobody moved.

The gang would be here in Hoback to see the local marshal and turn the body over to him for the reward. The lawman needed to sign off for the release of the money and that was whom the killers were waiting for now. It would be the marshal's duty to telegraph Jackson Hole for authorization,

16

and soon the money would be waiting for pickup by these bounty killers. That was their plan.

Noose meant to interfere with it.

He figured his presence was a fly in the ointment for these badmen and seeing him here they must figure he was brave or crazy. Noose figured he risked getting shot but not before the marshal came and the men got their reward money.

His spurs jingled as he entered the bar. Crossing the spare barroom built of unfinished pine boards, Noose saw that besides the gang there was nobody else present other than the bartender, and he wasn't much, just an old coot. The saloon was little more than a hut. A table and two chairs. A clock. The clock was ticking. Sauntering up to the other end of the bar from the bounty killer gang, the lone bounty hunter signaled the bartender.

"Buy him a whiskey. Least we can do," said Butler, smiling quietly.

"It's paid for," replied Noose, flipping a coin onto the counter.

The barman grabbed a bottle from the rack, eyes cautiously taking in his fearsome customers and the cool new arrival, and poured a drink. Noose stood tall at the bar, his ten-gallon hat tipped low over his forehead, boot braced on the wooden rail, taking a slow sip of his drink and staring straight ahead. He didn't need to look at the men to know they were watching him. Each and every last one of them. He'd made an entrance for sure, he figured, because he was the last man any one of these killers had expected to see. But Noose didn't fully know whom he was dealing with, at least not yet, and had to be careful that while he'd entered the bar on his boots, he didn't leave it in a box.

Time passed. Just a bunch of guys drinking.

Smells of dust and wood and sweat and leather filled Noose's nostrils, then the stinging tang of the cheap whiskey as he raised it to his face and sipped. His senses were suddenly more alert, as they always were when facing death. What if this was his last drink? he thought. He swallowed and felt the good burn of the liquid down into his gullet. It numbed him. Facing death made the whiskey taste better.

Noose took inventory of the logistics of a gunfight. He was in a good position at the end of the bar because all the gang were stacked up down the bar one past the other and if any one of them drew they would be distracted for a split second trying to shoot around the others between them and him — he just had to turn to have both his irons out and pump lead into the badmen and send them falling like a row of dominoes. Noose would most likely die in the shoot-out, but he'd kill or mortally wound most of the rest.

They were clearly thinking the same thing.

Two of the gunmen stepped away from the bar. One took a seat at a table to his right, crossed his legs, and leaned back, spinning a spur with a gloved hand. The other killer sauntered to the beam against the wall behind Noose, hands dangling near his holsters, casually eyeballing the hot dirt street out the window.

These men were professionals.

The clock on the wall ticked. The barman, growing more nervous, cleaned glasses with a cloth.

"What are you doing here?" Butler finally asked.

Noose just took another sip of his drink. He heard a few random hollow clicks of hammers pulled back on pistols under dusters, heard the clink of his shot glass on the wood counter as he set it down, heard flies buzzing, and he even heard the faint splat of a drop of sweat pouring from one of the posse's foreheads onto the bar. Still he stared straight forward, feeling the hard eyes on him.

"I asked why you're here."

"Same reason as you."

"We got business with the marshal."

"So do I."

"That boy slung over that saddle out there is our'n."

"You murdered him."

"Mean to dispute the reward?"

Noose sipped his whiskey, staring straight forward. He didn't answer. He wasn't unduly worried about being shot because the gunmen were not going to shoot him without sufficient provocation: it would be messy to explain when the marshal got there with the bartender as witness and might complicate getting their reward for Barrow. And Noose knew they knew he knew it.

Butler looked into his own glass. "Reckon you want a cut of the reward?"

Noose shook his head. "Nope."

"Want the whole reward?"

Noose finally looked at Butler and the others, and his gaze was sure and steady. "I brung him in alive. You boys murdered him and you're gonna pay."

The leader of the bounty killers reared up from the bar and swept a huge, incredulous look across the amazed eyes of the hardened grizzled gunmen lining the bar. A chuckle passed through the men like the sizzling fuse on a stick of dynamite, burning down to Butler, who laughed cold and mercilessly.

Noose didn't laugh. "You boys must be desperate. I figure the reward for Barrow comes out to less than a hundred dollars each. Maybe you should get real jobs. You know what they say, boys . . . you're worth what they pay you."

"Well, mister, what you got in mind to do about this here situation?"

"I'm gonna tell the marshal you killed Barrow."

"Twelve of us says different."

"We'll see." Noose just smiled to himself, which riled the killers. "Meantime, nothin' to do but wait."

CHAPTER 3

Bess Sugarland had woken at dawn as usual that morning in Hoback, a few hours before the men rode in with the dead body over the saddle of the horse, and somehow she just knew there was going to be trouble.

The young woman was twenty-one. She was pretty, hardy, and fit from a life spent out of doors. After brushing her teeth and combing her short auburn hair in the mirror of the small room in back of the U.S. Marshal's office where she lived, Bess splashed bracing cold water on her freckled face. It was a cold and crisp Wyoming morning, and the sharp sunlight blasted in through the window on her unmade bed. A woodpecker was tapping outside the walls and a squirrel scampered through the roof, and she promised herself to take care of both later that day.

Bess dried her face off and cast a glance at the old photo of her father and mother on the wall. It was all she had to remember her mother by.

She pulled on her jeans over her lanky hips, tugged on her boots, and buttoned her denim shirt over her firm young bosom as she finished dressing.

As she went to the door, she took the belt with rounds of ammo in the notches and the big Navy revolver in the holster and strapped it on.

Bess picked up the six-star silver deputy badge and pinned it on her shirt.

She left the room.

The marshal's office was empty in the early Wyoming morning, but she could already hear the old man puttering around in his shack next door. The young woman started the daily routine: she threw some wood in the stove, set it alight — two logs crossways, one on top, kindling below — and then put on a pot of coffee. The wood stove was empty so she went outside to the woodshed.

Bess breathed deep of the crisp, peaty morning air that refreshed her lungs. It was scented with pine and river water. Walking to the stump, she yanked the ax out, threw on a log, and cleanly split it with a graceful and powerful downward two-handed swing. Taking a look up at the thick-forested mountains and granite chasms that reared into the big skies around her, she inhaled the fresh and clear air and smiled. Then she gathered the pieces of wood under her arm and went back inside.

While making the coffee, she checked the telegraph to see if any warrants had come through.

The Hoback U.S. Marshal's office was out in the middle of nowhere, thirty miles from Jackson Hole. It was surrounded by some of the most spectacular and majestic scenery in the state — staggering mountain ranges and sweeping pine forests around the wending surge of the icy Hoback River that fed into the mighty Snake River a few miles on. The isolation suited her down to the ground. Usually they rarely saw a soul in these parts until the wranglers came down out of the mountains with their herds of sheep in the spring. But the occasional outlaw came through, who they were told to be on the lookout for, or there would be a posse or manhunt she and her father needed to do a ride-along with.

While the coffee began to boil and filled the office with the good smell, Bess took a seat and began stripping and cleaning the rifles in the rack.

That's when Marshal Nate Sugarland

walked in, washed and scrubbed with a big warm smile on his rugged, bearded face. He was a big, husky man of sixty-two years of age, heavyset but it was all muscle. He looked like a mountain man with a badge. The sight of her old man always warmed her heart as it had her whole life. "Mornin', Bess," he greeted her, blue eyes twinkling.

"Hiya, Pop. How did you sleep last night?"

"Terrible. Tossed and turned the whole time worrying about when you were going to get the hell out of here and move to Jackson, find yourself a nice man, settle down, and have a life."

"There's lots of time for that. Right now I got you to take care of."

"I don't need no taking care of. I need grandchildren."

"And I'm not fixed to be no housewife."

And so it went, affably. They had the same conversation a few times a week.

That was when they heard the horses.

"What the hell — ?" said Sugarland.

Sugarland and his deputy daughter went to the window, both of them looking out at the thirteen horses trotting into the outpost. Twelve of them were ridden by men in dusters. A body was slung over the saddle of the last horse.

"That man looks dead, Pop."

25

"Reckon."

"He's not wearing the same coats as the rest, so he probably ain't one of them."

"Good girl. Observant. Just like I taught you."

"Who do you savvy they are?"

"Bounty hunters, from the looks of them."

They watched as the gang tied up their horses by the saloon, left the corpse on the saddle, and went inside.

The marshal's eyes narrowed. "How do you like that, Bess?" Sugarland said in disgust. "Them bounty hunters got no respect. Don't bother coming here first to talk to us about claiming the reward. Just go to the bar and drink. Wait for us to smell the corpse and come to them. I got a bad feeling about these boys."

"How do you want to handle it, Pop?"

"They're taking their time. So can we. Let's have our coffee. Then we'll head over and sort 'em out."

They both poured their cups. Bess drank hers by the window, watching the bar.

Ten minutes later, she saw the big cowboy ride up, tie his horse, and go inside.

The first impression she had of Joe Noose was, he was very handsome.

CHAPTER 4

Fifteen minutes had passed since Noose had entered the bar. He and Butler never took their eyes off each other.

Now both men heard something else. Spurs outside.

The doors to the saloon swung open with a rusty creak and two silhouetted figures stood blocking the daylight.

A gleam of sunlight on a silver star flared on the bigger one's chest. "You boys brung in that dead man for a reward?" Marshal Nate Sugarland was an old man and did not move fast. Noose put him at under six foot two and on the better side of two hundred and fifty pounds. He was sweating profusely in the sun. He had a scruffy white beard, wore two Colt Peacemaker pistols on a weathered holster, but his eyes were sharp and observant.

His deputy was a girl, a lean and lanky auburn-headed kid who didn't look any older than a teenager. Noose registered her pretty tomboy face and gangly demeanor, but noted she had a good grip on the big lever-action Winchester rifle she held in both big hands.

"That's Jim Henry Barrow slung over the saddle outside. The bounty is a thousand dollars, dead or alive, Marshal," said Frank Butler, turning to stand with his back against the bar, facing the lawmen. "We're here to turn the body over to you and collect —"

Noose cut Butler off. "They murdered that man. He was unarmed. I'm a witness," he said.

Sugarland turned his gaze to the lone man at the end of the bar, standing apart from the others. He had not seen him ride up alone as his daughter had, and up until now had assumed he was part of the same gang. "I ain't with these men, Marshal," the big tough cowboy said as if reading the lawman's thoughts. "Name's Joe Noose. I am a bounty hunter but not a bounty killer like these boys. You can telegraph Victor and speak to the sheriff there and he'll vouch for me. I was following Barrow from Victor and I had taken him into custody unharmed when one of these men shot him dead and the gang stole the body."

Marshal Sugarland cut his narrow gaze from Noose to Butler, then cut it back to Noose again. "You sayin' this was an illegal killing?"

"Yes, I am." Noose nodded.

"Bull." Butler spat.

"That's a damn serious charge," the lawman said, shifting his gaze to the leader of the bounty killers. "Identify yourself."

"I'm Frank Butler. These boys is with me."

"I've heard of you. Not much of it good," Sugarland said, his eyes hardening in recognition.

Noose smelled liquor on the marshal's breath, which was worrisome. The bounty hunter slid his gaze over to the lady deputy. He picked up on the family resemblance. The young woman stood clenching her rifle with both hands, staying near the door, backing up her father, the marshal. Noose sensed her inexperience as a lawman but saw flint in her gaze.

"He's a damn liar," said Butler, nodding at Noose. "We were both chasing this boy Barrow, we got there first, the reward's ours, and he's just sore about it. I got eleven men right here swear that's the truth."

The eleven gunslingers gruffly murmured assent.

"Let's get to calling that reward in, Mar-

29

shal. I'm sure you're very busy so we'll take care of business and be on our way." Butler took out his wallet to pay the tab.

The wallet itself was a brown female severed breast, stitched into a tobacco pouch. A mottled brown nipple was on the side. "What the hell is that?" Sugarland asked.

Butler pinched a fingerful of shag tobacco from the grotesque pouch and licked a paper, rolling the cigarette one-handed. "Cut it off a squaw when I was in the cavalry back in the Dakotas." He lit the smoke.

Bess flinched at the obscene sight of the severed breast tobacco pouch.

The marshal saw the scalps. Hair and dried skin on the inside of Butler's open duster. "You boys scalp hunters?" His eyes hardened.

"Man's got to make a living." Butler snorted smoke from his nostrils.

"I don't like killers."

"It's legal."

The tension was suddenly so thick in the bar you could cut it with a knife. Noose's words had registered with the marshal. "Something don't smell right," the old man said.

Butler bristled. "My boys and me brought

in the wanted man. End of story."

Sugarland's mind worked slowly behind his eyes. He rubbed his beard. Then he looked at Noose. "Which one of these men did you see kill the man outside?"

The bounty hunter had to admit it: "I don't know."

"Don't know?"

"They ambushed us."

A strenuous chorus of argumentative objections and derisive grunts came from the gang of big dirty men in dusters who lined the bar.

"Don't make no never mind." The marshal turned to his deputy daughter. "Bess, get over to the office and telegraph Victor. Give 'em a description on this man Noose and check out his story." The fresh-faced girl nodded and hurried out of the bar, crossing the street and disappearing into the marshal's office.

"What about our money?" A testy Butler spoke through gritted teeth.

"Gotta be an investigation first. We're gonna take statements. Your story checks out, you get your money and you're on your way. His story checks out, there's gonna be a hanging. Maybe more than one."

Violence spread like stink through the assembled gang at the bar and they exchanged

31

surly glances. All frustrated eyes went to Butler, who was staring at the floor, thumbs hooked in his belt. "You're the marshal," he said in a controlled whisper.

"That's right," Sugarland said.

Now it was very quiet in the bar. Too damn quiet, thought Noose. He stayed rooted in place at the end of the bar, his eyes fixed on first the gang, then Butler, then the marshal. They were going to wait it out, and who knew what anyone was going to do. The bounty hunters had been dealt a bad hand and heavily armed as they were, they couldn't start shooting because they needed Sugarland's sign-off for the reward. In a few minutes, the deputy would be back from the marshal's office, where she was telegraphing Victor. Noose's story would check out. It would be a long two-day ride across the pass back to Idaho and they would all be in front of Judge Proctor. In the end, it would be Noose's word against these twelve gunmen.

Sugarland stood square in the center of the room, facing the dangerous gunmen at the bar, wearing his silver star and his crappy old pistol that looked like it hadn't been cleaned and would misfire. Butler peered over at Noose and they locked eyes. The gaunt, skeletal badman had death in his gaze. The clock was ticking.

"Marshal's got to do his job," said Butler finally. "I should know." With that, he opened his muddy black duster and pulled something out of his vest.

A U.S. Marshal's badge, dented and dull, gleamed in his gloved fingers.

Sugarland looked at it, confused. "You're a marshal?"

Butler's eyes narrowed. "I took it off the last one I killed."

The gun blast shook the room to the rafters. Suddenly, Butler had drawn his Colt Dragoon from his holster with one hand, pushing it under the flattened palm of his other gloved hand, fanning it, and fired five times, shooting Sugarland square in the chest, blowing fist-sized blood-spraying craters through his shirt. Each round hammered the old man back, his boots tripping backward, until he collapsed in a cloud of smoke and raining blood onto the floor.

The bartender should not have gone for the shotgun behind the counter. Butler whirled and shot him once square between the eyes. Blood and skull made an ugly splatter from the exit wound in the back of the proprietor's head. He slammed into the racks of bottles, falling to the floor amidst the shattering glass and spilling cheap liquor.

The room was filled with the deafening echo of gunfire and the smell of gunpowder and copper stench of blood.

It was over in seconds.

"Don't kill him!" Butler roared, and Noose knew that by "him" he meant Noose. All of the gang had their guns out. He didn't have a chance. Noose froze, hearing the hammers click back on the eleven gun barrels aimed at his head. He didn't breathe and moved his hands away from his pistol holsters. "I need him alive," hissed Butler again.

Noose just stood there, impressed at the cold-blooded efficiency of the murder spree that ended law — and witnesses — in Hoback.

Frank Butler spun his empty pistol into his left holster and drew the fully loaded second pistol from his right one. He faced the frozen, braced Noose and took a few slow, deliberate steps toward him, his bullet eyes squinted and his voice dangerously low. "You were right about one thing. One thousand dollars reward ain't much split twelve ways. How much reward is gonna be put up for the killing of a U.S. Marshal? I figure fifty to a hundred thousand dollars when we turn you in."

Noose's eyes narrowed. "Turn me in for what?"

"For the killing of the marshal." There was nothing to say as it sunk in. Right away Noose saw the fix he was in. He'd been framed. They'd killed the only witness to the marshal's murder. It was the word of twelve men against him. "Now you got two choices," Butler continued, pointing his gun point-blank in Noose's steely face. "You can stay here and we kill you, tell the deputy you killed the marshal before we did for you, and collect the reward. The other choice is you run, we come after you, and collect the reward."

Some choice, thought Noose bitterly.

Butler stepped closer, speaking through clenched teeth. "You get on your horse and you ride hard, boy. We'll be coming after ya. Just as soon as we get that deputy to authorize the reward in Victor. Make it all legit. Least we're givin' you a head start. This way you live a few more minutes. Move."

So Noose moved.

Bolting out the door into the fresh, dusty daylight that stung his eyes, he untethered his horse, swung into his saddle, and reined his horse around to charge off up the street at full gallop. As he rode out of town, he passed the kid deputy Sugarland rushing out of the marshal's office after hearing the gunshots, watching in confusion as Noose rode past and calling for him to stop, but then hurrying off with her rifle up the street into the bar.

Noose's horse left the dirt road at the end of town and galloped up the trail into the hills. He figured he had maybe a half hour before those killers got their reward authorized and would be after him to take him dead rather than alive. Noose figured he could get maybe five miles ahead.

He could already feel the noose tightening.

CHAPTER 5

Deputy Sugarland shoved through the swinging doors and took in the bloody scene in horror. Her face twisted in grief at the sight of the dead old man on the floor.

"*No!*" she screamed. Dropping to her knees by Sugarland's corpse, Bess stroked her father's body tenderly with a shaking hand and wept. Gathering the marshal gently in her arms, she cradled him and sobbed. "*Oh no, no . . .*"

In fury and anguish, she looked around at the hard men from where she sat on the floor. Frank Butler and his big, grim bounty hunters leaned casually against the bar. A long, shadowy and sinister line of duster coats and big hats. They impassively sipped whiskey and smoked cigars. "Who did this?" she shrieked, shaking.

Butler bit the tip off a stogie. "Warned you about that varmint."

"But — ?"

"We got a good look at him. Saw where he went."

"W-why didn't you shoot him?"

"Warn't none of our business." The leader of the gang fired up his cigar and shot the fuming deputy a chilling glance of his bullet black eyes. "Yet."

"What do you mean?" Naked confusion and dismay swam in her eyes. "W-why didn't you stop him?"

"Woulda had to kill him. It would have been murder. Can't kill him till it's legit, till there's an official reward and a dead-or-alive bounty."

The enraged young deputy leapt to her feet, drawing her revolver. "Then I'll get him if you won't!"

Butler didn't budge, maddeningly sure of himself as he regarded her patiently. "He'll kill you, ma'am. He's a professional shootist. You'll be dead before your gun leaves its holster. Killing him is a job for professionals."

She hesitated, in doubt. "But . . . somebody has to do *something,*" the girl stammered.

"Let me explain this to you. We're bounty hunters. We can bring him back, alive or dead, but we get paid. It's what we do. There ain't no reward on him yet."

Bess looked this way and that. "He's getting away."

Butler was implacable. "Then you best get that reward authorized."

"I can't authorize no reward."

"You got a telegraph, ain'tcha?"

"Yes, in the marshal's office."

"Then telegraph the Jackson Hole U.S. Marshal's office and get it authorized."

The confused girl thought a few seconds. "I guess I can do that."

"Then we'll get the killer for you. There's twelve of us, one of him, and we'll bring him back slung over his saddle. Just got to make the reward legal." He took a few slow steps toward her, cunningly manipulative. His testosterone-charged intimidating composure rattled the tomboyish girl.

"We'll take care of everything, missy. Don't you worry yer purty little head."

Bess nodded. "Okay, okay, I mean, sure, if that's what you think is best. So . . ."

"So you just need to telegraph in the reward."

"Telegraph the reward, right."

"To Jackson Hole."

"Jackson Hole, sure."

"Sooner the reward is authorized, sooner we ride."

"Right. I'll be right back."

"We'll come with you."

Bess was getting more flustered by the minute. "Sure. This way."

The badmen followed the pretty deputy out the door, twelve sets of eyeballs ogling her shapely posterior.

Moments later, the bounty killers escorted the deputy through the door of her own marshal's office. Butler eased the panic-stricken Bess into a chair by the telegraph. The gang leader sat down in the deceased marshal's chair, put his boots up on the man's desk, and snarled. "Telegraph Jackson Hole."

"O-okay," she replied. The deputy obediently tapped away. The other bounty killers hovered like buzzards. Their leader dictated the telegram:

MARSHAL SUGARLAND AND BARTENDER SHOT DEAD STOP KILLER ESCAPED STOP REQUEST AUTHORIZATION OF BOUNTY OF ONE HUNDRED THOUSAND DOLLARS STOP DEAD OR ALIVE STOP

The girl looked up, bathed in sweat. "A h-hundred thousand dollars?"

"Cash."

Deputy Sugarland tapped the telegraph keys.

CASH STOP

The clock on the wall ticked.

Deputy Sugarland gazed apprehensively around her at the big killers breathing down her neck, then looked over to the icy leader of the gang with his boots up on the desk.

"N-now what?" she asked.

Butler puffed his cigar, stretched his legs, and patiently regarded the clock. "We wait."

The bounty killers loomed, waited.

Butler didn't blink. Bess stared nervously at the telegraph. It sat quietly.

CHAPTER 6

Jackson Hole was a small town nestled in a valley at the base of the spectacular peaks of the Wyoming Teton mountain range. It was just waking up.

U.S. Marshal Jack Mackenzie, a leathery heavyset lawman in his early sixties, adjusted his hat and smiled at a few passersby on the unpaved dirt street as he walked to his office. Horse-drawn wagons with ranchers and frontier women in petticoats passed by on the street. It was a beautiful morning.

Mackenzie entered the U.S. Marshal's office and hung his hat, and his day went straight to hell.

His young, agitated deputy Nolan Swallows looked up from the telegraph as he urgently tapped out a message. "Sir, Marshal Sugarland's been murdered."

"What?"

"They want a reward issued. A hundred thousand dollars."

"Is this some kind of joke? Find out who's on the other end of this wire." Deeply shaken, the marshal watched as the deputy sent the transmission. Moments later came a response.

"Bess Sugarland."

"Aw, crap. His daughter. She's a good kid. Those two was really close, Sugarland and his daughter. That poor girl. She must be beside herself." Mackenzie thought things over a minute. "Ask Bess who killed Sugarland."

The transmission was a series of taps, and the deputy's pencil scratching on a piece of paper turned it into words.

"She says his name is Joe Noose."

"Noose. *That* Joe Noose? Get a description just to be sure."

More telegraph tapping back and forth.

"About thirty. Six foot three. Brown hair. Blue eyes. Scar on his face. Riding a painted mustang. Marshal, we know Noose. He's that bounty hunter came into this office three days ago saying he was chasing down Jim Henry Barrow."

"She know where he went?"

"East."

The Jackson Hole marshal rolled a cigarette and lit it. Smoke hung in the woodsy air of the fresh lumber of the structure. "Tell

43

her I'm going to organize a posse directly."

The telegraph went silent for a few tense moments.

It took a long time for a response.

When the unit finally started tapping again both lawmen's brows furrowed at what it said.

Swallows shook his head and moved his spectacles on his nose. "She doesn't want a posse, Marshal. Says there's a crew of professional bounty hunters in Hoback heavily armed, ready to go after the son of a bitch soon as the reward is authorized."

"Sounds to me like the Butler Gang that brought in Bonny Kate Valance the other day." Mackenzie indicated a slumbering female redhead locked in the small jail cell in the office. "Those were heading out to Hoback after the Barrow bounty directly. Ask Bess if the leader is named Frank Butler."

Deputy Swallows sent the message over the telegraph and when the answer came back he nodded affirmatively.

Pacing the room, Mackenzie thought hard. "How long you figure it would take us to organize a posse and ride out to Hoback? Four, five hours, something like that?"

Swallows nodded. "Sounds about right."

The marshal shot a hard glance at the

deputy. "Tell her to tell them I'll give 'em twenty-four hours to get their man. After that, I'm wrangling the posse."

Swallows tapped the keys furiously. The old man sucked smoke. "And tell 'em the money's authorized."

More tapping.

"They got their hundred-thousand-dollar reward."

CHAPTER 7

Thirty-two miles away in Hoback, the telegraph printed the response. Deputy Bess Sugarland desperately read it, looking frantically at Butler. "Authorized," she gasped breathlessly.

Butler reared to his feet with a metallic *clink* of spur. He regarded his bounty killers with bullet black eyes. "Let's ride."

The gang of bounty killers wasted no time going after the reward. They were out the door, on their horses, reins and guns in hand, loaded and locked down.

Bess came out of the marshal's office after them.

"I better come along."

The leader of the gang stopped the deputy. "This ain't no place for a woman."

She bridled at the condescension, swallowing hard. "I'm the law."

"Stay put."

They argued. She insisted that she come

along with the gang. The bounty killers and the scary man named Butler were having none of it, and the young female lawman wasn't sure where she found the nerve but she stuck to her guns.

But still they wouldn't let her come. It was no use. Bess backed down.

"Okay, I'll stay here," she said in a weak voice as she stood by the mounted gunmen, hating herself.

"We'll bring him back slung over his saddle by noon," the leader promised, tipping his big black hat. "Guaranteed."

Bess nodded.

Butler sniffed the air. Like an animal picking up the scent of his prey. It was all he ever had to do.

He pointed like a scarecrow into the hills. Twelve big men on twelve big horses spurred their animals' scarred flanks and galloped out of the town in a heavy cloud of dust, hooves pulverizing the ground. The leader's bullet eyes were black and unblinking as he perched fearsomely in the saddle, his gang in savage symbiosis like a terrible machine of horseflesh and duster and iron.

The deputy stood in the settling dust of the gang, feeling the ground shaking under her feet from their receding hooves, watching the tall riders ride up into the hot, mean hills.

They were an efficient outfit, Bess thought to herself . . . too damn efficient.

Something about them didn't smell right.

She had told them she would be going with them.

It was her job.

They had disregarded her, left her behind.

These men were stone killers for sure, but also professionals who intimidated her right down to her boots. Particularly the way the leader, Butler, radiated violence and hostility. Those feral eyes of his knifed right through your guts. Deputy Sugarland knew she was just a green kid and a girl at that. Only reason she was a deputy and even wore the badge was that her dad didn't know how to raise her any other way. She didn't have a mother. Probably her father deputized her, the young lawman guessed, because there wasn't anyone else out in these remote parts to take the job and keep the old man company. But raise her to be a lawman he did and she could ride and shoot and knew the job of a marshal, even if she'd learned it mostly by watching her dad do it. But now the marshal was dead. Murdered in cold blood by a no-account stranger who had come to town, and Bess was all there was left of the law. It was just her. The conflicted young woman stood on the empty street, watching the distant riders resembling a trail of ants as they rode away.

The scared kid in Bess wanted to just stay out of it and let the bounty hunters handle getting the killer. It was twelve of them against his one. They'd catch him for sure. Problem was she had this badge and the duty that came with it — the lawman she was raised to be knew it was her problem and the buck stopped with her. The old man would have expected nothing less of her. He never treated her with anything less than respect as a professional. Bess knew she better take a hand in this. With that resolve, she untethered her horse and heaved herself up into the saddle. Breaking open her shotgun, she saw it had two shells of buckshot chambered and checked to find eighteen more rounds in her saddlebags.

She fingered her badge.

It meant everything now.

"Screw it."

Bess Sugarland would ride after the gang directly.

But she had something to do first.

CHAPTER 8

Noose was a few miles into the hills by now, riding hard, the outpost of Hoback a tiny speck behind him.

Miles ahead of his pursuers, he peered over his shoulder to see the trail of dust at the base of the hill, clearly coming in his direction.

What had taken them so long? he wondered. What was their game? They had him dead to rights. Best Noose could figure, it was sport. But he knew for certain they meant to kill him. Only reason they hadn't done it yet was that inexplicable delay.

Then Noose realized he wasn't thinking straight.

The reward.

It would have taken a few minutes to autho-rize.

Meaning now they were coming after him, he had a bounty on his head.

Noose hoped it was a big reward, because

he damn well meant to be sure those sons of bitches earned every penny. As he galloped his horse up the trail, he took inventory: Right now he was okay. Unwounded. Fully armed. He needed to find some high ground where he could dig in and hopefully begin picking them off, strike fast with the element of surprise, thin their ranks.

Hell, with luck he might kill them all and claim the reward for himself.

But that would be a good trick.

What he needed was a river.

His tracks were clear and easy to follow. Even a creek would allow him to ride through the water in either direction if it wasn't too deep, concealing the hoofprints of his horse, eluding them for a time. But no water, creek or otherwise, showed itself.

Noose was going to have a hard time staying alive for even another hour. The heat was brutal, his horse was tired, and the pressures of the morning made it hard to think, but he had to stay clear.

He had a lot of killing to do if he was going to live to see sunset.

Now twelve horses galloped like black thunder across the landscape.

The bounty killers charged off into the canyons in pursuit of Joe Noose. Frank

Butler rode in the lead. He reined his horse. The killers gazed out at the dusty, empty horizon. Butler sniffed the air.

"West."

They galloped off.

Two minutes later Butler halted his men and pointed his finger like the Grim Reaper. The bounty killers looked where their leader aimed his gloved digit.

In the high rock formations, the lone figure of Noose was visible on the far bluffs under the baking sun. He scanned at the canyons around him, even from this distance his rugged face recognizable. Their quarry took out his canteen.

Looking down the gunsight of his Sharps rifle, Butler drew a bead on the back of the distant Noose's head. "Three hundred yards," he hissed to the others. "Wind from the east. Adjust an inch and a half up for trajectory."

Butler's black-gloved finger closed on the trigger.

It had been a bad week.

Noose lifted the canteen to his mouth. His eye caught a flash of metal in the reflection of the bluffs on the curved surface of the steel canteen.

He spurred his horse just in time to avoid the bullet that whistled past his ear.

Bullets exploded just behind his horse's hooves as he galloped up onto a ridge. Noose threw a look over his shoulder to see the twelve men in dark dusters blasting at him. He dug his heels into his horse and rode hard.

Butler and his bounty killers charged their horses off the high bluffs onto the plateau after the fleeing Noose, who had galloped up the ridge.

"Easy money," Butler chuckled.

Forty-eight horses' hooves pounded up the ridge.

In a gully, Noose leapt off his horse and took position behind some rocks by the entrance. He took careful aim with his pistols and listened to the approaching horses, aiming where he expected them to be any second now.

The bounty killers came on like a machine.

Noose opened fire on the gang as they rode in. He shot the gun out of one's hand. The ricochet of the slug off the pistol cylinder was a shower of sparks. Butler whistled stridently and secured his men behind some boulders as they took cover with practiced prowess.

They all traded fire.

Bullets *whined* past Noose's ears. His

slugs didn't reach the bounty killers. The pistols in Noose's fists *clicked* as the hammers struck empty chambers. Quickly he reloaded and shot back at what he could glimpse of the men in the dusters hiding behind the boulders, but he couldn't see much. They were in a good position and had him boxed in as they laid down suppressing fire. Volleys of slugs exploded against the rocks around the lone Noose.

Then Noose ran out of bullets. Cracking open his pistol cylinders, he saw both guns were empty. He thought fast and got an idea.

From his place of concealment, Butler grinned savagely at his gang. "I counted his rounds at the bar. He's used his twenty. He's empty." Butler saw Noose leap up from his cover and run for it.

"Gotcha." Butler aimed and fired once.

Noose dropped.

"Told you he was easy money."

A squat bounty killer named Slade went first. Butler and the rest of the gang followed close behind. Keeping his pistols up, Slade peered over a big rock, was pleased with what he saw, then looked back at his gang and nodded with a cracked-tooth grin. The gunman holstered his pistols and stepped over the rock.

Slade saw Noose sprawled motionless on the ground.

He approached. The scabrous thug stood over his fallen target and leaned down with a cocky smirk.

Suddenly, Noose's eyes popped open and he sat up blindingly fast, grabbing both Colt .45 pistols from Slade's holsters and shooting him point-blank with two guns square in the chest. The dead bounty killer's body was catapulted back ten feet through a red curtain of raining blood. His drilled corpse landed smack against three other bounty killers, knocking them down.

Before Frank Butler had time to react, Joe Noose had the twin hot muzzles of both .45 pistols jammed under his bristly jaw. Noose thumbed back the hammers of both guns, as all the bounty killers raised their weapons and trained them on Noose at point-blank range. The air was filled with a chorus of ratcheting *clicks.*

Noose didn't blink. "They shoot me, I shoot you."

Butler didn't, either. "Nice 'n easy, boys."

"Looks like we got us a situation."

"Reckon there's no such thing as easy money," Butler said.

"This is what we're going to do," Noose said, his face an inch from Butler's. "You're going to tell your boys to stand down. You're coming with me."

Butler smiled. "That so?"

"That is so."

"Let me guess. You're figuring on taking me to Jackson Hole. Turning me in. Getting it all straightened out."

"That's right." Noose jammed the muzzle in Butler's cheek, smearing a bloody crease in his salt-and-pepper whiskers. Then he shot a fierce glance to the gunmen drawing down on him with an army of firepower. "I said, *lower them guns or I kill him! Now!*"

Confusion and alarm flickered across the bounty killers' faces, wearing dangerous expressions that ranged from wary to stupid. The sound of the crickets in the area seemed to rise in a savage drone.

Frank Butler just laughed with the pistols in his face and looked Noose square in the eye. "That's your plan? Take me in, tell the law I killed the marshal? Your plan is crap. I got eleven boys here swear it was you."

"Ten."

"Well, you got lucky with that one." Butler's eyes glinted with mirth and he cut his gaze to his men holding their guns on Noose. "Slade wasn't worth spit anyway." He said to Noose, "You shoot me, they shoot you. Nobody gets paid. We're in it for the money, mister, ain't personal. Not yet anyways. I'll make a deal with you. Go on and drop your pistols and we'll leave off you. For now. Say we give you another hour head start."

Noose said, "You boys first."

Nobody moved.

Noose jammed the pistol muzzles harder under Butler's jaw. Butler's bullet black eyes didn't blink. "Boys, just kill him and be done with it," he snarled.

The bounty killers tightened their fingers on the triggers of the guns aimed right at Noose's head.

Noose whistled loudly.

A gallop of hooves.

The gang of badmen were caught off guard as Noose's horse charged into the gully. Noose threw Butler to the ground and knocked the men out of the way as he swung up into the saddle, escaping on horseback in a firestorm of bullets. Butler and his bounty killers ran to their horses and gave pursuit.

Noose rode for his life up the rocky arroyo. He looked over his shoulder to see the gang of men and horses charging after him in clouds of dust. They were still two minutes behind. Muzzle flash after muzzle flash appeared as bullets exploded around

Noose's horse's hooves.

His hand reached for a roll of sharp barbed wire he had in his saddle . . .

CHAPTER 9

The bounty hunters rode hell-for-leather onto the empty ridge at full gallop.

A length of barbed wire was suddenly snapped taut at saddle level at the entrance to the ridge.

The last bounty hunter, T-Bone, rode into it at full gallop.

The sharp wire sluiced through the flesh of his throat and his spinal cord like a knife through butter.

His head was severed.

The gunman's face was frozen in an expression of dumb surprise as his head spun through the air in a spray of blood jetting from the neck stump.

The decapitated body, guns and all, toppled over the edge of the ridge. His horse traveled on with a blood-soaked empty saddle.

T-Bone never had a chance to scream, just gurgle, and Frank Butler and his men didn't notice his absence until the leader pulled his horse up to look around the empty ridge and did a quick head count. "Where the hell is T-Bone?" he growled.

One of his men pointed grimly at the riderless horse.

Butler stared coldly at the bloody saddle.

"Now it's hundred thousand dollars split ten ways. Ten thousand each," he stated coldly with a trace of a smile.

It was sounding better to the greedy bounty killers every minute.

T-Bone's headless corpse lay at the base of the ridge.

Noose's hands smoothly removed the man's pistols, rifle, and bandoliers.

Then his fingers closed the eyes of the severed head lying nearby.

Frank Butler's black bullet eyes blinked. The bounty killers stared around them at the massive expanse of empty, desolate granite cliffs and pine forest.

Noose spurred his horse on toward the canyons and rode for it.

He looked over his shoulder to see the gang a mile back, gaining on him in a mushroom cloud of dirt.

Noose dismounted his horse.

He slapped its rear and sent it on its way, unmounted, into the canyons.

He ducked into the rock formations.

Butler reined his horse in the flats. Put up his hand. The bounty killers stopped. Butler smelled the air, handlebar mustache twitching — a human bloodhound. His head rotated like a gun turret as he scanned the canyons a half mile away, cutting sign.

He pointed with a black-gloved finger. "There."

They rode. Butler and his gang galloped into the low canyons, following Noose's horse's tracks.

The bounty killers rounded a bend.

Noose's horse was standing there, saddle empty.

"He's behind us!" Butler roared.

Before they could react, Noose leapt up behind them and shot a fat bounty killer named Sweet clean out of the stirrups. Half his face had been blown off. The dead man's gun went off into his saddle, crippling his horse. Noose ducked down and whistled for his own horse.

Frank Butler blasted Noose's horse with both barrels of his shotgun, killing it instantly. The horse collapsed where it stood and the bounty hunter was thrown from the saddle.

"Damn!" Noose cursed.

He leapt down a rocky incline, skidding

on the heels of his boots to get away. Then he lost his balance and toppled face-first. Noose somersaulted head over heels down the hundred-and-fifty-foot ridge, bouncing off rocks and boulders. He hit the bottom. Staggering to his feet, he scrambled away.

Butler shot a savagely triumphant glance to his men. "He's on foot now."

The leader reloaded and reseated his shotgun quickly and regarded Sweet's corpse under his lamed horse. "Hundred thousand cut nine ways. Eleven thousand 'n change each." The bounty killers exchanged avaricious glances. "Let's go get it."

They rode down the trail.

On the canyon floor, the nine bounty killers cantered on horseback to ledges at the base of the butte. They patrolled on full alert, riding past the spot where Noose landed.

Butler's eyes searched the area, machine-like.

They rounded a bend.

Noose jumped off a ledge above them, shotgun blasting, blowing the bounty killer Snake right out of his saddle. The corpse landed in a heap in the dirt with two huge steaming craters in his chest. Noose flew through the air, landed in the empty saddle, and spurred the horse onward.

Butler raised his pistol and drew a bead. He fired once.

Noose was hit in the shoulder.

He fell out of the saddle of the fast-galloping horse.

His boot caught in the stirrup.

Noose was brutally dragged across the rocks and tundra.

Bullets whined and exploded around his ears as the pursuing gang of bounty killers fired upon him. He tried to shoot back, but was smashed up as he was dragged by the hard-charging galloping horse. Painstakingly, amid volleys of rifle and pistol rounds, Noose sat up as he was dragged, and pulled himself hand over hand on the stirrup trapping his leg toward the saddle as he was jounced over the hard ground. With his last ounce of strength, the cowboy climbed back into his saddle and spurred the horse, escaping from his pursuers into a deep ravine.

Butler reined his horse. He put up his black-gloved hand for his gang to stop. Butler watched Noose disappear in the distance, and chuckled.

"Now, that, boys, is how to sit a horse."

He regarded his gang with his bullet black eyes full of fury.

"Hundred thousand split eight ways. Twelve thousand each."

The gang of killers masticated on that.

"Reload."

They did.

Butler's eyes darkened as he watched the cloud of dust that was his quarry melt into the waves of heat. The badman knew his prey was badly wounded, but that didn't change things. Because right now:

It was four, zip.

CHAPTER 10

If you are reading this I am dead. My body has been turned in by bounty killers run by Frank Butler and you have found this letter in my clothes. I swear I am innocent of the killing of the U.S. Marshal the reward has been put out for me on. Butler murdered the marshal in order to frame me and collect the money. Proof of this will be the bullets in the marshal's body are from Butler's own gun, not mine. These words are God's truth. Signed, Joe Noose.

Noose sat in the saddle writing the letter.

Finished, he folded the wrinkled, blood-splattered paper and stuffed it inside his coat.

Safe for now, he slumped in his stirrups and let his horse rest at the stream, where it drank thirstily.

Grimacing in agony, Noose unbuttoned

his shirt and fingered the oozing bullet wound in his shoulder. The slug had gone clean through but he had broken a few ribs getting dragged by the horse. The bullet hole had started to throb and was soon going to hurt like hell.

Noose was messed up. That was a fact.

His clothes were covered with blood, mostly his. In disgust, he wiped off some skull and brain fragments from the killer he shot with his own guns, rearming himself. The two Colts he confiscated were in pretty good condition and both loaded. Noose took quick inventory of his weapons and ammo: besides those two guns, he had the two Remington Peacemaker pistols, Winchester rifle, and bandolier belts filled with bullets taken from the second bounty killer he had killed with the wire. It was enough firepower to put up a fight and he was going to need it. Every last bullet.

Looking over his shoulder, Noose saw no sign of his pursuers but they were out there, maybe licking their wounds a moment but not far behind. And damn pissed.

Ironically, the more of the gang he killed, the greater was the share of the reward the survivors would split; the more bounty killers he took out, the more motivated the ones left alive were to kill him. Once they got him, these vultures would probably shoot one another in the back to get more money.

It was bad odds. He was still outnumbered. There were a lot more of them and sooner or later they would get him.

He needed a plan.

Jackson Hole was thirty miles away. Thirty miles of hard terrain lay between here and there. Noose knew he had to ride for town. It was his only option. If he could make it there in one piece, he could get to the marshal's office and tell his story and at least get out of the crosshairs of these bounty killers. There would at least be a trial and witnesses and evidence could be presented. He was an innocent man. It was a good bet that Butler and his thugs' reputation preceded them and doubtless some of that gang had warrants out for them. That was what Noose would do and was all he could do: ride for his life and make for Jackson.

Trouble was the town lay west and that meant turning around and heading back the way he came.

A bounty for the murdered U.S. Marshal would be serious money, probably a hundred thousand dollars. If he made it to town maybe he would take down all these bastards and collect the reward for himself.

Now, there was a thought.

It was the first time Noose smiled all day.

CHAPTER 11

The sun burned like a white bullet hole in the barren sky.

In a wash, the gang were watering and resting their horses.

Butler stood staring out at the gigantic pine forests and granite canyon breaks towering all around them in the Hoback wilderness.

His right-hand man, Sharpless, walked up, awaiting orders.

"He's not going far. We'll pick up his trail easy enough," Butler said without turning. "We need to kill him quick now. That marshal telegraphed he was organizing a posse tomorrow to catch him if we don't, and the clock is ticking on this reward."

"Where you figure he's heading, Mr. Butler?"

"Jackson Hole."

"But that's clear back the other way."

"He'll double back to Jackson directly. Try

to turn himself in to the law before we get to him, tell his story, take his chances they'll believe him. That's his only move. Hell, it's what I'd do."

The leader glared at his man and spat in the dirt.

"It's on us to make sure that don't happen."

Bess Sugarland caught up with the bounty killers just before noon.

Now as she reined her horse and looked down at the gang of eight riders grouped in the wash, she noticed there were fewer of them than there were an hour ago. On her ride to catch up, Bess had heard the explosive reports of gunshots and screams of agony echoing through the canyons and wondered if the bounty killers had run into an army because it sure sounded like a damn war had broken out.

From all the blood everywhere, it had: she had ridden past the corpses of four bounty killers getting here.

One individual had killed all those dangerous men.

Bess felt a twinge of admiration for the wanted man but then hated herself for finding any virtue in the man who killed her father. If she saw the murderer again and had the chance herself to shoot him, her finger wouldn't hesitate on the trigger.

A few short hours ago the young woman couldn't have imagined she'd have a crack at her father's killer given how fearsome a first impression the gang of twelve men had made, but so far they had been bested.

Thinking maybe these bounty killers weren't all they were cracked up to be, Bess suddenly felt less intimidated by the man-hunters and rode down into the wash to talk to them.

A twig *snapped* outside the camp.

Butler and the bounty killers quickly drew their guns in a symphony of cocking hammers. "Show yourself!" the leader demanded — his gloved hand was up, telling his men not to fire because he already knew it wasn't Noose.

The figure appeared, flashing a marshal badge gleaming in the sunlight.

It was that damn uppity girl deputy!

"Easy, boys. It's me," she said. "Acting Marshal Bess Sugarland, from back in town." The girl stepped out into the clearing, hands held open in front of her.

Butler was dumbfounded. He had not expected this. "Lower your weapons," he grumbled.

The gang did. The fierce leader gave the nervy young woman the stink eye. "What the hell are you doing here?"

Bess walked into camp, nervous but bearing up bravely. "The marshal was murdered by that man you're after. The law needs to be involved. Right now, that's me."

"That's you. I see." Butler regarded her blankly.

"I was his sworn deputy and now the marshal's gone, I'm in charge."

"You're in charge," Butler said mockingly.

"Yes, sir, I am, yes, I am in charge," Bess responded firmly, holding his gaze.

Butler's eyes glinted with mirth and he turned his back on Bess, huddling with his men and rubbing his hands. "Okay. She says she's in charge." He cut his eyes from man to man.

They all chuckled.

Bess went off and tied her horse to a tree across the wash, out of earshot. Behind her, the bounty killers whispered among themselves in a crouched circle that resembled a malignant kettle of vultures.

"How old is she, fifteen?" One smirked.

"You see the ass on that little bitch?" Another one leered.

"And them high, firm titties," added another bounty killer.

72

Across the clearing, Bess heard the mumbles and snickers — she knew they were talking about her and could guess what they were saying. Her back was to the bounty killers because Bess didn't want those men to see she was suffering an anxiety attack that froze her face into a taut mask. The sudden tension left Bess paralyzed and unable to breathe. Her sober realization of being one woman alone with ruthless armed men who could rape or kill her out here where nobody would ever know made her want to puke her guts out. Bess struggled to settle down. Truth was, she was scared spitless. But she had mettle and soon pulled herself together. Bess told herself she was a daughter who meant to have the man who murdered her father brought to justice and that trumped her fear. And she was the marshal now with the responsibility that came along with the badge. Her father had raised her that way and his strength came to her now. The anxiety attack passed as abruptly as it came on and Bess felt herself again.

The men kept whispering, out of earshot.

"We's gonna do her and kill her. Right, boss?" asked a scurvy killer taking a swig from a bottle of whiskey. "Each of us gets a turn, right?"

73

"Out here won't nobody never find the body," his equally scabrous friend seconded.

Frank Butler agreeably regarded his shootists and picked his teeth. "Reckon."

Bess piped up across the gully. "Just letting you men know before I left Hoback, I telegraphed the U.S. Marshal's office in Jackson Hole I was coming along with you to catch the marshal's killer, so they'll be expecting to see me when we bring him in for the reward."

Butler's eyes darkened. Foiled. For now.

"Relax, boys," he muttered. "She won't even be able to keep up."

CHAPTER 12

A few miles away, the wounded bounty hunter Joe Noose was cleaning his wounds. His shirt was off and his exposed chest and arms were horribly bruised and smeared with blood from the fresh bullet holes in his shoulder. The process was painful, but slowly he was getting his injuries cleaned. The part that was really going to hurt was soon to come.

Noose had put in by a burbling brook in heavy forest he had ridden deep into that the cowboy hoped would provide adequate cover from the posse on his tail — at least for an hour or so, allowing him to rest his horse. The freshwater would be useful. His own wounds were seriously in need of treatment or else he was going to be in worse trouble than he already was.

The tall pine trees crowned a steep switchback and mountain ridge overlook, affording a good view of the terrain below he had just traveled and from where the pursuing bounty killers were likely to follow. For the last few miles Noose had ridden in a zigzag pattern to elude them, traversing in and out of scattered patches of woods, attempting to throw Butler and his men off his tail. Soon enough, he would see how well that evasion tactic had worked.

It seemed safe enough here for now.

After tethering his new horse to a tree, Noose faced the physical challenge of getting off it. Stiffly and gingerly dismounting the saddle he was in considerable discomfort, the pressure of his boot in the stirrup when he put his weight on it sent stabbing pain up his sides where his ribs had been broken, and when his boots hit the ground, the searing agony of the bullet holes in him made him fall against the saddle with a gasp. The horse looked back at him with big eyes filled whether with pity or curiosity he couldn't tell. A few moments later the cowboy got his feet under him and found his balance but saw drops of his own blood on the pine needles crunching under his heels as he staggered away from his horse.

Noose limped to the overlook, leaned against a tree trunk, and took out his field glasses. He peered through them, mindful to angle them away from the sun so a glint of reflection wouldn't give away his position. A cursory scan of the landscape below through the magnified oval view of the small pair of brass binoculars revealed no other riders coming from the direction he had just ridden. To the left, a quarter mile out, Noose observed a lazy trail of settling dust from what looked likely to be a number of horses, so it appeared the bounty killers had gone just west of him. Noose couldn't tell how long it would take them to realize their mistake but had to figure they would wise up and double back soon enough — when they did, he better be elsewhere.

For now, Noose held the high ground. There he made a temporary encampment.

Returning to the tethered stallion, the cowboy took the canteen from the saddlebag to give some water to the horse. It jerked its head back when he brought the spout too close to its face to splash water in its mouth. The animal was high-strung and skittish, and Noose whistled gently to calm it. "Easy, boy. Easy. We both need us some rest. Got us a hard ride ahead. Got to get to Jackson Hole, turn myself in. They'll believe me. They'll have to. Need you to run fast, get us away from these guns, you hear?"

The horse, big in size and bronze of coat, regarded him warily with a cagey, dodgy look in its big brown eyes; it definitely didn't trust him yet. Noose could hardly expect otherwise, having shot its previous owner clean out of the saddle, though from the look of the raw spur gashes on the stallion's flanks and its overall abused and battered appearance, this was no great loss to the animal and he'd done it a service. Noose was good with horses and figured it was just going to take time to make friends . . . time he hoped he had.

If the stubborn horse didn't want to drink that was its business. Noose had to fix his wounds, so he rummaged in the saddlebags and found a roll of clean cloths and bandages, though nothing much else in the way of medical supplies. Staggering down to the brook, he knelt by the edge and refilled his canteen. Splashed water on his face. Then he peeled off his shirt, wet the cloth in the brook, and cleaned the bullet holes, both entrance and exit wounds. The cowboy reminded himself he had been lucky that the round had gone clean through and he didn't have any lead in him — cutting a flattened slug out of his body would have sorely put him to the test. When Noose had got as much dirt out of the skin as he could he dabbed the bloody wounds dry and reached reluctantly for his gun belt.

Pulled a .45 cartridge out.

Put the lead head in his teeth, gripped the casing in his fist, bit down firmly, and pulled — hard.

In a moment, the head came loose of the cartridge and he kept the bullet grit between his teeth so he'd have something to bite down on, because he was going to need it.

This was the part that was really going to hurt . . .

Turning the open shell sideways, Noose sprinkled a small pile of the gunpowder on first the gaping bullet hole on the front of his shoulder, then the hole behind it, like a saltshaker.

Tossing the empty cartridge, he pulled a stick match from his shirt.

Struck it with his thumbnail in a *snick* and flash of *hissing* flame.

Then Noose lit the gunpowder on the bullet hole in his upper torso, igniting twin sizzling explosions of sparkling flame that spat out the holes in both sides of his shoulder, instantly cauterizing the entrance and exit wounds by burning the flesh shut.

His agonized scream was muffled by the lead slug he bit down so hard on it nearly broke his teeth.

The stolen horse, startled by the spectacle, reared and whinnied in alarm, straining against the reins tied to the tree.

More fire suddenly flared, followed by another round of searing hot agony that made the cowboy reel from the pain as the wound was savagely cauterized. He was buckled over, clouded with the smoky discharge. Rocking on his knees, Noose coughed in the haze of rank smoke that stunk of burnt meat and gunpowder, waiting for the pain to subside and knowing the worst part was over.

Noose could get rid of the bullet in his mouth now.

He spat the slug out.

Wrapping the wound with bandages was the last step — once Noose finished the dressing it was the best he was going to be able to do for himself until he made it to a proper hospital in Jackson Hole. Good idea not to get shot anymore if he could avoid it.

A sudden wave of fatigue overtook the big cowboy, catching him up unawares. The peace and quiet of the forest lulled him with the pull of its solitude and tranquillity.

Noose stretched out on the ground, passing out from exhaustion. His pistol lay beside him.

"Just a few minutes' rest."

Soon his eyes shut.

■ ■ ■ ■

Noose heard the sound of the hammer of a pistol being cocked a second too late.

His eyes popped open.

Frank Butler pressed the muzzle of his Colt Dragoon between his eyes.

"Easy money," he chuckled.

Butler blew Noose's head off.

With a start, Noose awoke up from his bad dream, gasping for breath. He sat bracing himself, eyes wide. Soon he got drowsy and his lids started to close again. Noose forced himself awake. He reached over to his bandaged bullet wound.

And jammed his finger against it. His eyes bulged in pain.

Noose achingly staggered to his feet, grabbed his gun, checked it was loaded, and holstered it.

"Sleep when you're dead, fool," he grumbled to himself.

Climbing into the stirrups and sliding with a grunt into his saddle, the man untethered the horse and rode off into the vertiginous forest of lush green conifers.

It felt good to be on the move again.

■ ■ ■ ■

For the next few miles, Noose rode west, keeping the horse at a steady pace between a fast canter and a slow gallop, heading a little north of where he had last seen the Butler Gang turn south. Keeping a sharp lookout the whole time, he saw no sign of the eight riders and it appeared he had lost them for now. The trail soon left the forest and dropped down into an expanse of sprawling plain that opened onto a bend of the mighty Snake River.

The scenic tributary flowed on through Jackson Hole to points west, and Noose knew that by following the flow of the big river it would take him to Jackson . . . it was all the map he needed.

Man and horse rode into the shady glen to the gleaming stretch of the rushing expanse of river traveling by. Noose could see from the way the animal's chest was heaving and his mouth was chewing the bit that it was thirsty. What horse wouldn't be after a run like that in this kind of heat? The cowboy himself had to refill his canteen and it would feel good to splash some cool water on his face.

Noose dismounted, taking the horse by

the reins and leading it to the edge of the Snake River. As soon as his boots hit the ground, he felt the animal tense up. The stallion's face was lathered with sweat and its mouth around the tack was covered with froth. A taut furtive tension tightened in its muscles and stance, a high-strung nervous energy that Noose put down to tiredness from the chase or maybe an unease with his strange new rider now the old one had been shot off — you never knew with horses. The bronze stallion watched him anxiously with both big alert brown eyes as he led it to the river's edge to drink.

The horse dropped his snout into the flowing water.

Noose loosened his grip on the reins to give it some berth.

That was the moment the horse had been waiting for, apparently.

With a sudden surprise surge of strength and speed the stallion reared up on its hind legs and kicked Noose square in the chest with both front hooves, catapulting him clean off his boots into the Snake River. The reins tore out of his fingers. The cowboy landed in the drink with a wet splash and pained grunt, and when he had wiped the water out of his eyes he saw the horse was already off and running.

"Sonofabitch!" Noose swore as he rose to his feet, drenched from head to foot, and stepped to shore. There went his ride — the runaway horse was making a break for it, was already halfway across the glen to the edge of the tree line. Noose put both forefingers in his mouth and blew a piercing commanding whistle.

To his total surprise, the horse stopped running and came to a halt. It didn't come back, but held its ground, watching the cowboy by the river's edge in a defiant, cautious stare.

Noose came to a stop on the shoreline, his clothes dripping in a puddle around his sopping boots. The man didn't move a muscle. And he didn't take his eyes off the horse or break its stare. He was totally calm and patient. Minutes passed, and neither moved. Both just stood and took each other's measure.

Joe Noose knew that if he made any sudden moves that horse was gone, and he was on foot for good. He was just going to damn well wait the animal out if he could.

At least a hundred yards stood between the stallion and himself. Rushing it would be a fool's errand. If the horse had a mind to run and took off, he wouldn't get ten feet closer to it. He had to get the horse to trust him. That meant be patient and a little lucky.

It was thirsty. That he knew for sure.

Unslinging his canteen, Noose crouched down and dunked the nozzle under the water, letting the flow of the river fill it up, which it quickly did, gurgling over the spout. The cowboy rose.

He took one step closer.

By the edge of the glen, the horse shied, watching Noose warily.

The man saw the animal had been mistreated, badly so, by his late owner. The bloody spur marks on the stallion's flanks were fresh wounds, with a lot of scar tissue in the same area from a history of brutal kicking to drive it faster. Noose felt a surge of anger that anybody would treat a horse that way and felt no remorse he killed the man who did it. That man had it coming. Noose had always preferred animals, especially horses, to people.

Fifty yards away, the horse just stood and watched the cowboy testily. The steed appeared ready to bolt yet didn't. Not yet. One big brown eye filled with pain and distrust kept a close watch on the man it had just kicked. One hoof pawed the ground.

The cowboy took his time.

Didn't try to rush the horse.

It was a big, beautiful animal. Coat a vibrant bronze in color, mane and withers gold and long. The hue gave it the appearance of being armored, like a medieval knight's mount. Its mighty legs were long and muscular and it stood ten hands high at the shoulder. This horse was strong and fast and it had guts, Noose could vouch for that.

It wasn't a bad-tempered horse.

Just abused, was all.

A full thirty minutes elapsed before Joe Noose was able to walk across the glen to the animal's side. When he got there it was panting and shivering with dehydration, needing water in the worst way.

Noose opened his canteen and poured some cool river water in the horse's mouth.

Instantly, the stallion drank thirstily, lips opening and closing and head tossing back, as the cowboy poured the entire canteen down its throat.

When the canteen was empty, the horse was gazing at him with a warmer, more trusting gaze.

Guess we're friends now. The man smiled. *At least starting to be.*

Noose gently patted the powerful neck and warmly pressed his face against its shoulder, feeling the caution in the horse begin to melt. He spoke softly to it.

"C'mon, boy. You look like you're still thirsty and, hell, you drank all my water. Lucky for us, there's plenty to go around right over there. Let's go back to yonder river."

Noose took the reins and led the stallion back to the river's edge and it accompanied him without complaint. There, the animal dropped its snout in the rushing waters and slaked its thirst while Noose refilled his canteen and quenched his own.

The bronze of the horse's coat seemed almost metallic in the sunlight, Noose observed admiringly.

He named it Copper.

CHAPTER 13

Sun high.

The *scree* of a hawk.

A droning *buzz* of insects in the grass. The *swish* of a horse's tail brushing at flies.

Adjusting the brim of her hat, Bess Sugarland wiped sweat from her brow and shifted calmly in the saddle of her horse, eyeballing the eight mounted gunmen on horseback who eyeballed her back. Her gaze was even, purposefully direct: the last thing a lawman could ever do was show fear even when they felt it. The bounty killers were all resting their horses at the edge of a clearing for a few minutes . . . *ten minutes and not a second more, Butler had said three of those minutes ago.* The search for the man with the reward on his head had suffered a setback when their quarry had given them the slip the last few miles, and the men were all grumbling about having made a wrong turn somewhere, but where exactly they had gone in the wrong direction was the subject of some dispute.

The only one not offering up an opinion on where they *should* have turned back up the trail was the leader of the gang. A brooding Frank Butler sat on his huge black horse, glowering under the deep shadow of a tree, puffing a hand-rolled cigarette, snorting smoke out his nostrils as he impatiently checked the pocket watch on a fob in his black vest at regular intervals, noisily snapping it open and closed with a strident *snap* each time he did.

Snap. The timepiece opened . . .

The young female marshal was keeping her eyes open and mouth shut, putting names to faces of the eight men she rode with. The leader the men called Mr. Butler, the only member of the gang referred to by *mister,* she knew already; Bess was busy getting a handle on the other seven professional killers in the outfit — it seemed a sensible idea to familiarize herself with the dangerous and unpredictable types she rode with to know who she was dealing with and how better to deal with them in the hours to come. To this end, Marshal Sugarland paid close attention to what was going on around her and made a careful study of the gang.

Snap. The pocket watch closed . . .

There was the big and steady one named Sharpless, who some men in the gang called Will. He was heavyset, bearded, and swarthy, armed with two Remington Peacemakers he always kept cleaned and well oiled. In the pecking order of the gang, Sharpless appeared to Bess to be the closest Frank Butler had to a number two. Now and then she would observe the two men exchanging words out of earshot of the others, and Butler seemed to listen to Sharpless and consider his opinion when offered. Otherwise, the even-keeled, unassumingly authoritative Will Sharpless didn't talk much, except to disseminate his boss's orders to the other shootists, who seemed to respect this man of few words and look up to him. While Will Sharpless had about him a certain deadly air of violence, he also had one of reasonableness.

Snap . . .

Culhane — she thought his first name might be John — and Lawson — sometimes called Long Gone or Leroy — were another matter. The two were thick as thieves and stuck together like flies on crap, which both of them repellently reminded her of. These two vermin always rode side by side together, passing comments back and forth, and Bess knew from the dirty looks the scum shot her way at every available opportunity they genuinely hated her guts; whether that was because of her gender or her badge or both, Bess couldn't say, but among the entire gang she knew these two scrofulous vultures were the ones to watch out for. If she was going to have a problem with any of this crew, it was going to be with Leroy "Long Gone" Lawson and John Culhane.

The youngest, at least the most unsure of himself, was Jasper Weed. The whipping boy of the gang was often the butt of jokes about his emaciated reedlike build. Twice on the ride so far, Weed had to retrieve his hat from one of the other men who stole it off his head. Perhaps to compensate, he packed two enormous Colt Dragoons that appeared too big for his fragile feminine hands despite the big gloves he wore to conceal their smallness; the young woman marshal herself had less dainty mitts than this kid did. The other way Weed compensated Bess could smell on him . . . whiskey. The high-strung shootist took repeated swigs from a flask in his duster and acted visibly drunk. Bess had found herself watching Weed a lot the last hour or so — if the bounty killer gang had a weak link, she had decided, it was him; she had made up her mind to chat this one up at the first available opportunity.

The three others, Luke Garrity, Japeth Trumbull, and Earl Wingo, Bess Sugarland had names to faces for, but no real handle yet on individual personalities — other than they were, to a man, cold-blooded professional killers who would as soon deliver a man dead than alive for a reward. It made no difference to them whatsoever. The whole gang killed for money and it was what they were good at; a glue of raw homicide bound the group together and this made the justice-minded female lawman's very skin crawl in their company.

Bess switched her gaze to Sharpless as he made a *tsk-tsk* sound to his horse and trotted over to beneath the tree where Butler perched in the saddle. The leader had just gestured his number two over with a nudge of his jaw. Bess watched them casually out of the corner of her eye but couldn't hear what was said — none of the gang could. Sharpless's lips moved as he said a few words to Butler, who listened and nodded as Sharpless made a few finger gestures in his palm, then Butler pointed west, jerked his thumb sideways, then showed five fingers. Bess watched the exchange as without expression, Sharpless turned and rode his horse back to the gang.

"Five minutes, boys. Mr. Butler figures Noose intends on following the Snake to Jackson, so our plan is we're gonna head toward the river and cut him off. We move out in five and fixin' on riding for a good chunk of time. Finish your smokes. You got to piss, do it now and be quick about it."

Culhane dismounted, rubbing his crotch, and unzipped. Just before he whipped it out and pissed on the rocks, the marshal averted her eyes, blushing. He urinated a good long time and took just as long shaking himself. Finishing with a satisfied groan, winking at the other cutthroats, Culhane saddled up and took a swig of a bottle of whiskey. The others cleaned their guns.

Butler watched everyone with a steady gaze that missed nothing.

Bess felt uncomfortable suddenly. Sharpless had said that Butler said they would be riding for a while, and she was going to experience considerably more discomfort soon. It was now or never.

Swallowing, she dismounted without a word to the others and walked far out into the trees and undergrowth, looking back to be sure she wasn't observed. Bess went a good hundred yards, looked back, could still see the men through the branches, and figured that meant they could see her. Three minutes and another two hundred yards later, she was out of eyeshot and earshot of the gang of bounty killers. Unbuckling her jeans, she squatted in the bushes.

Making it quick, the marshal walked back into the clearing.

She stopped dead in her tracks.

The clearing was empty.

The posse was gone.

For a pack of ranch animals in men's clothing, they could move with skillful and quiet stealth if of a mind to.

"Sonofabitch." The young woman rarely swore unless she had cause to but now she did. Squinting into the horizon, Bess peered left and right.

No movement on the prairie or in the trees in the distance.

She leapt on her horse.

Galloped out of there.

Where were they?

Marshal Sugarland's mind swam with doubt, uncertainty, and the fear she had messed up letting herself get left behind but she kept her head screwed on straight. It helped that while Bess didn't get out here a lot, she had grown up in this territory so had a pretty good idea of the terrain from the times she had been here over the years.

She hitched herself forward in the saddle and rode hard, north for now, because the trail was better. Her eyes flicked right and left, looking for sign. She didn't like these men, but was gaining a grudging respect that they were good — able to vanish like ghosts. *Think,* she told herself. *Where would they have headed? Think like Butler does: Where would Noose most likely have headed?* The bounty killer gang could have gone in any number of directions but Bess logically guessed they were heading forward and north, not backtracking south. East lay the steadfast waterway of the Snake River and the gang wasn't likely to cross that without good reason. West was a possibility: big, wide-open country reducing their possible route in her mind to two directions — of those two options she made a mental coin toss and decided to keep riding north on the hunch the manhunters were following the path of the Snake River because they figured that was the direction Noose was heading. Bess spurred her horse again, galloping over a ridge, and once she cleared it saw she had guessed correctly.

A mile away on the open plain, the bounty killers were riding at a fast clip.

Bess caught up.

"Why didn't you wait for me?" she yelled.

Butler didn't look at her, slapping his horse with his reins. "Not my job."

"I told you I was coming along."

"We got a killer to catch."

"That's why I'm here."

"Then keep up. We don't work for you."

"Hey, wait a second." The young lawman recognized the familiar landscape. "Why this direction?"

"He's heading to Jackson Hole."

Frank Butler signaled his men to slow down to a moderate canter — they had been riding their horses full gallop and had to pace the animals. The terrain was becoming ruggedly uneven, the trail now erratic as the river dropped below a rise of canyon the eight mounted men and one woman had to scale and now rode carefully up. Hooves dislodged rocks that rolled over the edge of the cliff . . . with each successive few yards, it took longer and longer to hear the distant splash below.

"Why the hell would Noose do that?" Bess argued, riding up beside the leader. "He's wanted there. The marshal's waiting, armed to the teeth."

The gang boss rolled and lit a cigarette and did it with one gloved hand, no mean feat on a moving horse. "I savvy he got backup there. Extra guns to help him out."

"You mean partners?" Bess shot him a dubious glance.

"Yeah, mebbe. Heard he rides with Danny Dunbar and William Bob Robinson. Notorious shootists both, neither ever far from where Noose is. And they're in Jackson Hole as we speak. Last I heard they showed up last Thursday, was it not?" Butler glanced at his nearest man.

"Indeed." Trumbull nodded. "They was seen by several souls."

Garrity and Wingo nodded after Trumbull shot them a glance for confirmation, but Bess thought neither looked certain about seeing the men or even what they were supposed to be agreeing with.

Bess was suspicious. "You know this how?"

"They bought me a drink," Butler lied.

"Never heard of them. But good to know, I guess," murmured the skeptical woman.

"Don't worry there, Deputy. We'll nail this guy for you and make you look good." Butler's tone was patronizing.

"Marshal," Bess corrected him.

Butler looked at her testily, taking her measure again in the deliberate manner of a doctor routinely checking the pulse of a patient, but Butler seemed displeased that her pulse seemed to be getting stronger by the minute. The female lawman held his gaze bravely. "Since my fath— since the marshal's dead, until his replacement is decided, as his deputy I'm the interim marshal acting in his stead. That's the law around here and you damn well know it, Mr. Butler." She shot a bold glance at all the men in the posse. "You boys got that?"

Butler shrugged, jaw tightening, suppressing a yawn. "A badge is a badge."

"Thank you."

"Don't mention it."

Culhane suddenly pointed. "There he is!"

Butler snapped to attention. His gaze swung.

Sure enough, half a mile off, Noose's lone figure was on his horse, riding north atop a bluff over the bend in the mighty river.

"Get him!" the leader screamed.

The posse instantly charged after their quarry at full clip. The air was filled with a thunder of pounding horses' hooves.

Bess's blood was up. She dug in her spurs, regretful about the cinch of pain she felt in her horse's side but not regretful for the surge of speed her boots urged from her stallion.

There the blackhearted murdering son of a bitch was, not a half mile away, all but in her gunsights. She wanted him dead so bad she could taste it. Her eyes teared from emotion and the wind as she rose and fell in the saddle with the movement of her horse, keeping up with the posse and then some.

She loved her father, and this damn bastard was going to pay with blood for what he did!

Chapter 14

Noose whirled in his saddle at the sound of gunshots, bent in pain on his horse. To his rear, less than a mile off, he saw the wall of dust of the many riders tearing toward him out of the distance. He cussed. The bastards were onto him and they were moving like stink. *"Yee-ah!"* The big cowboy spurred his horse and galloped away as fast as his bronze stallion would ride across the bluffs.

On the horizon of the vast Wyoming vista, there was the tiny figure of the fleeing cowboy on the right, the cluster of pursuing gang on the left — two trails of dust, a small one and a big one, with space closing between them.

Clinging tight to the reins and saddle with his strong muscular arms and legs, Noose kept his eyes trained on the narrow, treacherous trail ahead. His horse was doing a good job negotiating the ragged switchback at the speed it was going. Damned if the steed didn't seem to be enjoying the chase. Copper was a stroke of luck in his favor as long as the gutsy damn stallion didn't get shot out from under him. The bullets coming in steady popping fusillades were wasted, not reaching him yet because his distance was too far from the shooters. Noose didn't need to look back to know space was closing and wouldn't look until the rounds were whistling past his ears. Noose figured that a man like Butler ought to know better than to waste ammo, so that had to mean he was trying to put on a big show, but for whom? As the cowboy leaned tighter into the charging horse, he swung his head left and right to check his options and quickly saw there were none: no place anywhere nearby to seek cover and dig in and pick a few of his pursuers off — just sheer ninety-degree granite face to his left, and to his right, a straight-down drop off the crevasse into the turbulent stretch of the Snake River, an unseen distance below. The cowboy drove his horse hard and rode for his life across the narrow, craggy canyon ridge. Noose charged relentlessly forward on Copper's broad back with the full knowledge they were in plain view of the Butler Gang, but for the moment there was no direction to go but straight.

Right up until they ran out of trail.

Suddenly the ground just dropped away.

"Whoa!" Noose vigorously pulled back on the reins of his horse just in time to stop its skidding hooves from plummeting over the edge of a dizzying hundred-foot ravine into the raging fork of the river.

Man and horse reeled on the stallion's dancing legs before a brink of canyon wall where the trail abruptly ended with the cessation of any solid ground. On any other occasion this majestic scenic view of a grand expanse of the great river rolling below might have been cause for admiration but now Noose stared around him in denuded desperation — nothing but the edge of the cliff lay ahead while directly behind the mushroom cloud of dust the advancing bounty killers made was now visible on the trail to the rear. The marauders were on him less than a quarter mile off and barely a minute away.

There was no choice.

Peering fiercely over the edge of the cliff, Noose eyed a perilous drop straight down into the boiling white water of the Snake River fork. With the blinding sunlight glinting off the sprays of surging froth, he had no way of telling how deep that water was at this junction or how close to the surface the big rocks surely beneath were. *Reckon I'm gonna find out right this damn second,* the cowboy thought.

"Sometimes a man's got to do what a man ought absolutely not *never* do," Joe Noose hollered. "Let's go swimming, boy! Go!"

He spurred Copper.

The horse was not stupid.

It did not budge.

"Go!" Noose spurred it again, hard. Copper reared and shied. Noose swung a look back over his shoulder, trying to wrangle the recalcitrant if sensible stallion. Now Noose could clearly make out the figures — nine, by his count — of the bounty killers. A thought came and went through his mind . . . *Nine? Hadn't he killed four of them?* Muzzle flashes bloomed in the oncoming cloud of billowing dust. Explosive ricochets rebounded and caromed off the granite of the rock ridge, showering his face with stone chips. Bullets *whined* past his ears. The air grew hazy and rank with the tang of cordite and gun smoke.

"Go!"

He took out his pistol and fired it near the horse's ear.

That did the trick.

The horse leapt.

Copper jumped off the cliff. Noose

hugged the saddle as the huge animal dropped through dead air, legs bicycling, head whipping to and fro, eyes wide with terror. Wind flapped the cowboy's clothes. His view was a spinning blur of sunlight and blue water. As the plummeting stallion's center of gravity began to shift, Noose felt the horse beginning to turn over during the plunge, meaning he would likely land beneath it — the cowboy prayed all the way down the water was deep and not shallow rocks whose impact would crush him beneath Copper's dead weight, for the stallion would die in the fall, too. Man and horse fell for what seemed forever until at last the river rushed up to meet them.

The impact came wet and cold but soft.

Noose and Copper hit deep water with a colossal splash, showering spray fifteen feet into the air. The cowboy was still astride the horse as both of them sank. The velocity of their dive and mass of their combined weight dragged them down under the river. His shoulder bullet hole screamed in searing white agony from the impact before the ice-cold water blessedly numbed it some. The cowboy was wrenched off his saddle. They sunk deep below the surface into the frigid current's propellant grip and got carried along with it. Noose managed to seize the reins as he and Copper were brutally swept downstream in the raging white-water rapids.

Still fully submerged beneath the fast-moving river, Noose saw he and the horse were moving in slow motion below the glassy roof of the water's surface glinting above with crenulated shards of sunlight slashing through the brackish murk. Copper's powerful legs ran uselessly in place, air bubbles from its nostrils joining Noose's in a column of cavitation rising up. Noose began to feel his lungs strain for want of air and felt sure the horse needed to breathe soon. The panic and disorientation in Copper's eyes was plainly visible.

It was good to stay down as long as they could, Noose knew — the cowboy could feel the mighty Snake carrying them swiftly away from their pursuers and putting distance between the men above on the cliff probably already taking aim on the river in anticipation of when Noose resurfaced. *Stay down. Stay down.* The cowboy gripped the reins and the saddle, hugging his body to the writhing, pawing horse as they traveled along with the river. They were safe below, but couldn't stay down much longer. It had already been a ten count and they were out of air. Looking over to Copper's face wreathed in the kelplike curtain of its own wet withers, Noose saw the stallion's glazed bulging eyes and knew it was drowning.

Time to go up and just hope to God they were out of range of the Butler Gang's guns.

Joe Noose started kicking his legs upward and tugging up on Copper's saddle, guiding the stallion toward the surface, ascending with it through brightening water until at last they broke into the open air in twin splashes of water, both man and horse gasping desperately for breath and filling their lungs with the glorious Wyoming high-altitude oxygen that had never felt or smelled so damn good.

As he looked up through the frigid water slapping his face, Noose saw the tiny stick figures of the posse appear at the high cliff edge, swiftly shrinking in size as they fell away behind.

Then he was just hanging on to his saddle horn for dear life, trying not to drown.

CHAPTER 15

Frank Butler halted his men at the edge of the cliffs. He took out his rifle, socked it to his shoulder, and fired round after round at the tiny figure of Noose as the man and his horse were swept around a bend in the river and disappeared from sight.

Lowering his gun, the fearsomely glowering leader spat bitterly. "Son of a bitch is outta range. We just missed 'im." A trace of spittle hung from his black handlebar mustache.

Bess felt a flash of panic and disappointment that the man she wanted dead got away again. But though she didn't admit it to herself, she secretly admired his sheer guts and the raw nerve it took to jump his horse off the cliff in a Hail Mary. Wind blew a gust of the foul body odor and unwashed stench of the possemen surrounding her that made her gag and nearly keel over. It was a smell of decaying meat and excrement. She put her hand over her mouth and nose.

The leader saddle-holstered his rifle and shot his gang a fierce hooded glance. "We're goin' after him."

"How?" Trumbull sputtered. "There ain't no trail!"

"We do what he done. We jump."

Lawson turned pale. "It's a hundred feet down. We'll be smashed to pieces."

"He warn't," Butler retorted, angrier by the minute.

"He was lucky, is what he was!" Weed whined.

Butler became livid and the veins bulged in his neck as spittle frothed his lips. "He's gettin' away! The money's *that way,* you gutless cowards!"

Bess felt her stomach clench, knowing what was coming even if the men, who knew their boss better than she did, did not. Getting a peek over the edge of the cliff, the female marshal began to make some quick mental calculations. Her hips squared in her saddle to get good balance and making sure her boots were secure in the stirrups, she took off her hat and clutched it tightly in her fist, gripping the reins so she didn't lose it in what was about to transpire.

"My ass ain't worth no hundred thousand

dollars," Culhane shouted, shaking his head like a wet dog.

Frank Butler thought a moment. He rode his horse back a few yards, putting the other seven bounty killers between him and the cliff.

He grinned savagely and said, "You got that right."

Quick-drawing both Colt Dragoon pistols, Butler fired straight up into the air over the heads of his gangs' horses: *Boom! Boom!* The startled bounty killers were so rattled at being shot at they rode around in circles but there was no room on the narrow switchback to do that. The panicked horses collided and reared. They had nowhere to go but off the edge of the cliff into the Snake River.

And over they went.

One by one, some at the same time, eight horses leapt or tripped or fell from the precipice. Some of the terrified bounty killers stayed in the saddles while others came off and somersaulted through the dead air, arms and legs grabbing and snatching at empty space. The first eight horses and riders plunged together in pell-mell, topsy-turvy formation until at last they struck the water with an explosive splash that sent a great fountain of spray fifty yards in all directions.

Bess went along with them, thinking the whole time down how thankful she was the dirty sons of bitches were going to get a bath.

As the female marshal plummeted, already securely planted in the saddle and stirrups, having anticipated the jump seconds before, she happened to look up.

Up on the cliff, Butler dug his spurs into his big onyx horse so hard they drew blood.

The stallion jumped over the cliff.

Above Bess, the huge figure of Frank Butler's black horse blotted out the sun in the overhead sky like a fearsome shadow of a monstrous vulture as it leapt off the edge — the leader was the last to jump but he did not hesitate nor did his ferocious horse.

Frank Butler clung to his saddle as his horse dropped through dead air. Down, down, toward the river.

He hit.

They all hit.

Everyone went into the river.

The Snake River surface was one tangled knot of horse and human arms and legs and asses and elbows bobbing above and below the surface in a chaotic aquatic maelstrom of confusion. A deafening cacophony of shouting and cussing and whinnying was almost but not quite drowned out by the thundering clamor of the river itself.

The two who were first in the saddle were the pair who never left their saddles in the first place: Frank Butler and Bess Sugarland were good riders who had taken the plunge in complete control of their horses and faculties, landing them hooves first in the drink with little fuss. Damned if while renegotiating his grip on his reins shoulder deep in the Snake, Butler didn't shoot Bess an admiring wink, she saw. *It struck her then the deadly killer was enjoying all this the way he enjoyed mayhem in general, for the simple reason it was when his kind of man felt most alive.*

In a single smooth movement in the water, Butler got out of the saddle and drew his gun, his other arm hanging on to his big black stallion as he was carried downriver alongside the others. Some of the bounty killers were flailing around up to their necks in the cold water. The nine riders were all swept swiftly downstream by the powerful current. The ones who stayed on their horses dismounted and gripped their saddles, riding along with their stallions. The ones who fell off, desperately tried to get back on their horses in the rough white water.

"I can't swim!" squealed Culhane like a drowning rat.

"Then hang on to your saddle good and tight!" the leader barked pitilessly.

As he floated, Butler helped Sharpless and Trumbull onto their horses, yelling over the roar of the rapids, "Keep your eyes peeled, boys!" The leader kept his pistol drawn and clung to his saddle, his bullet eyes searching the cliffs and shoreline above and around him.

Despite a lot of sputtering and water spitting, the floating posse had settled down some now they all had their drifting horses in hand and were keeping their heads above water . . . it was almost tranquil — like a holiday river outing except with a lot of guns.

One gun close by was dry.

Joe Noose stared down the gunsight of his Winchester rifle, drawing a bead on the rushing river and the heads of the men and horses coming around the bend. He levered the handle with a *ker-chack,* then was loaded and locked down.

A soaked Noose was crouched on a small ridge just above the river. His drenched horse was tethered beside him. Noose took careful aim with his rifle on the men in the river. "Fish in a barrel." He grinned with savage satisfaction. "Come 'n get it."

The crosshairs found a bead on the bobbing head of Frank Butler as it popped up and down in the white water.

Noose's finger closed on the trigger.

Pa-kow!

The shot boomed in a loud ringing echo amplified by the canyon walls.

A bloody flower erupted in Butler's arm. The water turned red. He grit his teeth in pain and aimed his pistol madly. *"He's up there, boys! Shoot him!"*

The bounty killers, struggling and deafened in the raging river, heard neither their leader nor the shot. Butler fired up onto the ridge.

The bullet ricocheted near Noose's head. He opened fire on the trapped bounty killers with his Winchester as they were swept past him in the river below. Cranking the lever fast, again and again, he unleashed lead mercilessly.

Weed was hit between the eyes. His limp corpse drifted away from his horse and was dashed against the rocks. His skull cracked like an egg, spilling his brains like red yolk.

Garrity was shot in the leg and dragged underwater.

Wingo was shot twice in the arm. Screaming in pain, he struggled to retain his grip

113

on his horse.

By now, the gang had all realized what was happening and the terrible danger they were in, busily grabbing rifles and pistols from body and saddle holsters. The river exploded with fusillades of gunfire and muzzle flashes as the floating shootists fired blindly in all directions on either shoreline. Their swimming horses panicked, unable to run or escape, trapped in the currents and treading water trying to keep their heads above the surface.

Bess's beautifully alarmed face swept one way then the other as she drew her pistol with one hand and gripped the saddle with the other. Wiping the wet strands of hair out of her eyes on her dripping face with the back of her gun hand, she scanned the rocks above, seeing nothing but the raging river. Around her was utter chaos.

As the bounty hunters bore witness to the water turning red all around them, they got the grim picture and set to business, employing their fearsome tradecraft as shootists. Clenching their guns, using their half-submerged saddles to level their aim, the gang blasted bullets into the surrounding cliffs in a relentless barrage, laying down a wall of suppressing fire. Hordes of heavy-caliber slugs ricocheted off the cliffs in clusters of sparks and rebounded back at them. Staccato strings of gunfire shot up from the river like a floating fireworks show. Noose's bullets exploded in geysers of water around their heads. A horse was killed and floated away. Butler alone got off surgical shots at the man on the ridge. The air was filled with screams, shots, ricochets, and always the omnipresent thundering surge of the great river.

Noose grabbed another rifle, this time a Henry, and blasted away. A bullet exploded off a rock by his ear. He wiped the dust out of his eyes and reloaded.

Just as the bounty killers were swept out of sight around a bend.

Noose rose and got to his wet horse. He and the animal were getting along just fine despite being newly acquainted and what he'd put the stallion through. Saddling up, he rode out along a narrow trail. Noose urged his horse along the path. He checked his diminishing supply of ammunition.

"Less than thirty rounds left, boy." he muttered to his horse but mostly to himself. "And there's still a lot more of them than there is o' me."

Unnerved and tired, Joe Noose reloaded his irons and headed on.

Due northwest, toward Jackson Hole.

Frank Butler and his gang rode out of the Snake River at a low point, soaked with water and blood. They stumbled with their horses over treacherous ground and struggled back into their saddles. Bess was one of the first back on her horse, and she could see the gang was in a foul temper. They were one less. With much groaning and grumbling and cursing, the drenched gang of killers fell into step behind their leader as he rode in the direction of the Teton mountain range that loomed over all.

Trumbull rode up alongside his boss. He took a swig of whiskey and offered the bottle. Butler just stared straight ahead.

"Us boys been talking," Trumbull said.

Garrity cleared his throat. "This stud is tougher than he looks, boss."

"We already lost five men," whined Lawson.

"Maybe this ain't a good idea, is what we're saying," Wingo said louder than he should have.

Butler's eyes clouded. Then they focused like a gunsight on Wingo. "Hundred thousand split seven ways is a lot of money," Butler said, and pulled up his horse. He turned it to face the six of his gang who were confronting him. "Course, a hundred thousand split six ways is even more for each."

The bounty killers exchanged confused glances.

"Ain't that right, Garrity?"

Garrity swallowed. He saw Butler's hand resting on his holster. "Reckon, but —"

"And I figure a hundred thousand split four ways is even more. Right, Lawson?"

Lawson eyed his fellow bounty hunters like a cornered rat. "Sure."

"Wouldn't you agree, Trumbull?

Butler shot Trumbull a brutal look. The gunman swallowed and nodded, eyeing the rest.

"And split two ways, that's even more money. Ain't that right, Wingo?"

Wingo nodded, mouth dry.

The leader's hand, gloved for fanning and firing quick-draw work, hovered over the holstered stock of his Colt. "But the most money is a hundred thousand dollars split one way." Butler's hand was now on his gun. He eyed his gang with psychotic fury. Wingo's saddle turned wet as he pissed himself. The bounty hunters withered under the brute force of their leader's murderous gaze. Then Butler cracked a slow, skull-faced smile. "But it's only money. Right, boys?"

His gang cracked up in hysterical nervous laughter.

"Only money," said Garrity.

"Just a lot of stupid money," agreed Trumbull.

"It don't buy you love." Butler's eyes were flat.

He gritted his teeth and the words were a hiss.

"Nobody quits."

Butler spurred his horse. "Now *ride!*"

The intimidated bounty hunters kept a fast clip behind their obsessed boss.

CHAPTER 16

Minutes later the chase was on again.

Joe Noose had gotten out of the Snake River on the eastern bank and had been riding sharply northeast, knowing the bounty killers in the river would soon be washed north of him — he was going to have to cut cross-country for now. The cowboy had no real idea where the hell he was, just a general notion of the area, but the north-flowing Snake turned hard east about fifteen miles ahead at Hoback Junction — that, he knew. By any sensible reckoning, those of the Butler Gang still ambulatory would pull themselves out of the water long before Hoback. Landscape permitting, Noose figured if he rode ten miles east, he could turn north and reconnect with the Snake, following it into Jackson, thereby hopefully avoiding his pursuers. Copper was galloping at a good clip, displaying admirable stamina. Noose would have paid good money for a horse like this but he'd gotten it for free, though Copper's previous owner had parted with the stallion at quite a cost. There was no trail, but the terrain was flat and solid hardpack, easy for the horse to traverse. Cyclopean clouds created an awesome vista in the vast Wyoming sky. The steady drone of insects in the fields was soothing to the ear, there was not another human being in sight, and Noose was feeling safe. But he had not made it half a mile, confident he bought himself an hour or two of lead time after blowing the hell out of the posse in the river, when the first bullet buzzed past his ear.

Swinging his head over his shoulder, Noose tossed a look behind him to face the unwelcome sight of men and horses hot on his tail, a lot of guns shooting in his direction, spitting off smoke and flashes. Even from the short glance, even at a sizable distance, he could see all of the men were very wet. Bullets screamed past on either side, blowing off chunks of clustered dirt near Copper's hooves. The fast stallion needed no spur to encourage it to hurry its pace as it lunged forward, charging ahead with everything it had.

Noose galloped across the huge landscape, a lone rider on his horse. The vast terrain was one big empty. The seven-man posse and the lawman rode in single-file formation in relentless pursuit across the breaks. A long trail of dust kicked up from their hooves' cleaves like a blade across the barren tundra. The lone hard-charging figure of the fleeing cowboy shot like a bullet across the valley, a smoke cloud of dust to his rear from the oncoming posse.

Noose rode up a steep hill into the woods.

Moments later, the gang appeared.

Pa-kow! Pow! Blam!

Shots rang out from the upper elevation where Noose had taken position.

Butler swung his arm with his rifle, ordering his men to seek cover. *"He's up there! Get down! Over there!"* All of the posse rode their horses into a wash and dismounted, crouching below the rocks. Nobody was hit, but the bullets kicked up the dirt very close. The bounty killers traded fire over the edge of the rise. Bess stayed tight beside them, reloading her pistol, Whatever she thought of these men, she felt safe in their company when the bullets were flying.

From somewhere behind the trees above the wash, Noose's voice boomed down at them. *"You boys had enough yet?"*

"Why don't you just lie down and die?" Butler shouted back, chambering a round.

"You can kiss my ass!" the hunted man's voice roared back. *"Tell you boys what I'm gonna do! Listen good! I'm gonna kill all of you and get the reward for killing the men who murdered the marshal and come out of this thing rich!"*

Butler's cynical laughter rang out through the ravine. He had one cautious eye on Bess, who crouched with them. *"That'll be a good trick!"* the leader shouted back. *"There's seven witnesses saw you shoot him, you lyin' sonofabitch!"*

The posse huddled in the low ground as their quarry's bullets came steadily at them, intermittent but lethally aimed — Noose had them pinned down and there was no getting away from his fierce, persuasive voice. *"You know you killed him, Butler, you murderin' bastard, 'n you framed me for the reward and you're gonna swing for it!"*

The female marshal looked perplexed. Sudden doubt shook her. Bess looked over at the leader. "What the hell's he talking about?"

Butler looked uneasy, she noticed, and so did the other men, judging by their shifty gazes. "He's just talking a lot of crap, Marshal."

Noose went on, his disembodied voice

somehow omnipotent and inescapable. *"You killed that man Barrow after I brought him in alive to steal the bounty and when I told the marshal the truth you murdered him just to get that big reward put on my head and it's all a lie! It's dirty money and dirty money you ain't gonna get!"*

Listening to all this, Bess wondered if it was the truth. *Why would this man lie at this point, make up some story to holler at the posse? He didn't know the law was riding with the gang. What would he have to gain by spinning this yarn?* Those no-accounts were giving her the stink eye and she could smell their guilt and fear by pure female intuition. Something wasn't right. But she couldn't be sure. Not yet. She had to play this out.

"I'm making you a one-time offer, boys! I'm speaking to your men now, Butler!" Noose's rough voice shouted, echoing through the woods. *"Any of you walks away right now, I'll let you live! You all know it was your boss man Frank Butler killed the marshal and the barman! Hell, for all I know, it was him killed Barrow! Walk away and I'll let you keep breathing! It's Butler I want! Reward's the same for one head as seven for the marshal so makes no difference to me. This is a one-time offer! I best believe you better take it before I change my mind!"*

The balls on that man, mused Bess.

Butler leapt up and boldly waited for the puff of smoke in the trees above before firing three shots into the position he had just gotten a fix on. *"There's still seven of us to one of you!"*

"I count right!" Noose tauntingly called back from his place of concealment. *"Hell, I got more bullets than the rest of you put together!"*

Huddling with her rifle, the marshal studied the bounty killers and saw that Noose's words were definitely getting to them, and their leader saw it, too. They had a chink in their armor. Noose was getting in their heads.

Something was wrong here. Something definitely stunk about this whole entire situation.

And suddenly, a bad fear shot through her.

Butler gestured to Trumbull to move out. "I'll keep him talking. Get his ass."

Drawing two razor-sharp bowie knives, Trumbull loped off like a wolf out of the wash. Bess had her heart in her throat as she watched him move silently into the trees, following the sound of Noose's voice.

Fifteen minutes transpired before Trumbull came out of the woods empty-handed, a black look on his face as he shook his head side to side. Bess didn't hear him speak, but the meaning was clear.

Noose was in the wind.

CHAPTER 17

Marshal Jack Mackenzie stood by the window of the Jackson Hole U.S. Marshal's office looking out at the distant mountain range toward Hoback, thinking about the twelve bounty hunters chasing down Joe Noose and remembering he hadn't liked those men when he'd met them a week ago. Those boys had the smell of homicide all over them.

Mackenzie thought back to a week before when Frank Butler and his gang of shootists had brought Bonny Kate Valance to town and delivered her to the U.S. Marshal's office for the reward.

It had been a quiet morning and the old man had been sitting at his desk filing warrants when he heard a woman's voice cussing and hollering and carrying on out in the street, so he had grabbed his pistol and gone outside to see what the hell all the commotion was.

The twelve-man gang had ridden straight up Broadway, looking like an invading force of marauders: heavily-armed big, dangerous men wearing dusters and hats set astride strong horses that looked like they didn't shy from gunfire. People were getting off the street, fast. A thirteenth horse was escorted in between them. And that was the first time Marshal Mackenzie laid eyes on Bonny Kate Valance.

She was roped like a prize hog, tied over the saddle on her stomach, her face covered by long red hair of the brightest shade he had ever seen. The woman had stopped hollering because at that moment one of the gang had stuffed a gag in her mouth, which only made the hellion wildcat struggle and thrash about even more. She was dressed in worn denim trousers and a work shirt but her shapely form was apparent. Bonny Kate's face was flushed bright red with rage and her eyes bulged with a crazy fury. The woman was beautiful to begin with but with her blood up and high color, she was positively astonishing to look at. Mackenzie thought he had never seen in the flesh as primal a female force of nature as this woman was.

Thinking he'd picked a hell of a time to send his deputy Nolan Swallows on an errand across town, Mackenzie had been about to grab a rifle and deal with this army of ruffians holding a helpless female captive when he recognized the unmistakable face of the lady he had seen on a good many wanted posters the last few years. Recognizing who she was, the marshal realized these men were bounty hunters who had captured the notorious outlaw Bonny Kate Valance and were bringing her in for the reward.

The posse stopped their huge horses directly in front of the marshal's office and the leader of the gang looked up at Mackenzie from his saddle and doffed his big Stetson with a respectful nod, fixing him with eyes as dark as night above a black handlebar mustache. "Good afternoon, sir. I'm Frank Butler," he drawled. "These are my men. We caught Bonny Kate Valance and brung her here for the reward. That's the merchandise back there on the horse."

Butler had taken a folded wanted poster out of his duster and proffered it: the sketch was clearly the bound and gagged woman hog-tied on the horse behind him. The handbill read in bold block print letters:

WANTED.
FIFTY THOUSAND DOLLARS
For the Capture of Outlaw
BONNY KATE VALANCE
For the Crimes of
MURDER, ROBBERY, ARSON, ASSAULT.

In a smaller font it read:

CAPTURE ALIVE.
Deliver Only to Local
U.S. Marshal's Office.
approach with extreme caution.
Fugitive Is Armed and Highly Dangerous.

Giving the gang a hard once over, Marshal Mackenzie just grunted. "Looks like it took twelve grown men to capture one little lady."

"That it did, Marshal." Butler grinned. "We're ready to turn her over to you at your pleasure. Then we'd be grateful if you could get that reward authorized so we can be on our way."

The old lawman nodded. "First, let's get Miss Valance locked up. We have a cell inside the office here. You boys get her off that horse and bring her inside and we'll get her behind bars where she belongs. Then you can sign the paperwork for her and I'll authorize that reward. How's that sound, Mr. Butler?"

"Agreeable, Marshal." Butler rotated his head like a gun turret and shot a glance back at the scurvy band of cutthroats he had riding with him. "Get this trollop off the horse and haul her into the marshal's office so he can jail her pretty behind. I want guns on her until the marshal locks her cell with his key. Watch this bitch. She's tricky. You men know the drill with her." The leader swung out of his saddle and tethered his horse to the rail in one smooth, muscular move.

Mackenzie watched from the office porch, quietly impressed by the professional precision and coordination this large posse of bounty hunters operated with, making them like a well-oiled machine; the other eleven men dismounted in unison, boots sledge-hammering the ground on landing as four swiftly drew Colt Navy and Peacemaker pistols from their holsters and pressed the muzzles against Bonny Kate's forest of red tresses as three other men used big knives to cut the ropes.

A crowd of Jackson Hole pedestrians was gathering around now, and twenty-five locals stood watching the prisoner handoff. Whispers passed like a lit fuse on a stick of dynamite through the crowd as they recognized the infamous woman outlaw.

Frank Butler slid out his Colt Dragoon and rotated the cylinder with as fearsome a rattle as any snake ever made as he slowly walked up to his captive and glared at her with hooded eyes. "Remember, woman. Only reason you ain't dead slumped over that saddle is the reward for you is delivered alive. Would have saved me fuss handing you over as a corpse even at a discount. But you was just delivered alive to the U.S. Marshal's office, cut and dried and in front of witnesses, so if you do anything to make us kill you at this point we still get paid either way. Point being this: don't test me." Still face forward, four guns against her head, Bonny Kate just watched him blankly.

"How about you take that gag off her now?" Mackenzie said from the porch.

"I would not recommend that, Marshal. The lady has a dirty mouth on her and nothing to say you want to hear." Butler swept his hand at the crowd of disapproving ladies in the crowd of rubberneckers. "Nor fit for the ears of polite society." The female outlaw's eyes were red-hot coals staring over the gag at his face. Her face was the color of fresh strawberries.

"This is Jackson Hole, not Tombstone nor Dodge City, and we don't treat prisoners in our civilized town that way. Untie her. Ungag her. Do it now. That's an order." Mackenzie took a hard tone.

"Have it your way." Butler tore off Bonny Kate's gag.

She spat in his face.

"You bastard!" the woman screamed now her mouth was untethered. Gasps and a few titters of laughter rose up from the crowd of onlookers. The pistols aimed at Bonny Kate's head got cocked back in unison by their handlers. The laughing stopped abruptly and there were more gasps from the locals, because watching a women get her head shot off became a distinct possibility.

Butler wiped the saliva off his face with a mean smile but dead eyes. "That's as close as I ever want to come in this lifetime to tastin' a kiss from you, Bonny Kate Valance." He nodded to his boys. "Cut her loose. Keep her covered. Get her inside. Let's get paid."

Twisting her arms behind her back hard enough to strain the joints in her shoulder sockets, two of the bounty hunters slashed off the ropes on her bound legs and wrists. Jamming rifles and pistols in her back, the shootists force-marched Bonny Kate Valance up the stairs onto the porch with her cussing and cursing them to hell and gone the whole time. "I'm innocent, Goddammit! I didn't do none of what they say I did! I'm an honest God-fearing, good woman and you can't treat me like this! You filthy heathens are all going to hell! Took all twelve of you to get me, it did! I'm more man than any of you are! Get your dirty hands off me! Help! Somebody, help!"

Standing at the door as the hulking gang of gunmen shoved their prisoner inside the office, Marshal Mackenzie and Frank Butler exchanged forbearing glances as they followed last and closed the door behind them.

In the crowd, lips flapped like flocks of ducks. All anyone standing outside could talk about was how at long last the notorious outlaw Bonny Kate Valance, the most dangerous woman in the West, had been apprehended and was being held prisoner in their town!

"Now shut up," Marshal Jack Mackenzie said as he eased Bonny Kate Valance out of the fierce grip of the armed bounty hunters and ushered her into the cell. The small but solid iron cage in the corner of the room was built to hold two. Once she was inside, he stood in the doorway and unholstered his revolver. Still staring straight at the infamous lady outlaw, Mackenzie said quietly, "You men can put those irons away now."

"Stand down," Butler told his men firmly, and they reholstered their pistols and lowered their rifle barrels.

"I have to pat you down for weapons." Mackenzie snapped his gaze back to Bonny Kate. He took one look at the soft curves filling out his guest's blue jeans and button shirt and swallowed hard. His face was coloring with embarrassment. "It's U.S. Marshal regulation when we lock somebody in one of our cells. I can do it or I can ask Mr. Butler here, but I think you would prefer somebody more professional."

"Be my guest," Bonny Kate, with a saucy smirk, said to the lawman.

With a sharp intake of breath, Mackenzie stepped into the cell with Bonny Kate. "Sorry, ma'am," he said. "Spread your arms and legs, please." The marshal did a brisk, professional pat-down of her armpits, bosom, belt of her trousers, butt, crotch, each leg, ankles, and boots. The woman submitted, nonplussed and unoffended. Looking very relieved to be finished, his face slick with sweaty embarrassment, the marshal stood and nodded at his prisoner. "You're clean."

That brought a smile to her lips.

Mackenzie left the cell. "Step back," the marshal said, and the lady outlaw retreated three steps as Mackenzie closed the cell door and turned his key in the lock.

"Let's get you boys out of here," the marshal said to Frank Butler and his men, who stuffed the confines of the lawman's office like buzzards in a gulch, filling it with malignance. Mackenzie took a seat at his desk and opened a file cabinet, pulling out a reward requisition form. The gang stood patiently, not saying a word, as the marshal took out his pen and began scribbling information on the sheet, including the name of the felon brought in for the reward, the time and place it happened, and his own name and office information. The process took about five minutes and during that time there was not a jingle of spur or creak of leather from the posse, so still they stood. Finally, Mackenzie looked up and lifted the paper. "Okay, boys. Last thing we need are all your signatures at the bottom here, all of you who are claiming the reward."

"You boys go first." Frank Butler had walked several paces to the big board with the reward notice handbills pinned up. Mackenzie could see he was studying the one for a bank robber named Jim Henry Barrow.

In turn, the bounty hunters walked up and

signed their name on the official reward requisition form. A few seemed to be having a problem writing their own name. "Any of you boys don't got a proper signature, an *X* will do," the marshal told them to their visible relief.

"This bank robber Barrow has a thousand-dollar reward, dead or alive, it says," Butler stated, his back to the lawman as he regarded the poster.

"That's what it says," Mackenzie replied.

"Says here he was last seen making off for the Hoback area. That's 'bout thirty miles due south of here, right?"

"Yes, it is. It's the jurisdiction of my counterpart, Marshal Sugarland." Mackenzie did not care to bandy words with obvious brute killers like these men, especially their leader, who looked to be the worst of the bunch, but the man was a dog with a bone.

"Being as we're here, and my boys and I are presently unemployed, so to speak, think we might go on after this Barrow fellow."

"Well, you're a little late, Mr. Butler."

At this, Butler turned to face Mackenzie, and his eyes had that hooded look back again. "He been caught, you mean?"

"Will be. What I mean is another bounty hunter named Joe Noose checked into my office a day ago and is already hunting Barrow. He's worked with our office before and he always gets his man."

The last bounty hunter scratched his name on the reward requisition form and a silence descended on the room. There was a tambourine metallic chime of spurs as Frank Butler crossed to Mackenzie's desk, bent at the waist like a gentleman, and signed his name.

The marshal glanced at the ornate cursive of the signature and was surprised at the elegance of the penmanship. This was an educated man who was kin but not kind to the mad-dog killers he had riding with him; someone who projected an air of intelligence and cunning far superior to his minions. The marshal got the distinct impression Butler came from a different gene pool altogether — an enigmatic, mysterious, and highly dangerous background Mackenzie couldn't guess and didn't want to. The leader of the gang set down the pen respectfully and plucked up the requisition form in his gloved fingers. He spoke with a calm and eloquent formality to his drawl as he said to the marshal evenly, "My understanding is if this other bounty hunter hasn't caught his man yet he can't lay claim to the reward and it remains an open bounty."

"You understand correct, sir."

"Then my boys and I intend to go after it. The reward is dead or alive, correct?"

"Correct. You may take that reward requisition form in your hand to Jackson Savings & Loan just down the street and they will cash it for you and give you your money."

"Much obliged." Butler tipped his hat and he and his gang departed.

When Butler was halfway out the door Mackenzie stopped him by saying, "We prefer alive."

"Of course you do," Frank Butler retorted as he departed.

Not much later, after as much time as it would take to stop at a bank, there was a loud martial thunder of horses' hooves that swiftly faded south toward Hoback, and the men were gone.

It was the last Marshal Mackenzie had seen or heard of these bounty hunters, men he would characterize more as bounty killers, until the telegraph came from Hoback requesting authorization for the reward for the murdered marshal Sugarland. Mackenzie didn't like Butler or his gang then and he liked them less now with each passing hour, knowing they were out there,

knowing there was some bad business going
on.

Those boys were just wrong.

CHAPTER 18

"Where's your mother?"

Bess looked over, surprised, to Butler, who she saw had fallen back and was riding beside her. His head was tilted as he regarded her with interest in his hard eyes that, she now saw, were such a dark shade of brown they only appeared black.

"She passed when I was six," Bess replied.

"I'm sorry," Butler said.

"Never really knew her."

"You father, God rest his soul, he raised you, then?"

"Yes, he did." Bess smiled sadly.

"Brothers? Sisters?"

She shook her head tightly. "Just me. And him."

"And he taught you the family business. Raised you to be a lawdog." He peered at her from under the brim of his black Stetson.

"It's what he knew." She shrugged.

The gang leader looked ahead and nodded to himself with approval. "I think that's good. A woman makes a fine lawman."

Frank Butler seemed a lot less threatening all of a sudden. Bess didn't want to admit it to herself but it felt good to talk to someone after all that had happened today and was still to happen. The big, hard man beside her gazed at her watchfully with a nonjudgmental regard. He radiated a forceful, implacable masculinity that she found oddly reassuring. He was easy to talk to when he wanted to be, it seemed. "I apologize for the manner of my men. They're not as socialized as they might be. These boys are a little rough around the edges, I admit. Spend most of their time out on the trail. But they're all good men and can be counted on. Handpicked them myself. We'll get your father's killer, that you can be sure of."

Bess just nodded. She thought about the five of the gang that had already been killed by the man accused of killing her father and decided not to mention that inconvenient detail. "Where do you and your boys come from?"

"All around," Butler replied.

"You work in Wyoming."

"We're manhunters, Marshal. We go where

the men we're after are. New Mexico. Utah. Arizona. California. Even Mexico. We've worked all those places."

"Anywhere there's a fat reward, you mean."

"It's our job. Somebody's got to do it."

"I suppose you're right."

"Some of the men we hunt, sometimes there's gangs of them and often they cross state and territorial lines. Local law can't follow and coordination with their counterparts is disorganized. That's where we come in. The men we hunt are often heavily armed and dangerous and don't think twice about killing women and children. The local law sometimes is simply plain outgunned. We're professionals. We hit what we aim at. And we always get our man." Butler sounded pretty damn sure of himself.

"Good to know." Bess meant it.

"This may be out of turn, Marshal, but I think your daddy would be proud of you."

"You're right," she said. He looked at her. "It is out of line."

"No offense, Marshal."

Butler rode on ahead.

The trail took a downward turn and widened out, the horses' hooves crunching on slippery rocks. A clatter of tumbling stones into the ravine made her stomach clench. Beneath her backside, the horse felt unsteady. Bess kept her eyes straight. Ahead, a high plateau loomed with arrowheads of pine trees like green lizard scales covering the skin of grass and granite. It was going to be a rough slow climb. Bess couldn't imagine how the fugitive Noose was staying ahead of them by escaping up this rugged terrain with a bullet in him. She couldn't help but wonder if the bounty killers were going in the wrong direction — a fast glance at the body language of Frank Butler, tall and confident in his saddle with the steady to-and-fro turns of his head almost ma-chinelike as his keen eyes swept the land-scape for sign of their quarry, calmed her doubts. The man was like a human blood-hound on a scent, his perseverance relent-less and his entire presence a little frighten-ing in its raw obsessiveness.

It was almost like this was personal.

Like it wasn't even about the money.

The rest of the pack of mercenaries were all about the money, though, she had no doubt of that. They smelled of murder and blood, a bad scent emanating from their rot-ten pores. Bess swung her gaze across the faces of the gang behind her, holding their stares when they met hers and not showing fear. She was protected by her badge, and these jackals would do her no harm.

She was a U.S. Marshal.

So why did she have to keep telling herself that?

CHAPTER 19

A week before in Jackson Hole, Deputy Nolan Swallows had been out running an errand for his boss, Marshal Jack Mackenzie, and had just left the gun store after buying a few boxes of .44 ammunition and dropping off two Henry rifles to be overhauled and have their sights checked. He hadn't been gone from the marshal's office thirty minutes and had been in the store half that time. The town of Jackson had been quiet and Broadway mostly empty when he went in the establishment but fifteen minutes later when he left, the same street was bustling with activity; the sidewalks were jammed with people and the air filled with urgency and excited talk, so the deputy immediately knew something big was happening in Jackson.

Whatever it is, Swallows thought, *word travels fast.*

The lean young lawman knew he better

get back to the office with all possible haste so he hurried with his parcel of bullets down the dirt street, dodging past horses and wagons as his sharp ears caught snippets of passing conversation from a few men.

"— in our own damn jail —"

"— hear she's twice as much of a looker than they say she was —"

"— Naked, I tell you! Had her bosoms hanging right out catching the breeze, was what Joe told me —"

More confused than ever, Swallows quickened his pace, turned the corner onto Pearl Street, and was greeted by a large crowd of local businessmen and shopkeepers leaving their stores and throwing up CLOSED signs as they joined a burgeoning crowd of pedestrians heading like a herd of steers toward the U.S. Marshal's office a half a block down.

When he heard the name, spat with venom and disgust by a passing woman, it dawned on Deputy Swallows what in fact was going on as he heard the loud voice of the female citizen. "Bonny Kate Valance! Right here in our good town! I don't care if she's going to be hanged, hanging's too good for the likes of her. What I want to know is why they brought her to Jackson in the first place and what she's doing here!"

A few local men not looking where they were going bumped into the deputy and jostled him. One of them, a bartender Swallows knew named Jim Peters, instantly apologized, then was tugging on Swallows's sleeve, pumping him for information.

"Deputy, is it true what they're saying?" the barman stammered. "You got the real Bonny Kate Valance in your jail?"

Deputy Swallows had left the office before Frank Butler and his gang rode up and delivered the prisoner for the reward so at present he knew nothing about any of this. Right now the deputy had no idea what anybody was talking about. Careful not to undercut his own authority by sounding like he didn't know something he ought to, Swallows simply gave his standard reply, "The marshal is straightening this all out and he'll let everyone know everything they need to when he's good and ready to 'cause he's the marshal and it ain't my place." With that, the junior lawman shouldered past the onlookers and moved on down the street.

Three minutes later, Swallows pushed through the crowd in front of the single-story building that housed the U.S. Marshal's office and there Jack Mackenzie was standing outside the door, his face red as he looked at his deputy, shook his head, and

147

quipped, "Well, Deputy, you got the worst case of bad timing in history, going out on an errand the last fifteen minutes. Close the door behind you and lock it, then I'll fill you in."

Right after Swallows was inside and had bolted the lock he saw the notorious outlaw Bonny Kate Valance in the flesh.

The deputy was tongue-tied, couldn't get a word out.

There she stood behind the bars of her cage, flaming fiery red hair tumbling like a mane around her shoulders, voluptuous figure beneath a work shirt and blue jeans, softly pressed against the bars of the cell while on her angelic healthy freckled face her heart-shaped lips were curled in something in between a smile and a sneer as her magnetic blue eyes fastened, then locked on the deputy's.

Swallows felt like his insides had just been turned inside out as his knees got weak and legs went numb. The legends and stories were true: the infamous renowned woman gunslinger and bank robber had all the raw, wild, untamed beauty and seductive charisma the legend said she did. Bonny Kate just stood, there more animalistic than ladylike, watching him with equal parts randy amusement, aloof detachment, and affable disregard. That the woman hadn't bathed in some time was apparent: weeks of sleeping outdoors were manifest from sullied layers of caked trail dirt, grubby saddle grime, and dried sweat smeared over the exposed soft skin of her face and hands. Yet lack of soap and water hurt Bonny Kate's looks not one bit, Swallows observed, for she was the rare woman who looked better dirty, as if it was supposed to be her natural state and cleaning her up would wash off the animal magnetism she so sensually radiated, and to do so would wipe away the natural endowments her clothes barely kept under wraps. And there was her perfume — Swallows could smell the female outlaw's pungent body odor from across the room, an arousing sweet musky lady funk that had the lawman breathing through his nose to better inhale her scent. Because of this powerful first impression Bonny Kate Valance made, Deputy Nolan Swallows had formed his opinion of her character in the brief five seconds he first set his gaze upon her.

That Bonny Kate was a savage.

The deputy decided she was the same as a jungle cat that belonged in the wilds, not a cage, and seeing Bonny Kate behind bars caused him regret until he realized those hungry eyes of hers now fastened to his had, like a jungle cat, the predatory sheen of killer instinct.

"Stop staring, Deputy, ain't you ever seen a dead woman before?"

"She don't look dead to me, Marshal."

That got a grin and guffaw from the prisoner. The deputy thought her teeth were the whitest he'd ever seen, even though they looked sharp. To Swallows, her short little laugh sounded like whiskey tasted or would sound if single malt made noise.

"Might as well be," Mackenzie said. "Her neck's gonna be swinging at the end of a rope in a month's time. First woman ever executed in this territory. That is a historical fact." Mackenzie sounded unimpressed with their famous prisoner but behaved with a professional equanimity. "Deputy Swallows, meet Bonny Kate Valance. Making history like she always has, right to the bitter end."

Swallows took off his hat. "Good afternoon, ma'am."

Bonny Kate actually curtsied, and the graceful gesture looked proper and genteel. "Every time of the day is good to me, Deputy, being as I only got thirty of 'em left, so they tell me," she retorted in her husky, honeyed voice. "That is, unless I can convince you two lawmen that what I have been saying all along is the truth, that I did not kill those men they say I done but I damn well know who did and can prove it, and the fact is, I am an innocent woman unjustly convicted and about to be wrongfully hanged!"

CHAPTER 20

Noose was getting more friendly with the horse he had dubbed Copper with each passing hour.

The cowboy took pains not to push the animal too hard, saving up its strength until he needed it, and never used his spurs on its scarred flanks.

The trail wended through hilly olive green and dun brown terrain steepled with verdant pine trees. For now the coast was clear. A monolithic barrier range of clouds formed jagged massifs in the vast slate blue sky overhead, blocking the sun so the air had cooled down.

Riding straight and tall in the saddle, Noose sat the horse well, patting it on the withers and chatting with it. The conversation was one-sided but didn't feel that way, because Copper would look back and shoot him a glance now and again to indicate he was listening and maybe even understood

— at least Noose liked to think he did. In a few minutes he would dismount and let Copper rest and drink from his canteen.

It was a great horse, tall and strong and muscular with a beautiful line to its back. But the months or years of violent maltreatment from the dead no-account prior owner had taken its toll on the brave piece of horseflesh. The first hours Noose rode Copper were difficult and he had expected the stallion was going to be a heap of trouble. The cowboy had felt the fear and tension braced in the stallion's clenched muscles between his own lower legs like the wary horse was expecting to be struck or hit at any moment. In those moments, Noose would hush it and pat it with his big, strong, gentle hands and the quivers inside the animal would cease and a longer and longer calm descended upon the steed.

Joe Noose was slowly gaining the horse's trust — a good thing because both of their lives depended on it: the murderous bounty killers on their tail would not hesitate to shoot horse or rider or both, depending on what was most expedient for them at that given moment; Noose knew he and Copper needed each other to survive. The funny thing was, the cowboy had begun to suspect the animal figured the same thing — he felt their growing bond intensify with each mile.

Copper was incredibly responsive to his every physical and verbal command; Noose had a hunch it had been an army cavalry quarter horse or at least begun life trained in a military stable, due to the fierce clockwork precision of Copper's movements. Farm horses just didn't act that way. Or might be the horse was just special.

Plus, there was a natural warmth and affection the bronze and gold stallion exuded, wholly unlike any army mount Noose had come into contact with. This horse had a big damn heart.

Now it had an owner who appreciated it.

Noose was going to never forgive himself if he got Copper shot or lamed or otherwise injured in the journey that lay ahead. If that came to pass, he would personally murder the son of a bitch that harmed his horse and make sure he hurt that man tenfold. Didn't matter whether it was right or wrong.

This horse had known suffering. Joe Noose knew his strong connection with Copper came from that, since he himself carried considerable hurt and pain beneath his tough exterior. Copper sensed it because horses are sensitive creatures. Always good with horses, Noose had been called a horse whisperer by some, and all true horse whisperers carried a lot of emotional scars around inside that the animals responded to from their own inner sensitivity. The connection was intimate and intricate. Both Noose and Copper were fine-tuned animals and each understood the other with an easy, natural communication.

The best part of riding Copper was Noose did not feel alone. Here, now, outnumbered and outgunned and hunted like an animal, the cowboy had every reason to feel isolated but the horse kept him company. He had a friend. A companion and a comrade he hoped to keep for a long, long time. It wasn't just his own life Noose worried for, it was Copper's. But Copper had his back, too. The worst part of being hunted down like a lone wolf was you felt so wretchedly solitary and insignificant, always trying to just save your own sorry skin. It made a man feel small, and his courage and strength shrank with that self-perception. When you felt responsible for something outside yourself, the need to protect it made you stronger. That's how Noose felt about this horse and he was feeling stronger than he had since this whole damn thing began.

As they rode along the crest of a ridge, Copper kept a strong vigorous pace, not needing to be rested or provisioned. Noose kept a semi-relaxed gait in the saddle, one hand on the reins, one hand clenching his Colt .45 — his head made a steady rotation, his gaze swinging from mountains to valley, then back again, repeatedly looking over his shoulder. Undulating drab green grassy slopes rose and fell like a woman's backside, the swells spiked with deep blue-green steeples of pines covering the mountains on either side like reptile scales.

Noose was wishing for trees.

Right now, he was riding in an open quarter-mile area with only the sky to cover him, exposed to sight and the line of fire of his enemies. He was starting to sweat as much from nerves as the heat and felt like a sitting duck. Trouble was, this was the way the trail led. He needed to get himself and his horse under some tree cover and fast.

To his left, the ground dropped off sharply into a granite gorge, so that wasn't going to do him any good. Two hundred yards northeast, to his right, there was a dense forest leading up a treacherous ravine too steep for Copper to climb, but if he could get inside the tree line his ass wouldn't be hanging out. Problem was, between the trail and those trees were piles of rocks and rubble, and the horse would have a hard time finding footing and could break a leg. They were between the hawk and the buzzard, as the saying went, but the trees were the only safe option so they had to try and take cover there.

Noose used his knees and reins, not his spurs, to steer Copper slowly and carefully off the path and toward the pines, and his horse's hooves left the trail and crunched over the rocks. The cowboy patted its neck and whispered reassuringly to his steed, and all the while his own eyes cut back and forth over the area and then to the ground to see where his mount was stepping. It was slow going, but they made safe progress and the wall of trees drew steadily closer — close enough to see that past the branches parts of the mountainside might be scalable on horseback after all.

His saddle felt wet and when Noose looked down, he saw a spreading crimson red stain in the browned leather. His bullet wound had opened and was beginning to smart again, but he put the pain out of his mind and kept a sharp lookout.

Looked over his shoulder at the trail behind.

Empty.

He shot a glance behind him again, saw nothing in the direction they'd be coming from, the only direction they could approach.

The tree line grew ever nearer. Copper's hooves skidded on the rocks with an unsettling abrasive sound, but it kept its balance and put its feet right, trotted evenly, and kept going steadily forward.

A damn good horse.

The hills were quiet but the killers were out there, Noose knew, and not far behind.

He just couldn't see them.

Maybe that meant they couldn't see him, either —

A bullet buzzed past his ear close enough to singe his scalp, the loud *crack* of the rifle reaching his ears an instant later.

— then again, maybe not!

All of a sudden, the shots were coming fast and close, just missing him, so the bounty killers had to be just out of range, a few hundred yards back.

Lips tightly compressed over gritted teeth, Noose cocked his pistol and twisted in the saddle, sending a stabbing pain through his midriff. Yes, they were coming from the direction he thought. There was movement and rustling in the trees a few hundred yards back up the trail and a second later, the seven bounty killers broke cover and charged out of the forest, guns blazing. They

158

were on him like flies on dung.

Whirling forward, Noose didn't even try to get off a shot — it would be a wasted bullet and lead he could scarce afford to spare at this distance. His hard gaze fixed forward, the cowboy focused all his attention on Copper, knowing now was the moment to use the time he had banked to get all the horse had to give. *"Yee-ahh!"* Noose shouted loud enough for the steed's respect but not loud enough to scare it, driving his legs but not his boots against the animal's flanks, galloping it forward and half-blind into the trees.

Branches and nests of twigs slapped his face, and the green curtain of pine brushed aside as the man and horse rode into the trees. Once inside the shady forest canopy, the ground appeared to go straight up — the steeply slanted mountainside was rough, uneven, and rock strewn. Rows of big pines stood in their way like giant fence posts.

"Go, boy!" Noose shouted again. *"Yee-ah!"* The horse took the hill, and the fearless stallion ran at a ninety-degree angle as it climbed up the incline in long forceful strides, powerful hind and front legs galloping in unison. The precipitous grade and pull of gravity sent Noose sliding back in the saddle and he grabbed on to the pom-

mel with both hands as his horse determinedly ascended the steep mountainside. Its hooves plowed the dirt. Copper's face was turned dead straight ahead, eyes taking quick measure of the uneven ground and ditches and ruts between the trees — Noose did not have to tell the horse a damn thing because if there was a way to go and get up this pass, Copper was going to find it and take it.

By now, the bounty killers had reached the tree line, and when the gunshots came they were plentiful and close by.

A roaring fusillade of bullets fired up from below punched ragged holes in the trees around Noose, plowing craters in the trunks, splintering chunks of bark, and showering wood chips all over man and horse. The air filled with clouds of blasted timber fragments. Strings of rifle and pistol reports crackled through the forest in a deafening directionless echo. *"Go, don't worry, boy, just go, we can do this!"* yelled Noose, his face a savage mask. With relentless effort, Copper kept jackknifing his back and front legs, carving his way higher and higher into the hills. A lot of ground had already been covered.

Swinging a glance over his shoulder, Noose saw to his grim satisfaction the

Butler Gang was not having as easy a time getting up the mountain as he and Copper had now the posse was trying to give pursuit. The horses were having none of it — the hill was too damn steep. The sounds of yelling men and protesting horses and cracks of whips faded below. Soon, Noose would be out of range of the guns.

Suddenly there was a percussion of pounding hooves — Noose looked back to see that Frank Butler had taken the lead and charged his ferocious black horse straight up the hill following in Copper's footsteps. His mean stallion was big and fast and looked as evilly determined as its rider — its frothing mouth chomped at the bit, yellow teeth bared carnivorously . . . Noose could swear that damn steed's eyes were red!

The cowboy thought if there was ever a horse he might shoot this would be the one because this four-legged son of a bitch looked like it wanted to eat him.

Butler was a crack horseman and sat in the saddle shooting two guns up at Noose with both gloved fists, using his legs to stay on his tilted horse. He loosed off one bullet after another — left, right, left — the slugs whizzing past Noose's and Copper's heads. Butler's black stallion did the rest of the work. And it was gaining as it scaled the mountain face.

The intimidating initiative Butler's horse displayed by taking front position proved sufficient psychological motivation for the other horses and got the rest of the gang moving. With their brutal armed riders in the saddle, the rest of the stallions charged straight up the incredibly steep hill in single-file formation right behind Butler now they saw his horse could do it . . . and the gang of bounty killers came on like a relentless, inescapable killing machine whose only purpose was death-dealing.

The trees parted and Noose saw past Copper's head the beginnings of a trail on even ground heading northwest into the forest. They had to get off the slope, so he yanked on his tireless horse's reins and once they had ascended to the ledge, galloped it down the trail even though he didn't know if it would lead anywhere except a dead end in the brush and the trees.

For a few precious seconds, the man and horse put distance between them and the posse giving them chase of a few hundred yards. Noose just rode hell-for-leather, riding for his life and hoping he and Copper didn't get shot in the back.

Mostly Copper.

CHAPTER 21

Galloping around the bend, by the time Noose and Copper saw the edge of the ridge they were going too fast to stop. The trees suddenly parted and there was just big sky and a ninety-degree drop down a hundred feet of slope into the surging expanse of the Snake River wending around the mountainside. *"Whoa!"* Gritting his teeth, the cowboy yanked back on the reins as hard as he could, trying to turn his horse, who was already scrambling to a stop and rearing on its hind legs, but it was too little, too late . . .

Copper went sideways with Noose in the saddle as the stallion's rear hoof slipped in the soft dirt of the brink of the declination and gravity did the rest. Over they both went . . . man and horse toppled off-balance down the sheer face of the ravine, the horse's hooves pawing and stomping as it slid down the incline toward the beckoning white-water rapids of the Snake below. To his credit, Copper did not fall, at least at first, and stayed upright on all four legs for about the first twenty-five feet they slid.

Joe Noose gripped on to the saddle for dear life, looking down, thinking if the toppling horse could stay up then he could stay in the saddle. It wasn't the landing he was worried about because it was just water below, deep and fast — they were both ending up there in a few moments anyhow and it was going to be wet, but landing in the river wouldn't injure either of them and they could just ride the Snake a few hundred yards or even a mile or two, then ride out. Everything would be okay if he got lucky and the horse could just stay on its feet a few more yards.

He didn't get lucky.

Luck hadn't been with Joe Noose all day.

Copper's shoe caught a rock and knocked both front legs out from under the stallion and it toppled like a felled tree onto its side. The cowboy saw it coming and threw himself out of the twisting heaving saddle so the horse didn't fall on him and break his back or neck. The stallion rolled over and over, whinnying, its legs bicycling and pawing the air and dirt as the horse rolled like a log down the long steep slope, kicking up clouds of dirt and brush as it fell toward the river.

Noose watched his horse go. He had grabbed on to one of the small trees poking out of the ridge and broken his fall but now could do nothing but watch as Copper tumbled helplessly the last few yards and hit the river with a huge turbulent splash, exploding a geyser of freshwater into the air. The cowboy felt the cool spray on his face fifty feet up. Copper was instantly swept downstream in the rapids, bobbing his head above the water, four hooves pedaling in the river as the stallion was carried away. The bright bronze of the horse's face was easy to make out, gleaming like a gold coin against the deep river blue even though the rest of it was deep brown now its coat was soaked. Noose could see the animal was unharmed — it had made a safe soft water landing and likely wouldn't drown in the Snake. The cowboy could see all four legs pedaling, so the horse hadn't broken a leg. Noose was relieved about that. They both could have been killed in the fall, so maybe they did in fact get lucky. Somewhere downstream when the river got shallower, Copper would climb onto the shore and be just fine.

But it was the last he was going to see of

this fine horse, that was certain. Noose clung to the root of the tree jutting from the slope, watching the horse's head shrink smaller and smaller as Copper was washed away into the spectacular scenery and deep blue band of the stretch of the river.

The horse was looking back at him the entire time, making eye contact the whole way.

Damn, that was a hell of horse.

It was his friend.

Joe Noose was going to miss it.

A crumble of hooves above him, a lot of hooves of a lot of horses, made Noose freeze statue-still. It was the posse. He clung onto the tree on the side of the slope, huddling out of sight below it. Dirt spilled down on him. From the shade of the small branches he figured he was likely shielded from view and if he didn't move and if the damn tree did not pull loose of its roots he might survive. Right now, the cowboy just stayed quiet and listened to the disgruntled chatter of the voices twenty feet above him.

"— They went in the river." Butler. "River goes west. Saw the horse for a second fore it went around the bend. Looked like it was alive and kicking. Don't see Noose. Do any of you boys?"

"— No. Just the horse —"

166

"— Mebbe he drowned. He'll fetch up sooner or later —"

"— We need the body. No body, no reward." Butler again.

"— I don't see anybody floating in the Snake, boss."

"— Gimme those field glasses."

Twenty feet below the bounty killers, their quarry huddled close to the side of the hill, keeping himself small. The chit-chat had stopped and though Noose couldn't see them, he figured the gang was making a thorough scan of the river with a pair of binoculars. The cowboy hoped they wouldn't check the hill. If he were in Frank Butler's position, he'd lower a man on a rope tied to a saddle up top, having him check the whole slope where the horse took the fall just to be sure — but he wasn't Butler . . . these cutthroats were impatient and trigger-happy, short on deliberation and diligence, and that hotheadedness had gotten their asses in a sling many times this day.

Just to be careful, Noose put one hand on his holster.

It was empty!

His Colt .45 revolver was gone. It dropped out of his holster when he and his horse fell down the hill. That and the fifteen rounds in his belt were the only protection he had, and bullets weren't of much use without a gun to shoot them with. The cowboy regretted losing the two Winchester repeater rifles and ammo bags on Copper's saddle that got washed away with the horse, but regretted losing the horse more. For now he didn't move a muscle, one hand gripping the tree trunk, the other holding onto a boulder as he hid out of sight.

So far, Noose didn't hear any of the men above him dismount. No squeaking of the saddles. No jingle of spurs or stirrups or sounds of boots hitting the ground. As the minutes ticked by, he grew confident none would dismount. In a few minutes they'd turn their horses right around and follow the northerly direction of the Snake River's flow, looking for his body washed up onshore. These vermin were nothing if not predictable.

Problem with these boys was they were lazy, Noose knew . . . they wanted the easy money. Good chance that was going to get them killed in the end.

"I don't see him. Take these damn field glasses back," Butler's voice growled from above. "Let's ride down and check the river."

You do that, partner, Noose thought, grinning not a stone's throw away. *You just do that.*

As he'd surmised, there was directly a clamor of reins and hooves and bumping of men and saddle that sounded more confused than menacing, followed by a clopping of hooves as the riders retreated back the way they came and their noisy departure faded into the country stillness.

Good. His arm was getting tired.

The day was hot, the raw heat of the hard Wyoming skies bearing down hard.

Joe Noose peered out from beneath the tree, squinted upward, and saw nothing but the ridge above against the harsh glare of the sun. He began to scale his way back up the steep incline, using the bushes and scrub for hand- and foothold. The cowboy made swift progress, wanting to be on top of the hill and off the side of it before the bounty killers rode down to the river — one look up and they'd see him and shoot him right off the side of the ravine.

A few minutes later, Noose's fingers clung to the lip of the roof of the hill. Lifting an eyeball over the edge, he took a cautious glimpse at the surroundings . . . the coast was clear. The bounty killers looked to be long gone. Nonetheless, he was careful as he swung his legs up, and quickly surveyed the area as soon as he was atop the hill in case Butler had grown a brain and left one of his boys behind as an insurance policy.

Nobody was up here with him except a small lizard darting under a rock, so Noose crawled all the way back up. He turned his head slightly and adopted an intensely listening attitude — in the distance, maybe three hundred yards west, he could just make out the sounds of the gang riding out of the trees far below at the edge of the river. Voices could be heard, but the bounty killers were too far away for him to hear what was said.

Dropping silently to his stomach, he inched forward on the dirt and peered over the edge of the hill he had just recently fallen over on his horse.

The outfit had assembled down at the river's edge, all present and accounted for. Eight horses. Eight men. Eight hats. They were discussing something he couldn't hear or make out. The ring of hat brims tipped together against the sun looked as sinister as a clump of poisonous mushrooms. Butler was pointing north — presumably ordering a search of the shoreline for Noose's body in that direction whether he was alive or dead, because that's where the river would have taken him. The riders departed in

170

powerful lockstep like a vile, dangerous mechanism of murder, a machine just as likely to kill the man that used it. Above, a scud of clouds passed over the sun at the precise moment of the gang's hegira, casting a forbidding shadow over the land escorting the bounty killers on their northward journey.

When the horses and riders were out of view, Joe Noose finally rose to his feet. He was tired. He was hurt in a dozen places. But flowing adrenaline fueled his busted body. That would last only so long. The cowboy knew his energy was not limitless, and he could not elude these men forever. Wiping clammy gritty sweat from his brow with the back of his aching hand, Noose stared out toward Hoback Junction, now hidden from view behind the towering jagged tree-carpeted mountains on either side of the river, where the distant blue line of the Snake would fork east toward Jackson in a few miles.

An eagle swooped overhead and spread its vast wingspan coasting on the thermals; it banked and dove and coasted above the river in magnificent flight. Noose admired the sight, reflecting that some animals had no natural predators because they were too damn tough. He was not one of those animals, the cowboy knew, and right now he was prey for a whole gang of nasty predators.

But once as a boy Noose had seen a small dog get snatched up in the claws of a big hawk that flew away with it into the sky. The boy Joe had watched, riveted, as that hound had fought savagely, clutched in the talons of the hawk ascending on big flapping wings way high into the sky. The dog had bit and clawed and fought for its life so hard that suddenly it must have got in a lucky bite because that hawk suddenly screeched and stopped flapping and bird and dog fell, dropping from an immense height. Young Joe had watched them plunge forever, like a dream, locked in a death embrace, sure that tough little dog was alive all the way down but the hawk sure wasn't and the canine had won the fight. When the bird and dog hit the ground, both were instantly killed on impact. It was a mess. But all the boy Joe could think about was what that hound had been thinking on his way down . . . knowing it had killed that hawk so much bigger and tougher than it was. The dog had to know the fall would kill it, but Noose felt in his heart that even though that scrappy little hound knew it was going to be dead in a few seconds, it savored its victory against something bigger than it was, satisfied it took that son of a bitch with it.

That dog had a good death, the way Joe reckoned things.

Right now, Noose felt trapped in a no-win, lose-lose situation just like that dog had been, and his hawk was Butler and his gunmen. Death was a certainty but if he was going down he was going to take those sons of bitches with him . . . *every last one.*

It was time to go. He had to get a move on. The big solitary figure of Joe Noose stood on the vast lip of the canyon cliff, feeling outnumbered and alone. He was still breathing but he wished he hadn't lost his horse. It was a long, long, walk to town and those who were chasing him down had horses — he didn't and that put him at a sizable disadvantage.

For now, the good news was, they were looking for him in the wrong direction.

The bad news was, the eight gunmen were heading north and now stood between him and Jackson Hole, the only civilization for fifty miles. To get there, he was going to have to get past them.

Nothing had changed.

173

CHAPTER 22

The sun was going down, and Bess Sugarland knew they were going to have to camp soon. And she was going to have to camp with them. The rookie marshal figured on sleeping with one eye open but also figured she probably wouldn't sleep at all.

Bess was fifth in line of the eight horses and riders trotting down the trailhead. The shadows grew longer on the big dusters and weathered saddles of the rough individuals she rode with, and darkness was not far off. Bess could hear the mumbled whispers of the posse about that very thing. In the lead, Frank Butler swiveled his head back and forth in machinelike repetition; from where he was looking Bess could tell he was searching for a place to camp.

On the right, a heart-stopping steep granite ridge ribbed with lush conifers shot up two hundred feet into the sky. The clouds were low right now, so the tops of the mountains and tall hills were sheathed in a misty evanescence. The blue-greens and olive greens of the grass and tree tundra were a dark and ominous shroud of color blanketing a terrain that, depending on the light, sometimes appeared almost black-and-white in aspect. The atmosphere was foreboding and dank. The sun had fled behind the grayish murk overhead, visible now only as a sickly boil of a glow in the hazy pallor of the unrelieved skies.

To the left, the sprawling wending stretch of the churning Snake River carved a rumbling slash through the valley floor like a wet cold wound. The progression of the trail hugged the shoreline following the direction of the river's powerful, inevitable flow — a course that ran through Jackson Hole, where Bess Sugarland knew all this was somehow headed.

Everything boded ill.

But at least she had a horse like the others did.

This was no place for a man on foot like Bess knew the man they hunted to be. Against her better judgment, she almost felt sorry for him but quickly remembered he murdered her father, or so they said. The man Joe Noose was out there somewhere, the female marshal thought as she looked left and right alertly, her uneasy gaze traveling over the ruggedly forbidding Wyoming terrain the company traversed. It was going to be a bad night for him. Maybe her, too.

Butler whistled. "There." The gang all looked where he was pointing: a clearing by the shoreline fifty yards ahead. "Looks like a good place to camp. Night's upon us, boys. Noose ain't going no place in the dark. With or without no horse. Let's fetch us up some grub and catch some shut-eye and we'll set out before dawn and have this sumbitch slung over a saddle by lunch tomorrow." With a click of his teeth, Butler spurred his horse into a canter along the dusty trail and reined it around in the clearing below. There, he swung smoothly out of the saddle and tied off the reins on a large tree so conveniently positioned that it might have been left there for that exact purpose.

The gang rode their horses down into the open area by the shoreline, dismounted, and began to unpack and set up camp.

An hour and a half later the sun had set.

The sky was full dark.

Four tents had been pitched. The female marshal had one to herself. The men were to bunk with one another, taking shifts sleeping while the others stood watch. The horses were tied off on two trees at the edge of camp. They were dimly seen in the gloom, jaws working in the feed bags strapped to their snouts as they stood together against the cold. A large campfire in between the tents cast a glimmering glow on the tents and the trees at the edge of the perimeter but barely reached the river just a few yards from camp. The firelight died after twenty feet and everything was swallowed in darkness and empty negative space where the breadth of the mountains could be felt and heard from the wind in the trees but not seen.

A deep country silence descended, broken only by the occasional *clop* of a hoof or *clink* of a bullet belt or *squeak* of leather. Many of the men had already eaten and retired to tend their wounds, clean their guns, play cards, or sleep.

Across from Frank Butler, Bess Sugarland hunkered by the fire.

"How's the food?" he inquired cordially.

"I've had worse," she responded, forking a mouthful of beans and squirrel meat.

"Culhane can shoot the feather off a bird at four hundred yards but can't cook to save his life," the leader of the bounty killers said to the marshal in a tone that approached apologetic for him.

Bess bit on something hard, winced, and spat a grain of buckshot into the palm of her hand. "Culhane, that's his name? You should tell your man to shoot squirrels with a .22, not a scattergun."

"I'll tell him that."

"How did you get into this line of work?" she asked Butler straight out.

"Pay's good. And I'm good at it. Might say I got a talent for it."

"Killing?"

"Hunting men. Catching 'em. Killing comes with the job. But the job is catching men. Can't kill what you can't catch." He caught her eye, the firelight dancing in his corneas. "But killing men, if and when it's required without hesitation, is a job description of this here line of work. When it's legal."

"Dead or alive."

"The notices sometimes say that, yes." He nodded.

"You prefer dead, I'm betting."

"The choice is up to them."

"Sure it is." She smiled.

He held her gaze. "They can surrender. They can not do the crime and get the reward put on their heads in the first place. Once they do, it becomes my business. I like my business to be neat and clean. The less fuss, the less hassle, the better."

"Bringing a man in dead is less hassle, I imagine."

"Sometimes."

"Mind if I ask you another question, Mr. Butler?"

"Ask me anything you want, Marshal."

She indicated the other bounty killers around the camp with a sweep of her hand with the fork in it. "Why do you need all these men?"

"Can't have enough good men." He shrugged.

"Fair enough. But today you're only after one man. It seems excessive. Like a pack of hounds after one jackrabbit."

"The more dogs you have, the more likely you are to catch that hare. The one sure way to win a battle is with overwhelming force. I learned that in the war and I apply those lessons to my job. But this ain't no rabbit we're after, ma'am. This is a dog. A mad dog. A rabid cur of a dog that I remind you murdered your father."

"I have not forgot, sir. Yes, the man that killed my father is a dog, that is a fact."

"Yes, ma'am, he is."

Bess regarded Butler a long moment. He held her gaze, watching her back with something in his eyes she didn't like —

something she couldn't put her finger on. Finally, she said, "Well, you know what they say."

"No, what do they say?"

Bess stood, scraped her plate into the fire. She fixed Butler in a direct stare down where he sat below her and said, "It ain't the size of the dog in the fight. It's the size of the fight in the dog. I'd say that, fight-wise, this dog you're after, he's got some size on him. Hope yours is as big."

With that, she turned and headed toward her tent, disappearing behind the flap.

Frank Butler didn't watch her go. He just stared into the fire, the light gone from his ugly eyes. He spat the rest of his mouthful of food into the flames, wiped his mouth with the back of his hand, and took a sip of coffee.

"Bitch," he muttered.

CHAPTER 23

Being swept down the rough, rock-strewn flow of the Snake River was dangerous enough during the day but it was suicide at night.

The current was deep, icy, and powerful. The swift surging breakwaters coursed and smashed against large rocks all the way through this stretch. And Noose couldn't see the river, only hear it — all his eyes could make out was a deeper black in the already pitch black of the rural countryside. In the sunlight, a man might be able to swim or at least reach out and push away from the big wet boulders if he was lucky. Not so in the dark when you couldn't see what you were heading into. But the cowboy could smell the river a few yards away and feel the cool coming off the water, sense the huge unseen force of weight and gravity of the Snake River barreling past.

The moon was faint behind murky clouds

in the gloomy sky tonight and while there were stars aplenty, little light shone down on the Snake. The river, that of it that could be discerned, resembled a big black void. It was a jagged dark ribbon like a yawning crevice in the valley floor.

But Noose knew this river afforded him an opportunity to slip past the eight armed and trigger-happy men now positioned between him and Jackson Hole — a town where he might find sanctuary if he could make it the twenty miles to get there. First, Joe Noose had to duck past the bounty killers and get ahead of them if he was going to survive. He didn't dare try it on dry land. During the day, they'd spot him for sure and pick him off quickly and easily. His only chance was to try and make it past them at night, when the gang was unawares, camped and resting. Even so, they might hear him. Could have a guard posted he didn't see. These professional killers were bloodthirsty and ruthless but they weren't stupid and were full of animal cunning. Noose could count on them setting alarms with empty cans and chains on wires near camp to make sufficient racket to wake the whole bunch if he tried to sneak past. His only way to get past them was to go down the river, and he was going to have to float so they didn't see him.

A canoe or a raft wouldn't do, even if he had one, and he wouldn't risk using it if he did. A watercraft they could spot from shore. A man alone up to his neck in the water in the black of night, maybe, hopefully, not.

That plan at least he felt confident of and had made up his mind to try.

The bounty killers were camped on the shoreline but would not see a man in the river getting washed by. It was just too damn dark. Noose himself couldn't see the rocks and boulders glistening shiny and black ten feet ahead as he took his first steps into the freezing Snake River. This might work if he didn't get his skull cracked open and his brains splattered on a rock, or knocked out and drowned in the rapids. It was easily possible. Or he could crack his ribs open again and if he made one noise, let alone let out a cry of pain or a scream, those shootists would hear him and start blasting.

There had been no easy ways the last twenty-four hours and his options were no less difficult now.

From where he hunkered by the eddies knee-deep in dank fragrant river mud,

Noose could make out the distant fire of the bounty killers' camp a quarter mile ahead down the river on the shore past the flowing water. He could vaguely smell burning wood and smoke and a faint whiff of coffee. A few tents and eight tethered horses were visible. The gunmen were mostly out of sight, probably in the tents. A couple of men hunkered by the campfire and smoke rose off it into the air to be swallowed in the darkness. There wasn't much going on. A lot of the men might be asleep.

The gang clearly figured they could take a load off because there was no way a wounded man like himself would try to travel this country in the dark. Under normal circumstances, his enemies would have figured that correctly, but these circumstances were anything but normal and improvisation was required.

Noose couldn't hear anything from here because this close the sound of the loud river surging by shattered the stillness and drowned out most other sounds.

It was as good a time as any.

The cowboy waded into the Snake. Cold shot up his legs and he instantly felt them go numb. The rocks were slimy with moss and algae, and his footing was slippery. The ground dropped away below the surface quickly, so it hardly mattered that he lost his footing because within a few seconds, Noose was up to his waist then his chest in the river. The strong surge of the swift current exerted its quick firm pull and he was off his feet, up to his neck in the river and being swept downstream. The bracing cold was like being dropped in a box of ice, but it felt good once he got used to it, refreshing against his aching wounds. The sense of deep power of the great river filled him with awe as he was carried downriver with the sweep of the current. Noose kept his body below the surface, paddling with his hands and feeling ahead of him for any surprise rocks that might crash against him. His nose and eyes were above the rapids, and remained unblinking and fixed on the fire and tents of the camp that were coming up quick on his right side as he sped past the shore.

The figures of the bounty killers, three, then four, were visible now, sitting around the fire, carrying their rifles and tossing their coffee dregs into the flames.

The tableau of the camp, like a chiaroscuro oil painting of golds and browns against a black canvas, grew closer and closer as the submerged man came up on it. There were silhouettes of people inside the tents, elongated shapes against the glowing amber canvas lit from the inside by kerosene lamps. Joe Noose was floating in the middle of the river, steering a straight trajectory as he was carried downstream, and he kept a sharp eye on the shoreline of the camp he was about to pass. None of the men were looking in his direction. Sparks floated bewitchingly up into the darkness above the dwindling fire, and the cowboy smelled burning wood clearly now.

Noose switched his gaze to the river ahead. A twenty-foot-wide stretch of firelight fell from the camp onto the river like an illuminated band directly ahead about a hundred yards. The men cleaning their rifles by the tents could see if and when he was washed downstream through the light. After that, the Snake flowed past the camp and all was darkness again.

Taking a deep breath, Joe Noose ducked his head below the surface of the water and tried to swim deeper. He kept his eyes open, but all he could see was pitch-black murk. Then gradually a dim illumination came and went as he traveled through it, and Noose knew he was past the light and the camp itself so he came up for air.

No bullets hit him in the head as his mouth and jaw burst through the surface and he gulped down oxygen. Swinging his gaze behind him as he was washed down-river, Noose saw the tents of the camp shrinking behind him upstream, a few of the horses tethered to a tree on the outskirts giving him the side-eye as they somehow noticed him in the river, but none of the horses sounded an alarm and they, too, soon were lost from view.

The last thing Noose was looking at that caught his attention as he floated past the camp was the silhouette in the last tent, which he assumed was a trick of the light, since other wise one of the bounty killers had grown a nice set of tits.

Breathing a sigh of relief that he was safely past the gang's camp, Noose turned his face forward into the river a split second too late.

The wet rock sledgehammered his skull and he passed out.

CHAPTER 24

Bess didn't go back to her tent like she planned. She had been walking that way but was jumpy. Her whole body ached but her heart hurt worse than anything physical. Tiredness hung like a lead blanket over her shoulders and limbs and she wanted nothing more than to lie down and get some sleep but her guess was she wasn't to get a wink tonight because she wasn't going to risk closing her eyes for a second on these men.

Her being a U.S. Marshal kept these rabid dogs on a leash only as far as it went.

A marshal's badge was just a piece of metal.

She had one, but bullets were pieces of metal, too, and they had a lot of those, these men did.

The female lawman walked alone through the darkness away from the glow of the fire where she had left that man with the killer's eyes, Frank Butler, sitting alone. She didn't know anything about him but that he was a very bad man. Bess had heard people talk about evil . . . preachers in church, her father when he read her the Bible before bed, but that was just a word for *bad.* She had never seen evil up close until now. Butler was evil in the flesh. You felt he was capable of anything. Even though each step took Bess farther from the comforting glow of the fire into the deepening darkness of the camp perimeter, it also took her a step farther away from Butler, and that made her feel safer.

Bess wandered across the campsite toward the river.

She didn't feel safe around any of these men.

It was good to be alone.

There would be no sleep tonight, this was a certainty.

It was a clear night. She looked up. The vast canopy of Wyoming sky loomed above her, black as pitch but beaming with millions of blinding stars. Bess smiled. *That's where her dad was now.* Up in heaven. Because if ever a man deserved . . .

Bess's throat suddenly constricted with choked grief and sorrow, eyes burning with stinging tears as she felt a racking sob wrench up out of her guts. Quickly, the young woman wiped her tears away and forced composure on herself — she better not cry in this bad company. But she wanted to weep. It had all happened so fast today, from her father's murder to her riding with the bounty killer gang to her being here. Bess realized she hadn't had time to cry at all for her father. She had gotten into action right away, grabbed a gun, saddled up, joined this motley crew to go after the man responsible and get justice for her father — she hadn't had time to think, and now Bess realized she hadn't wanted to think, because if she did she would have to think about the lost parent she loved so much . . . and she would cry.

Maybe if she hadn't been so quick on the trigger to bury her grief beneath ill-considered action she would have done a little thinking, thought things through a bit, not gone off half-cocked. Because now that Bess had a few minutes of reflection in all the peace and quiet, she saw clearly how unwise her decision that brought her here to the remote wilderness, one woman alone with this gang of mongrel killers who would shoot her, or worse, the minute she got in their way or they had a mind to. Her marshal's badge wouldn't protect her any more than it did her dad.

She should never have ridden with these men.

Hadn't Nate Sugarland always told his hyperactive tomboy daughter to think things through, to measure twice and cut once, to look before you leap? He had been full of dozens of such homilies.

Don't just do something, stand there was her dad's favorite.

By God, Bess was going to miss him.

Might see you sooner rather than later if I spend any more time with Frank Butler, Dad, she thought, smiling up at the stars. That at least was a comforting thought.

Until a voice suggested now might be the perfect time for the reunion.

The marshal swung her head from the riverbank into the camp and saw two men standing in the dark by a tent talking . . . about her. She couldn't see their eyes but felt their rodent gaze on her. The young woman's ears were keen and damn sure heard what one of them said loud enough that he wanted her to hear it.

"Excuse me, boys. I heard that," Bess said sharply, turning in their direction.

Yellow-toothed grins flashed like knives in the dark.

She took a step toward them. "You want

to say it again?"

"Nobody was talking to you . . . Marshal." She knew the voice. Culhane. One of the surlier of the shootists.

"No, you were talking *about* me. I heard what you said."

"What was it you heard?" Lawson. The other dirtbag. She was keeping track of names.

Bess felt herself experience an adrenaline dump. Her body tingled and her heart pounded as her pulse raced. She was sick of feeling scared around these men and needed to show them she was not to be messed with. Only way to do that was kick some ass so they respected the badge and the woman behind it. Looked like now was that moment.

The marshal walked up to the two bounty killers and stood toe-to-toe. "What I heard one of you say was, 'That bitch lawdog gets a bullet in the skull way out here, nobody would . . .' Didn't catch the last part but caught the first and can guess the rest." Both gunmen held her gaze defiantly. She held theirs right back. "You just threatened a U.S. Marshal."

"You ain't no real marshal, you just some little lawdog's bitch —" Culhane didn't finish his sentence. Pulling back her arm, her fist closed, Bess Sugarland punched him in the jaw, putting her whole shoulder into it. With a cry of surprise and pain, the bounty killer was knocked to the ground. His head shot up in fury as he spat a tooth. "You're dead."

Feeling sudden movement to her right, Bess ducked a roundhouse swing by Lawson, and as his balance wavered when his fist went over her head, she straightened and kicked her left leg up into his groin as hard as she possibly could. Her boot slammed into his crotch with crunching force and Lawson screamed in a high-pitched porcine squeal, clutching his pants and dropping to his knees, face contorted in agony as he started to puke. Bess, untouched, stood over the man and stared down at him in pure disgust and disregard.

"Looks like you need a new set of balls. Want to borrow a pair of mine?" she said.

"Bitch!" Culhane drove himself off the ground, going for her throat with both outstretched hands, spittle frothing from his lips. Bess dropped to a fighting stance and brought up her fists, but Culhane didn't get another step before four of the other bounty killers leapt out of the dark onto their fellow shootist and held him back, restraining him by the arms and in a choke hold from attacking Bess. It was Sharpless, Trumbull, and she thought the others were named Wingo and Garrity.

"What are you doing, you stupid fool, you don't hit a marshal!" Sharpless yelled, his arm wrapped around Culhane's neck as he throttled him and dragged him to the ground with the others, Culhane kicking and thrashing the whole time. In moments, he was subdued by the other bounty killers.

"You okay, Marshal?" Sharpless asked, worried, coming up to Bess and touching her arm, his eyes filled with worry and concern — *about me screwing up your reward for you with the U.S. Marshal's office,* Bess thought cynically as she lowered her fists.

"I'm fine," she retorted. "They were the ones got hurt, not me."

"That's a fact." Sharpless grinned appreciatively. "Where you learn to handle yourself like that?"

"My father."

"I'm sorry for the actions of my men, Marshal." Bess swung her gaze to Frank Butler standing by the campfire, his eyes reflected in the dancing flames. "I take full responsibility. You have my word it will not happen again."

With a dismissive wave of her hand, Bess let Butler know with that gesture it was no big thing. "Been a long day for everybody." She took a deep breath and started walking back toward the river, a good fight being just the thing she needed to get her blood flowing, because now she had landed a few punches she felt less afraid of these men.

The marshal looked back over her shoulder to see Lawson and Culhane were now on their feet but Butler hadn't moved. The rest of the bounty killers had gathered around and trouble was stirring . . . but not for her.

"I want a word you with you boys in private." Butler stood tall and formidable in the gloom, backlit by the campfire that carved his jagged shadow in a jigsaw of darkness on the ground.

"Yes, Mr. Butler." Culhane and Lawson exchanged nervous glances. They had a good idea of what lay in store.

Butler nudged his jaw for the two men to follow him across camp into the darkness. Then he turned his back and walked grimly in that direction. The bounty killers followed their leader, jumpy in stride. The three walked about thirty paces until they were out of eyeshot and earshot of the rest of the gang and the marshal, then Frank Butler stopped and turned to face his two men, his eyes glittering blackly above his thick mustache. His voice was low. "I told you boys not to make trouble with that marshal, didn't I?"

"But she had it coming, Mr. Butler, I — we —"

"I run this gang and I gave you an order," Butler snapped, cutting off Culhane.

"Yes, sir, you did."

"Did you follow it?"

"Nossir, we didn't." Lawson looked at his boots, fingers worrying the brim on his hat.

"Damn right you didn't."

"We're sorry, Mr. Butler," they both said.

The leader adopted a reasonable tone. "I can't have any trouble with the U.S. Marshal's office in Jackson Hole when we deliver Joe Noose slung over his saddle, and this woman can make some. I don't like having some nosy uppity lady marshal riding with us and getting in our business any more than any of the rest of you do. But those is the cards we been dealt. The reward hangs in the balance. We need her on our side or, failing that, we need her not to screw things up for us, which she can do because of that badge. If she gets wind of what really happened back at the bar, or if the U.S. Marshal's office thinks this ain't anything but a legal bounty, we don't get that money. That means we play it smart and we play it cool and what I don't need are any of my men acting like fools and blowing this reward and taking money out of my pocket."

"We understand, Mr. Butler."

"You damn sure better. You boys disobeyed an order. You know the rules when one of my orders gets broke." The fearsome leader of the gang reached into his vest and took out a pair of metal pliers he gripped in his glove.

Culhane and Lawson turned pale, their faces clammy with squeamish fear.

"Which hand you shoot with, Culhane?"

"Please, Mr. Butler."

"Which hand?"

"Right. Right hand."

"Your left, then."

"Oh crap."

"Pick a finger."

Miserable, Culhane raised a trembling left fist and stuck out his shivering little finger.

Butler used the pliers.

The sound of the muffled scream thirty yards away in the dark caused Bess Sugarland to look up sharply from the reflection of the stars in the rushing water. She couldn't see what was happening from where she stood at the river's edge but a moment later there came another shriek and whimper, muted, like somebody was biting down on a rag. Troubled, the marshal took a few steps back into camp, her hand near her holstered Colt Peacemaker. A few of the bounty killers were hanging around smoking and drinking from a bottle of whiskey and if they heard the screams, they weren't paying attention or knew something she didn't.

Bess peered ahead into the country gloom as she saw three men step out of the darkness.

The one in back was Butler, which she could tell from his height and mass. The two in front were the ones she just had the fisticuffs with, Culhane and Lawson. Both were cradling hands covered by a single glove and it looked like there was blood on those gloves. Both men's faces were screwed up in pain, and as they walked past they studiously avoided her gaze as they slunk back to their tent.

As she stood and watched them retire, Bess was wondering what the hell happened, then Frank Butler passed her and tipped his hat in a courtly manner. "Have a pleasant evening, Marshal," he said with a gentlemanly tone in his gravelly voice and was on his way.

These boys sure have their own way of doing things, Bess was thinking as she watched Butler swagger past the campfire, emblazoned briefly by its flaming glow until his figure melted into the ubiquitous darkness, where he seemed right at home.

CHAPTER 25

Noose's eyes blinked open.

His head hurt very badly.

His vision was red and bright.

Blood was in his eyes.

And sunlight.

Something was all over his hands and face.

He heard hooves — very, very close.

The bounty killers were riding past him on the trail.

A steady clop of hooves so close he felt the ground shake with the drop of each horseshoe in the dirt.

He didn't move.

He didn't breathe.

Just counted.

One, two, three . . . eight horses.

Why eight?

Why the hell wasn't he dead?

When were the bullets going to come?

All Noose moved were his eyes. He couldn't see the horses that were so near him their shadows fell across his face as they trod past. This meant it was dawn, because the sun was low to the east. The sound of the river rushing north was his compass. Every instinct Noose had urged him to look at his enemies to see what he was facing, but to do that he would have to turn his head and he didn't want to risk that.

The cowboy lay prone in what he knew was the muddy riverbank, wondering about the weight he felt in his hands and arms and legs and boots and face. Rolling an eye to his left hand, keeping his fingers frozen still, the cowboy instantly realized why the nearby bounty killers didn't see him: mud from the river covered his entire body, caked him from head to foot where he had washed ashore into the eddies. Unless somebody was really looking hard, to the casual glance he would appear to be part of the shoreline.

Sounded like the bounty killers weren't paying attention.

In fact, it sounded like they were just waking up, still half-asleep in their saddles.

"— the hell did he get to? —" A weaselly high-pitched whine of one of the gang.

"— He's behind us." Butler. Unmistakable. "Couldn't have gotten past us last night."

"— We turn around, then? —"

"— No, not just yet. He'll be comin' this way 'cause that's the only way he can go. We don't spot him in the next few hours, we'll split off a crew to go back and check to see if he died, then gather up the corpse before the vultures get at him and take his face so we can't identify him for the reward —"

The voices were growing distant to the north now, percussive hooves fading off up the trail. Butler's voice carried back in the wind.

"— Keep an eye out for vultures, boys. Eyes to the sky. Man in his condition, they'll be tracking 'im, too. Might be the buzzards'll point him out for us. Lead us right to him."

Then the bounty killers were out of earshot.

Noose didn't move a muscle for the next fifteen minutes except to breathe regardless, taking no chances. That was a narrow escape.

Butler was right about the vultures.

Noose needed to keep moving, because the minute he got lazy and started giving off the stink of death the buzzards would start circling, putting a target in the sky on him for those damn mercenary killers.

After a moment, Noose rose to a sitting

position, looking through the weeds to be sure the coast was clear. The men hunting him had ridden on and were out of sight. That meant the Butler Gang had gotten ahead of him again and he would again have to find a way past them to get back out in front. But it might not be that bad this time: it looked from where he sat that the trail they were riding turned east, so he could head straight north on foot and hopefully regain his advantage and position if he got a move on.

His body felt very heavy. The dry mud that covered his head and hair and torso and everything else felt like a heavy blanket of cement. The cowboy saw the water rushing by not three feet away so he just rolled right over into the Snake River with a splash and let the current clean all that dirt and crud right off.

When he stepped out onto dry land again, Joe Noose was soaked head to foot and his wet leather boots *squeaked* and squirted water with each step he took — but he was good and clean, his wounds clean, too, and when he looked up he smiled, seeing the skies were bright and clear.

No vulture would come near him.

CHAPTER 26

Marshal Jack Mackenzie had never seen Jackson Hole in such a damn uproar.

The capture and incarceration of the notorious outlaw Bonny Kate Valance currently locked in the cell of his U.S. Marshal's office had ignited the local passions and touched off a powder keg of heated political debate in the town of Jackson. Her celebrity status and intoxicating charisma as a gunslinging libertine lady outlaw were a tonic for the town residents. The tales of Bonny Kate's wild exploits in both gunfights and the bedroom were the stuff of legend and it was hard to tell what was true and what wasn't. What *was* truly indisputable was she was the biggest thing to hit Jackson since the lightning storm of '87 that blew up the munitions dump. All day long and into the night folks would come to town and surround the marshal's office just trying to get a glimpse of the female prisoner in the flesh, like she was a circus animal in a cage. Mackenzie and his deputy Swallows had their hands full keeping the crowds back and last night had had to sleep in the office, taking shifts standing guard. Locals were yelling and carrying on. Men were throwing love letters and sending flowers, and women were tossing eggs and notes telling the vixen to burn in hell. The lawmen had remarked to each other many times it was like they had Jesse James himself or Geronimo in the cell. But Buffalo Bill's Wild West show or Barnum & Bailey's circus wouldn't have stirred such a brouhaha; instead it was because this particular outlaw was a female, a hot tempestuous one, and the historical significance that in a month she was going to be the first woman to be executed and hanged in the United States, Marshal Mackenzie knew.

Jackson Hole was a town where women were a major political force. They ran businesses and were outspoken, their opinions respected. They held political office and had influence in the community. Not that Jackson was a bad place to be a man, but the power was shared. Marshal Mackenzie was just fine with that. He felt men screwed things up all the time and believed women possessed innate common sense about the world so he welcomed their strong stabilizing presence in his town.

But everybody in Jackson had gone crazy with the arrival and lingering presence of this legendary lady outlaw in their midst. Her being here was creating not only hullabaloo but social friction as well. The town was in anarchy.

Clean as the chop of an ax, Bonny Kate Valance had divided Jackson Hole straight down the middle into two divisive factions split along clear gender lines of male and female: if you were a woman you hated Bonny Kate and wanted her hanged, and if you were a man you lusted for Bonny Kate and damn sure didn't want her executed before you had a chance with her. Mackenzie saw the lady outlaw had such an effect on males some would have done the deed even *after* she swung at the end of a rope. The local ladies had made their position a political one: with women's rights came accountability. Therefore, if the law could execute a man for certain crimes it was a woman's obligation to be executed for the same crimes a man was. The men predictably adopted the gentlemanly if equally hypocritical position that it was not genteel for a civilized society to execute a member of the fair sex. Mackenzie knew this was all posturing and hogwash and actually thought it was funny as hell — the women-folk hated Bonny Kate because all their husbands and boyfriends wanted to bed her, and the men, well, the women were right . . . the men did want to bed her. The marshal already knew of two divorce petitions filed with the county clerk's office in the last twenty-four hours and guessed a lot of husbands were going without a home-cooked dinner and sleeping in the barn tonight.

The marshal stood looking out the window at the mob of Jackson Hole women carrying signs and chanting slogans in the street. They had just elected the first city council in the growing town and the entire membership was women. Normally this was a good thing, but now they were all out there on the street giving speeches and shouting the same slogans painted on the signs.

"Hang Bonny Kate! Hang Bonny Kate! Hang Bonny Kate!"

"The right to a vote means the right to swing on a rope!"

Through all this, Bonny Kate Valance just sat in her cell, twirling that flaming red hair of hers around her finger, her blue eyes twinkling, knowing all the fuss she was causing and probably enjoying herself. She was like one of those dogs that riled other dogs just by walking down the street. She had that pheromone. Mackenzie guessed that her whole life Bonny Kate had been stirring up trouble just by having a pulse. Every so often she would catch the old marshal's eye and he'd feel an electric current run through him as her blue eyes flashed in his. If Bonny Kate was afraid of her upcoming date with the hangman she wasn't showing it.

It was going to be Marshal Mackenzie and Deputy Swallows's job next month to put Bonny Kate Valance on a horse and ride with her, giving the outlaw an armed escort over the towering Teton Pass mountain range that bordered Idaho into neighboring Victor, where the gallows had already been set up for her hanging scheduled in thirty days. It was a gigantic pain in the ass, but this hanging was a historical event, with the state senator coming in from Washington, D.C., no less — the politician had run on a hard-liner law-and-order platform promising to lead Idaho and Wyoming into the twentieth century by running the outlaws out. Bonny Kate Valance, the first women in U.S. history to be hanged for murder, was of great symbolic significance to his campaign, and reporters were coming from the big papers all over the country. All this to say, the date of her execution was fixed. But since it would be twice the ride to get marshals from Idaho to come over the pass to Jackson and take her back across to the waiting gallows, political pressure had been applied and the U.S. Marshals' headquarters in Cody had sent orders to Jackson Hole Marshal Mackenzie that since she was delivered for the reward in Jackson, he was to take her over the pass. Everything about this assignment pissed the hell out of the cantankerous old Jack Mackenzie. It was all politics and horse dung. If they wanted to hang Bonny Kate Valance they could do it in Jackson just as easy as Victor — simple as throwing a rope over a tree, putting that lady outlaw on a horse with the noose around her neck, and smacking her horse on the behind. But because some big politician wanted to exploit the execution to get votes and because Victor had all the money pouring into the hotels and saloons bolstering their local economy, the damn execution was scheduled on this specific date . . . and *his* office had to drag her shapely butt all the way over the Teton Pass. Marshal Mackenzie had better damn things to do and the more he thought about it the madder he got.

The marshal would be glad to get Bonny Kate out of town and be rid of her, so Jackson could get back to normal.

The murder of his oldest friend, Hoback Marshal Nate Sugarland, weighed heavily on Mackenzie. He knew a capable posse of manhunters were chasing the villain responsible and would bring him in dead or alive for the reward but *they were doing his job for him.* Jack Mackenzie was the U.S. Marshal here and a fellow marshal had been gunned down and Mackenzie's job and his sworn duty was to catch the man responsible and deal with that individual directly.

His job was not to babysit some sexy female over the Teton Pass just so some Washington politician could look good and neither was it his damn deputy's job, not when his best friend and fellow marshal's killer was in the area and there was a chance they could help catch him.

Mackenzie looked at his watch and did some mental time estimation and calculations. He had twelve daylight hours at least that he and Swallows could arm themselves up and ride out toward Hoback and possibly intercept Nate Sugarland's killer, because last he heard the bounty hunters and the man they were tracking were heading this way.

And if it took them more than a day, that was tough. Bonny Kate wasn't going anywhere and that peacock of a senator could kiss his behind. The Cody U.S. Marshals' headquarters were going to be mad as hell and Mackenzie was going to hear it from them, but screw them, too. It was time for him to retire anyway.

What they should do is thank him because if he caught the Hoback marshal's killer he would be doing more than his job.

He would be saving them the reward.

The great thing about getting old, Jack Mackenzie believed more and more, was you did what you wanted and you didn't give a damn, and the only thing he gave two bits about right now was riding his way.

"It don't feel right just sitting here twiddling our thumbs doing nothing," the marshal said irritably. Mackenzie stood restlessly by the window, staring out across the plain at the distant looming mountain range of Hoback wreathed in a low cloud bank of the lowering sky . . . Somewhere out there in the thirty miles between Jackson and Hoback were the man with the price on his head and the bounty hunters on his tail. From his vantage at the window, the lawman could not see anything but trees and mountains and big sky, but they were out there somewhere.

Seated at his desk, Deputy Swallows was busy filing reports and doing paperwork. He seemed preoccupied with his duties and didn't respond. A pot of coffee bubbled comfortably on the small stove in the corner.

"They're coming our way," Mackenzie added, still looking out the window.

"We don't know that, sir," Swallows replied, putting down his pen on the pile of papers and looking up. "We don't know which way Noose went, do we? He mighta headed east toward Alpine."

"Maybe. The Snake River limits his options, though. Hard to cross it just on a horse. Easiest escape route is toward Jackson, maybe try to get over the pass."

"You're probably right."

"I guess I just don't know. You never know what a desperate man might do."

Swallows could see his boss was perturbed and tried to reassure him. The young man was of an agreeable, helpful nature. He said, "They'll catch him before long, these bounty killers. That kind of reward is a big incentive. They'll catch him, all right."

The marshal grunted, rubbing a hand through his thinning gray hair. "What if they don't?"

"Somebody will. Reward like that."

"I feel like we oughta get out in it. Do some tracking and hunting ourselves. It's our job, after all. Brother officer shot down like that. We might get lucky."

"Sure would piss them bounty hunters off if we catch Noose our own selves. Make 'em miss out on that reward money. I'd like to see their faces then."

"Would myself."

Walking to a map on the wall, Marshal Mackenzie studied it for a few moments. Swallows got up from behind his desk and walked up beside him. The lead lawman put his finger on the area marked HOBACK. "This is where Sugarland was shot yesterday," he said as he then traced his finger north, down on the map, to where the black wending line marked SNAKE RIVER bent east across mountain and valley topography cut by the river toward the marking for JACKSON HOLE. Mackenzie nodded to himself. "I say this is the way that killer is coming and those men after him is coming, too. Somewhere roughly along this route, anyway. We're here." The marshal tapped his finger on their town. Then he drew it along the map west in the other direction toward Hoback. "I say if we ride out now, good chance we'll intercept him."

"I follow you, sir."

The marshal grabbed his hat and his gun belt and swung his pale-eyed gaze to his deputy. The even-keel young man looked up, awaiting orders, and got one delivered with a toothy smile.

"Swallows. Grab your guns and saddle your horse. We're riding to Hoback."

Marshal Mackenzie walked to the rack by the door and got his hat. "Load up, Deputy. Let's ride." His spurs jingled as with a snap to his step he walked across the creaky floorboards to the gun rack and snatched two Winchester rifles, cocking and loading each.

Opening the ammo chest, Deputy Swallows grabbed two boxes of .47 caliber and one bandolier belt of .45 caliber ammunition. He took his bolt-action Henry rifle from the gun rack and screwed on his own hat.

"Make sure this place is locked up tight so nobody harasses our prisoner while we're gone." The lawmen went around locking and bolting the windows and closing the steel shutters, which took them a minute or two and then they went to the door.

"Behave yourself, Bonny Kate," Marshal Mackenzie said on the way out.

"I never do." She smiled saucily. "Don't

hurry back now. I got no place to be."

"After you, Deputy," said Mackenzie as he held the door and both men left the marshal's office. He hung up the CLOSED sign inside the window on the way out. Then he bolted the triple locks.

The lawmen stepped out into the fresh air and strode around back to the stable where their big hardy quarter horses were tethered. Each loaded their saddle holsters with their rifles and filled their saddlebags with ammo. They double-checked the loads in the heavy irons in their belt holsters. Saddling up, the marshal and deputy untethered their stallions' tack, heading off at a full gallop out of the stable toward the big empty of Hoback Junction ten miles to the west.

CHAPTER 27

Yesterday the horse had climbed out of the Snake three miles farther down from where it fell in.

The bracing chill of the turbulent river waters had refreshed the stallion while it was swept along the fast rapids, a relief from the brutal heat, but being off its feet had alarmed the steed desperately treading water with its hooves, struggling to keep its nose above the surface, snorting air.

When unseen rocks crashed against its flanks the horse bellowed, and there was a bad moment in a rough patch of white water when blows of the stones below the surface and suffocating frigid water going up its choked nostrils to surge down its throat made the bronze horse feel certain it was going to drown . . . until seized by raw panic it pawed and twisted and righted itself, big brown eyes bulging with fierce determination to live, and so it did.

Moments later, the cool water had turned deep and slow, current now smooth and stately in flow, easing the stallion's lengthy passage downriver from up-country. The bronze horse rotated its sleek and strong body rightways up, legs not finding footing but hooves slowly pedaling underwater as if running in place and soon it was swimming. The motion kept its big head above water, the animal sucking in air as its hammering heart beat less quick until its feet at last met resistance of soft mud and the horse could walk and this it did . . . all the way out onto dry land.

The bronze stallion stood on the plain dripping wet and shook itself dry. The soaked riderless empty saddle felt heavier on its back than it had before. Catching its breath and feeling a pang of hunger, the horse nibbled on the straw on the ground, then lifted its handsome head to look around its quiet, vast, unfamiliar surroundings. The horse had never been in this place before. It did not know where it was.

A horse will always return to the barn or head home, wherever that home happens to be. This is instinct.

This particular horse had no home; for as long as its equine brain recalled, its traveled life had been perpetually in transit, forever journeying to new and different places down distant trails the stallion was unacquainted with and never saw again, always headed where it hadn't been before.

But a primal instinct to return home stirred in the stallion. Not knowing where such a place could be, the horse experienced an urge to go back where it belonged.

Which was?

Where was home?

At first, the animal didn't know.

Then it did.

Doubt became certainty as the horse recalled the face of the rider who rode it last — the man who understood the stallion and treated it well, the friend whose heart beat in time with the stallion's own, the partner who made it feel an equal; the horse had become reborn with his new friend in his saddle, had felt alive for the first time in its entire existence. Unlike the old rider who hurt and beat the horse until it felt enslaved, abused, and dead on its feet, this new rider was a friend who made the horse feel special and valued and free . . . and gave it strength.

Home. The horse did not understand exactly what this *home* was that the pull of instinct was compelling it to return to, but the rugged stallion's strong heart said the man was the closest thing to it.

His friend was home.

And that was where the horse must go.

Last thing the horse remembered was watching his friend's face looking back on the hill while the stallion was getting washed down the river . . . then the man was gone.

The bronze-colored coat of the mighty stallion Joe Noose had dubbed Copper was drying and as the sun came out gained the color and hue of a glorious suit of armor.

Besides a keen sense of direction, Copper had plenty of what is for good reason commonly called *horse sense.*

The river had carried the horse in this direction.

His friend was back the other way.

Breaking into a quick trot, Copper set out and headed up-country.

That was a day ago.

CHAPTER 28

As she sat on her horse amid a gang of bad men she distrusted, Bess Sugarland remembered the last time she had laid eyes on her father before riding after the man who killed him . . .

Bess had closed his eyes before she left.

Her soul had been reeling after the bounty killers left town to give chase to her father's killer. The young woman didn't know what to do. She was all alone and had never been alone. Bess had always had her dad, but suddenly, horrifically, no more. Marshal Nate Sugarland lay sprawled in the saloon, shot full of holes, covered with blood.

She couldn't just leave him there. Not in the bar, bleeding on the sawdust.

Yet she had to go after the man responsible. Bess could not let her father's murderer escape, even if a formidable gang of killers were already hot on his heels. And she was the marshal now.

The thought of her father's corpse going ripe in the heat if she was away for days curdled her stomach. It was wrong.

But Bess knew if she did not saddle up in the next hour the gang of bounty killers would be long gone and she would not catch up.

Standing in the empty saloon that still reeked of cordite and the coppery stink of blood, Bess stared down at the marshal. His blank eyes were open, staring up at the ceiling. His ruddy, pudgy face and white whiskers were peppered with spackles of drying blood. His cheeks were already turning pale. The entrance wounds on his chest were raw and gushing and his shirt was soaked red. Her father had died a sudden, violent death and his last moments on earth were agonizing, this was clear, yet his expression was peaceful, Bess thought. There was no expression, she then realized, for the body was just a shell. His soul had departed.

The clock on the wall ticked, reminding Bess of the minutes slipping away where her time for action would quickly pass.

Her father would need to be properly buried but she had no time to do that now. The heat was going to get fierce in the next few hours. Bess thought what to do. There was ice in the cooler in the back of the bar in an oiled wooden trunk. Her first thought was to stow Marshal Sugarland's body there, keep it on ice, thereby preserving it until her return.

Her vision blurred as she saw the moisture on her hands and felt the hot wetness on her face, blinking away the sting of the tears. This was no time to cry. Crying would come later, when this was done. Right now, she had decisions to make.

The ice cooler . . .

No, not that.

Bess saw in her mind's eye the blue stiff figure of her father lying in a pile of ice and it was such a cold, bleak, lonely picture she knew that just wouldn't do.

He needed to be home.

Among his things.

In his own bed.

Cleaned up.

At rest.

Home.

She swung her gaze through the swinging doors of the saloon and saw the U.S. Marshal's office across the dirt main street of Hoback, the family quarters visible to the rear, and she made up her mind.

"I'm sorry, Daddy," Bess whispered down to the body at her feet. "I'm gonna get you home."

Decision made.

Couching down, she tenderly got both hands under his armpits and heaved with all her strength. The corpse was heavy, limp but starting to stiffen with rigor mortis. Bess Sugarland bent down, using all her might to heave her father's head and upper torso over her own shoulder, then rose and stood with a grimacing grunt. Nate Sugarland's dead body was slumped in her strong and healthy young arms and for a moment Bess stood there holding him up, like a dance partner who had collapsed from exhaustion. The young woman felt his blood, the same blood as hers, splash over her shirt and trousers that became wet and sticky and the moisture of it was against her skin, but this only galvanized her further. Gritting her teeth with a determined gasp of effort, she bent her knees, got her own weight under the heavy body, and slung it over her shoulders, clinging with all her strength to the arms slung around her neck, and leveraged her father's corpse onto her back.

As she staggered with him across the floor, the old wooden boards creaking below her boots, the blood splattering the leather and leaving a bloody trail of bootprints in the sawdust, Bess caught a quick glimpse of the morning's other victim behind her.

The barman, blasted to pieces behind the counter, lay twisted in a pile of busted glass and was soaked with spilled whiskey from the shattered bottles. Him she would have to leave. Bess had never liked him anyway.

Family came first.

Each step she took broke her heart.

Her dead father was on her back.

His blood was all over her.

Keeping her unblinking gaze fixed on the back door of their house behind the marshal's office that drew ever closer with each step, Bess trundled on and focused on just putting one boot in front of the other. The flat heat of the Wyoming sun baked down. Bess heard only her own ragged exhalations and crunch of boot steps on the dirt. Once, somewhere far off, came the *scree* of a hawk but the woman didn't notice.

These were the hardest steps Bess ever took.

She could smell her father, the familiar manly scent of soap and the outdoors coming off her skin as his cold face pressed against her cheek but it was fading now. Bess breathed the scent of her father in deep before it fled forever.

"We're going home, Dad. Almost there. I got you." She heard herself repeating this over and over as she carried his lifeless heavy bulk across the street from the bar toward their shack until at last she was at the door.

Shouldering through the door, Bess gasped in relief departing the suffocating heat as the cool of their rooms embraced her. The shades were drawn. The place was quiet and dark.

She would not rest until she had him in bed.

Her legs were ready to give out but Bess made it the twenty paces through the door of Nate's room and with her last ounce of strength, carefully lowered her shoulder and eased his dead body onto the mattress of the bed. The springs squeaked. Relieved of the great weight, the young woman stood up and stretched her aching arms, gasping for breath. Looking down, she saw the bloody, peaceful body of her father lying half on, half off the bed. Her heart swelled knowing at least he was back home, in his bed. It seemed restful. Bess stepped forward and took both his legs and lifted them onto the mattress, straightening him out on the sheets.

She pulled off his dusty, weathered boots and set them on the floor by his dresser. The boots were retired now, having walked their last step with Nate Sugarland.

Then she removed his gun belt and slung it over the bed frame. He wouldn't have to worry about his shooting anyone anymore.

Going to the kitchen, Bess drew a bowl of water from the sink and fetched some soap and a few washcloths and towels. Returning to the bedroom, she set the bowl and cloths on the dresser. Then she quietly sat on the bed beside her father.

And she cleaned him up.

Washed the blood from his face.

Removed his shirt.

Gently used a wet soapy washcloth to wash the blood from his big torso and from around the bullet wounds.

She cleaned him up with loving care.

The tears rolled down her face.

Soon the blood was gone and except for the ugly black holes in his chest, Nate Sugarland seemed like he was asleep except his eyes were open.

Reaching out two fingers, Bess gently closed the lids.

Nate's eyes were now shut.

His daughter rose and went to the closet, fetching the folded quilt, his favorite, that her mother had sewn for him when she was alive. Bess laid the quilt over her father and drew it up to his neck like a blanket.

Last, Bess Sugarland leaned forward and kissed Nate on his cold forehead. She whispered in his ear, "I love you, Dad. I'm going to catch the man that killed you and have him hanged. I'll pull the trigger on him myself if it comes to that. I have to go now."

Her job was done here.

She straightened up and buckled on his gun belt, checking the loads in the pistols. The Colt Peacemaker revolvers were very heavy but the heft felt good in her hands. They would knock down whatever they hit and what they hit would stay down.

They were big guns but she had big hands.

One of the many strong things she had gotten from her father.

Then she turned and left the room.

A minute later, acting U.S. Marshal Bess Sugarland had saddled up and was riding hell-for-leather out of town after the gang of bounty killers.

Here, now, twenty-four hours later, Bess rode on her horse with the gang of assassins hunting Nate's killer. She switched her gaze left and right at the big, filthy armed men on horseback on all sides. Homicide radiated off them. She could smell murder on their dirty hides.

And Bess knew that she might already have found who killed her father.

The question was, what was she going to do about it?

She had a few ideas . . .

CHAPTER 29

Making doubly sure he stayed out of sight before he chanced a look at his pursuers from his position behind the rocks, Noose peered over the edge of the boulder, squinted through the trees, and made out the distant specks of the men and horses.

It was the bounty killers, all right. Hot on his trail.

He counted.

Counted again.

That couldn't be right . . .

There were twelve to start, Noose recalled. He'd taken out five of the gang over the last day and had been certain those vermin were dead . . . yet the distant figures of men and horses across the ridge clearly numbered eight.

Didn't make sense.

Seemed highly unlikely they had hooked up with more of their confederates way out in this remote stretch of wilderness that was a long way from anywhere else.

It occurred to Noose that one of the gunmen he thought he had killed had survived and maybe these bastards were tougher than he thought.

He needed to take a closer look and be sure he wasn't seeing things. Rummaging in his jacket, wincing from the shooting pain in his ribs, Noose fetched up his small pair of field glasses. Lifting them to his eye, he peered through the binoculars, panning them left and right until he got a fix on the gang, magnified now large enough in his view to count the cartridges on their bandoliers.

The faces were all recognizable from the up-close look at them he'd had yesterday back at the saloon . . . there was the leader, Frank Butler, the only bounty killer whose name Noose knew, the hooded cold-eyed gaze over his black handlebar mustache making him instantly identifiable. Noose recognized the others easily enough: the small one that looked like a rat; the bald one with the scattergun slung over his shoulder . . . face after face was familiar as he scanned his field glasses across the men and horses.

Then he saw the woman.

And now he knew why there were eight.

Noose recognized her, too, from the saloon. The marshal's daughter. Auburn-haired and uppity, full of juice. *What the hell was her name?* He disremembered. While the woman had been a deputy back at the town it looked like she had switched badges, because that was a shiny silver seven-star U.S. Marshal's badge now pinned on her pert bosom. So that was it: the marshal's daughter was riding with the bounty killers to oversee the hunt for her father's killer. Now it all made sense.

Lowering the binoculars, Noose rubbed the stinging sweat out of his eyes and raised the field glasses to look again. He settled the oval view on the female marshal. She had sand, this one. Noose had picked up on that back in the bar but he truly respected her grit now. Hell of a day she must have had dealing with her father being shot and now taking it upon herself to ride with this dangerous bunch — one woman alone in the woods with seven heavily armed professional killers. And she didn't look afraid.

From the gang's glowering countenances and the tension he could pick up even from this distance, Noose knew that she hadn't been invited. The woman came on her own volition and was sticking to them like glue. This pack of vultures did not appreciate her presence, that much was clear. It wasn't tough to figure out why: Butler and his brutal crew wanted to kill Noose out in the middle of nowhere where there were no witnesses and bring him back slung over the saddle for that fat reward they meant to collect.

This woman marshal complicated things.

In a lot of ways.

In spite of himself, Noose's mouth cracked in a narrow grin as he chuckled quietly, thinking about all the ways the lady was messing up Butler's evil plan just by the simple fact of being there.

Reckon those boys are learning there's no such thing as easy money, Noose mused. *Probably thinking about that a lot once she showed up. Serves them right.*

She may be only one woman but she had the badge.

She was the law.

This could save him. If he could get to her, Noose could tell her what really happened back at the bar: how Butler had murdered her father, the marshal, and framed him for the terrible crime to get the fat reward put on his head. *But would the marshal's daughter believe him?* It would be his word against seven bounty killers. Noose knew he had proof of his innocence and

Butler's guilt if he could live long enough to get it in front of the proper authorities: the proof was in the bullets in the dead lawman's chest — Butler had shot the marshal with his own gun and that Colt Dragoon was a different caliber than Noose's Colt .45, so those fatal rounds could not have been fired by Noose's pistol. The cowboy's one slim hope was getting to the woman marshal somehow without getting gunned down by the bounty killers and then spilling his guts to her. But he wasn't stupid. Noose knew that right now the woman wanted his head and it was very personal and she would be the first to shoot him on sight — but if she was any kind of sworn law enforcement officer with a shred of integrity, she would do the lawful thing: she would use her authority as U.S. Marshal to call off the bounty raid and take the whole situation in front of the judge in Jackson Hole, where the matter could be investigated and adjudicated. Noose knew full well that Butler and his gang were not going to like that, and maybe not stand still for it. It was long odds, but about the only chance he had.

The woman showing up could be a stroke of luck yet for Noose.

But not for the lady marshal, he quickly concluded.

She could easily wind up dead, shot in the back or worse, if she got in the way of the bounty killers and they decided to be rid of her. These cold-blooded killers had already murdered one U.S. Marshal and would not hesitate to murder another. This was a certainty. Out here in this vast wilderness, the shot wouldn't be heard and her body would never be found. Noose doubted this woman truly knew the kind of men these were, but Noose definitely did.

And now suddenly it wasn't just his own hide he was worried about, it was hers.

If she died it was on him.

In a way, Noose felt responsible for the murder of the U.S. Marshal. Even though Noose didn't see it coming, had he not been such a stubborn self-righteous cussed son of a bitch and trailed the bounty killers to town, that lawman would still be alive.

And his daughter wouldn't be out here in grave danger.

So if she got killed it would be on his head, was how Joe Noose looked at it.

Right then, he felt his ingrained stubbornness kick like a mule in his gut.

No way he was going to let anything happen to this woman.

Not while he was still breathing and had bullets left.

If he could just contact her in some way even if it meant getting too close to the gang for his own safety.

He had to warn her.

CHAPTER 30

Bess needed to relieve herself.

Had to for the last fifteen miles.

She'd been holding it in for the last two hours and was in considerable discomfort with the bounce of the saddle. The country they had been riding through the last two hours had been wide-open prairie that did not afford any privacy. She could have ridden off by herself, gone a few miles, and probably found a suitable spot, but something told the canny female marshal it was a good idea to stick to these villains like glue and not let them out of her sight. At the same time, she didn't want them to watch her drop her drawers so she had bitten the bullet — literally had stuck one of her .44-40 rounds between her molars, grinding against it, riding out the cramps in her bowels that came and went.

Five minutes ago, to her indescribable relief, fortune smiled on her. Luckily for her, the grim dogged procession of tired horses and bent buzzard figures of bounty killers rode up an incline and the posse was in the trees — rows of pines in dense walls of branches and trunks in both directions were on either side of the narrow trail. Both sides gave Bess ample forest cover to do her business shielded from sight of the men. To her left, the landscape angled sharply upward in a sheer slope of hard granite and lush conifers jutting at obtuse angles to the grade — that would be a hard climb and the woman didn't think she had that kind of time. To her right, the slope looked level for a few hundred yards past the tree line, then appeared to drop off into a ravine of some kind. That was the preferred direction she would head for.

When she could stand it no more, she spoke up. "Mr. Butler," Bess called out to the man in black riding directly before her on his giant mean stallion. "Can we take a ten-minute break? Nature calls."

"As nature will do," he amiably replied without looking back. "Take your time. We'll rest the horses 'n wait for you here."

"Much obliged," Bess said with a relieved exhale. Descending out of her saddle and tossing the reins to Butler, she loped off the trail across the wild grass toward the dense tree line ahead. Her pace became even brisker as soon as she crossed into the cool, dark, peaceful canopy of pine forest. Once she felt the comforting embrace of its solitude, only then did she look back — to her great relief, after a few paces the posse was soon lost from view altogether past the branches.

Bess was thinking, *Ought to have told Butler twenty minutes,* because she intended to walk as far as she could into the woods and put a considerable distance between herself and the men behind her before she did what she came to do . . . even the next state would not be private enough for her.

A wave of relief washed over Bess, who experienced a sudden flood of euphoria — *it felt so good to be alone finally.* It had been suffocating having no breathing space to herself and her own thoughts riding with these bad men the last day. She had not realized until this very instant the degree of tension and paranoia she experienced every single moment she was in the company of Frank Butler and his bloodthirsty gang . . . the always having to look over her shoulder, always having to watch her own back, needing to keep her eyeballs on them every second of every minute of every hour with her hand always near her gun, constantly on guard expecting the unexpected, knowing anything could happen with killers like these who were capable of anything. She was alone. Truly alone. *With them.* The debilitating clenched guts and stomachaches of tension never ceased. Bess's head swam as she felt a rare panic attack coming on. In the anxiety of the moment, she just wanted it to stop, wanted it over with . . . *this whole damn terrible business had to end.*

Something blinded her for an instant — a metallic flash in her eyes. A ray of sunlight through the high branches had glinted off the marshal's badge on her breast and her eye caught the quick reflection . . . she took that as a sign.

Bess understood the U.S. Marshal's badge was worn on her shirt for a reason, so she settled down immediately. She had a job to do.

The female marshal knew she was better than all of these bounty killers put together and would prove it. *Don't let the sons of bitches get you down,* Nate Sugarland always said. Bess then added to herself, *especially dirty sons of bitches like these.* A murder of crows these men were, a kettle of vultures. Bad business. Very bad company indeed.

Bess stopped walking. Where was she going and what difference did it make? *Not going to feel safe until this thing is over and better accept it.* So she sucked it up.

This was as good a place as anywhere.

"Shouldn't somebody go with her?" Lawson asked, unsure.

"Any volunteers?" Butler quickly shot his boys a dry, sardonic glance, like it was the worst idea in the history of bad ideas.

No hands were raised. Nobody spoke up. All thought better of it.

"I would not want to be in the boots of the man who found that filly with her drawers around her ankles," Butler said with a snort of laughter, a roll of his twinkling eyes, and a merry grin on his face. He shook his head. "Nossir, I would not."

That supplied the bounty killers with a brief, cheap chuckle at the lady marshal's expense.

CHAPTER 31

She was coming his way.

Noose could not believe his luck when the posse stopped and the marshal dismounted and headed into the woods. He knew he could count on her getting well out of earshot of the bounty killers, and the cowboy wasn't going to get a better opportunity to catch her alone and tell his story. The time for him to make his move was now.

He hunkered down on a high ridge above the forest line, the Butler Gang to his left sitting on their horses on the trail with the western mountain face on the other side. Below him, south, the forest was flat and continued a few hundred yards to his right where it dropped off in a gradient pine-covered slope that spread out west for close to a mile where it met the twinkling blue line of the Snake River.

The small, blue jean–clad figure of the woman disappeared into the trees, and Joe

Noose broke from his place of concealment and descended toward the woods.

She buttoned up and washed her hands in a brook. Bess didn't want to go back, not to those men, but knew she had to. This thing wasn't done by a long shot. *If I could only stay here by myself a few more minutes,* the marshal had been wishing. Suddenly she realized she was not alone, sensing a presence that quickly made itself known when it spoke from a few yards away.

"Marshal, I'm unarmed and I'm turning myself in," a husky, unthreatening drawl softly whispered.

Whirling around, Bess drew her revolver, cocking back the hammer on the huge figure of the man standing under the shadows of a tall pine ten feet away. His shoulders were broad, his posture erect, and his clothes were covered with old blood. *"You!"* She instantly recognized Joe Noose from the first time she laid eyes on him when he rode into Hoback yesterday — the young woman had thought Noose was good-looking then but right now, as violence consumed her and she aimed her pistol between his eyes, she wanted only to blow the handsome out the back of his head.

"No!" he said.

Her finger began to close on the trigger, and he cleared the ten feet in less time than she had to squeeze it and his big fist wrenched the Colt Peacemaker out of her palm, flipped it around, knocked open the cylinder, dumped the bullets on the ground, closed the gun, and handed it back to her before she had a chance to breathe.

Joe Noose now stood two feet from her, his craggy face wearing an expression of animal intensity, both his hands up, palms open and empty. "I didn't shoot your father, Marshal. As God is my witness. Just let me ex—"

Bess's eyes were wild with rage and she heard herself screech like a cat as she lunged forward, drawing her bowie knife from her belt, stabbing and slashing at Noose with the blade. Her face was twisted in feral savagery. For a very big man, the cowboy was quicker than he looked, stepping out of the path of the knife with cat-footed grace and avoiding her furious swings and jabs with little apparent effort. Bess hissed: "You killed my father and I'm gonna cut your heart out, you son of a bitch!"

"Now, that ain't what happened," Noose retorted with an unrattled calm she had to credit him for, even in her agitated state. He easily dodged and ducked her thrusts with the knife, keeping his hands out in a placating gesture, trying to talk her down. "Think about it, Marshal. I'm one man with one gun. You ever stop for a minute to think how I walked out of that bar, me against twelve men and twelve guns, if I had killed the marshal, your father? Think logical, ma'am. You figure I had me the drop on twelve men? Twelve professional shootists? I did not. I walked out because they let me walk out. Hell, they ran me out. Gave me a head start, in fact. Why do you think they did that, Marshal?" Cool and slow, Noose backstepped in a slow retreat as Bess kept coming at him with the knife — but Noose got away from her blade easier than Bess did from his words, and her slashing strokes had less and less punch behind them, listening to what Noose said: "They did that because they didn't have no reward on me yet. There was no money in it. They needed to get you to get the reward authorized before there was any profit in hunting me down." Bess stopped, lowering her knife hand to her side and just stood there, gasping for breath and staring wildly at Noose. He said, "Startin' to make sense to you now?"

She just glared at him, winded, but the anger was gone from her gaze. Her breath came in hard, rough bursts.

Noose looked her straight in the eye. "I didn't kill your father, Marshal. Frank Butler did. While his men stood by and watched. And he did it to frame me for the reward he and his pack of jackals could hunt me down and collect. That's the truth. Those are the true facts. And *that's* what happened."

Bess sheathed the knife. It seemed to her like she had always known something like that was what really happened. The big, rugged cowboy in front of her fixed her square with his blue, unblinking eyes the color of winter sky and she knew he spoke the truth — and knew he knew that she knew now.

"I kinda figured." Bess nodded.

She sat down on a rock. Threw a glance to the trees in the direction of where she left the posse but didn't hear any movement. Every part of her body hurt. Bess looked over at Joe Noose and saw the blood on his tattered and dirty shirt and pants and knew the tough man had taken a lot more punishment than she had and was holding up pretty well. She forgot her own pain, feeling ashamed.

The handsome chipped-granite unshaven face regarded her patiently. "Question is, you're the marshal and what do you plan to do about it? There's still seven of them, but there's two of us now."

"We got to make it to Jackson Hole. That's the nearest U.S. Marshal's office," she said quietly.

"Mackenzie and Swallows. Met 'em four days ago."

"That's them." She nodded.

Noose crouched down in front of Bess so he was eye level with her even though the effort hurt his wounded side. "You know that gang's got to kill the both of us now. Me, they still got the reward on. You, you're a witness and if you talk, that reward is history and their necks are in nooses. They need both of us dead. You understand that?"

She nodded again.

"I'm sorry about all of this," he said softly.

"How is it your fault?" She looked confused.

"I stirred things up, I suppose you could call it. Butler and his boys shot a man I had captured alive for the bounty and they stole his body at gunpoint, brought it to your father in Hoback for the reward. Thing was, I went after them. Came to that bar, confronted them, and told the marshal what they done, and, well, that's when Butler shot your father. So in a way, this is my fault. If I'd have just let it go, your —"

"Stop." She cut him off. Bess looked Noose in the eye with a sad, unaccusatory gaze and shook her head sympathetically. "Sounds like you were trying to do the right thing."

He shrugged. "I was. But it turned out wrong anyhow."

"I don't blame you."

"Just trying to say I'm sorry I got you into all this."

Bess had a thought and, brow furrowed, looked up at Noose. "This whole thing, it ain't just about reward money."

"Sure it is."

"That man Frank Butler wants your hide."

"There's that, too, I reckon."

"What did you do to make him hate you so much?"

At that, the cowboy paused and laconically scratched the back of his head and after he thought it over, half grinned. "I showed up, I guess."

Bess thought Noose looked damned handsome when he smiled, and she did, too. "What does that mean?"

Noose shrugged. Considered his words. "It's like this, I suppose. Take the world. There's men like me on one end, men like him on the other, and all the rest of the folks in between. I ain't saying I'm all the way good but Butler, he's all the way bad. The two of us just can't breathe the same air. Can't be on the same planet. Before we met, we didn't know of each other so there was no problem, but two days ago we did meet and the world, you see, it just ain't got room for the both of us. One of us has got to go. Don't mind saying I'm hoping that's him."

"I hope it's him, too."

"Let's make damn sure of it, then. You ready to move?"

"I am."

"Let's go."

Turning his back, Joe Noose returned to where the .45 cartridges he'd dumped out of Bess's pistol lay and picked them up off the grass. Walking up to the lady marshal, the cowboy handed them back. She reloaded her gun, saying, "Obliged."

Noose smiled. "I didn't get your name."

She laughed. "Bess. Bess Sugarland." The young woman held out her hand and the cowboy shook it.

He smiled again with a wince of pain. "Marshal Sugarland, my name's Joe Noose and it's a pleasure to make your acquaintance even if I'd prefer it was under better circumstances."

The Butler Gang took a smoke break.

Others had a drink from a bottle of whiskey they passed around. Killing time.

Waiting for the lady marshal to come back from answering nature's call.

Frank Butler checked his pocket watch. She'd been gone ten minutes.

He'd give her another ten.

Against the vast green wall of the canyon ravine, two people made their way down the jagged slope. The descent was difficult and the man had been wounded, so the woman was helping him along.

"Nobody's gonna hang you. I'm the law. It's my word. You're off the hook."

"Nice to hear. But right now hanging's the least of my worries. Those killers back there are my worry. Ought to be your main concern, too." Noose grimaced in pain. Blood was seeping through his shirt. "I'm messed up."

"I know," Bess said.

The lawman eased the cowboy to the ground and sat him against the rock. She opened her canteen and gave him water.

"Drink."

Noose gulped it.

"Let me look at these." Bess examined his wounds and winced, squinting. "How is it you're still alive, mister?"

The cowboy shrugged. "Stubborn, I guess."

The marshal took out her handkerchief, poured water on the cloth, and cleaned the bullet wound as best she could. His chest was covered with dried blood and as some of the caked gore came off she saw the bruised swelling on his right side. She whistled through her teeth. "Not only do you have a bullet in you —"

"It went clean through."

"Okay. Not only have you been shot, you got a few broken ribs."

"Sounds about right."

Rubbing the balled wet handkerchief on Noose's chest over what she thought was another wound under the dried blood, the bare skin was cleaned . . . what was revealed in the center of his chest made her recoil in shock. With a startled gasp, Bess took an involuntary step backward when she saw what was on Joe Noose's chest. *Is that what I think it is?* She choked.

He sighed.

Furrowing her brows and leaning in for a closer look, Bess cleaned the blood off around a savage burn scar seared into the flesh of his muscular torso, the pale mottled flesh in the center of his hairy chest a disfigurement where no hair would ever again grow, a mark roughly the size of her fist:

The letter was upside down.

It looked like a noose with a piece of rope attached.

And it had been made by a red-hot cattle brand.

The man had been branded.

Like an animal.

Noose just watched her face evenly, his eyes unreadable.

Bess was mortified. "Joe Noose. You got *branded.* Somebody branded you like a damn steer. Who would do such a thing to a man?"

She had only glimpsed the mark for a few seconds before Noose noticed she was staring at it and his eyes flashed with unease as he quickly pulled the shirt over his torso to cover himself up and the branding scar was now lost to her view. But that was long enough for Bess to see the weal made by a red-hot branding iron that had happened years ago, for the mark had long since healed over.

The subject plainly made Noose uncomfortable, so he changed the topic as he buttoned his shirt. "We best get moving."

Bess, being young and forward and impulsive, couldn't take a hint. "How did you get branded, Noose? That brand looks like a noose. That how you got your name?"

"I don't want to talk about it."

"But —"

Avoiding her gaze uncharacteristically, for the big cowboy was a man who looked you straight in the eye at all times, Noose just muttered evasively in his laconic drawl, "Don't matter. Nothing to do with our present situation." The cowboy didn't want to talk about it. This much became clear to the marshal so she dropped the subject.

"I need you to stay alive, Noose. We're just ten miles from Jackson. You got to stay alive to tell the law there your story. Think you can do that?"

Noose nodded.

"You saw them kill the marshal, you said."

He nodded again. Bess poured some canteen water on his head to refresh him, and he asked, "How many of them are left?"

"Seven. You got the rest."

Noose's grin was mean. "Good start."

"That's a fact. You shot the hell out of those boys."

251

"They had it coming."

"That is also a fact."

The bounty hunter's mind was working behind his eyes. "The reward. How much is it?"

"Hunnert thousand dollars."

"Paid to the man brings in the man killed the marshal."

"In cash, dead or alive."

"The reward belongs on Frank Butler." Newly energized, Noose rose fearsomely to his feet. "I intend to collect."

"I'll help you," she said.

"You want a cut?" he asked.

The female lawman just shook her head.

"What do you want, then?"

She looked at him true.

"Justice."

Then she added, "And I want the rest. I want to know everything that happened yesterday."

The bounty hunter and the lawman pressed on side by side across the rugged tundra of the ridge and over the next five minutes he told her.

After Bess had heard his story, she said, "So they ambushed and murdered the man you'd already caught, then stole the body for the reward. That's how this whole thing got started."

"Right, that's the way it happened."

"And you went after them. Alone."

Noose shrugged. "Reckon."

"Couldn't just drop it? Cut your losses?"

"They killed an innocent man."

"What was that to you?"

"He was in my custody. I was bringing him in."

"Took a big risk. One against twelve."

"Didn't think too much about it. Figured I'd get the marshal involved and things would get straightened out. Never figured them for killing the marshal nor framing me." He chuckled. "But I gotta give 'em credit. Was pretty smart. Makes you wonder if it's the first time anybody tried it."

"But now I know the truth, it ain't gonna work out so good for that man Butler."

Noose shot Bess a flinty glance. "Unless you're dead and can't be a witness. Something for you to think about."

They locked eyes.

"I can take care of myself," she said, sticking her jaw out brashly.

"Due respect. Just sayin'."

"I hear you."

"Keep your eyes open. Ears, too."

"They're gonna be after us soon."

"Stake your life upon it."

They traveled in silence for a few minutes

253

without discussion until at last he spoke up. "You're one to talk."

"What do you mean?"

"How long were you riding with that gang?"

"Since three miles out of Hoback."

"One girl. Seven of those bastards. You have any idea what could have happened to you?"

"I was lucky, I guess."

"Just saying. You're one to talk to me about going up one against twelve."

"It was different. That man they killed who you had the bounty on was a stranger. Didn't mean nothing to you. The marshal was my daddy."

"You didn't know they killed him then."

"No, I thought you did."

"So why not just let them do their job? They were plenty good at killing."

She was reflective for a moment, ashamed and defiant. "I guess I know what it was. Because I wanted to be the one pulled the trigger on the man that killed my daddy. I wanted to do it with my own hand, not let somebody else do it. I wanted to kill that son of a bitch myself."

"And you thought that was me."

"Yes, I did."

"When did you figure it out?"

254

"The men were talking. I heard you in the rocks. I don't know. Maybe somehow I knew all along. I was thinking about you a lot on the trail. First I hated you, waiting for you to die. Then all you went through I was seeing firsthand, the odds against you, you sticking in there fighting and giving it right back to those bastards, that got my respect, made me even root for you, and, Joe Noose, that riled me. But somewhere deep down I knew a man like that couldn't be no yellow-bellied killer. And I could see just the kind of yellowbellies that gang is."

"Thanks." His eyes flashed with warmth.

Noose grimaced and choked, buckling over. Alarmed, Bess grabbed hold of him and ran her hands over his torso. He groaned. "You come this far. You gotta make it. If you die, there ain't no witness to who killed my father."

He nodded and stood straighter. "I know you don't want Butler to get off."

"He won't get off. One way or the other. Even if I have to shoot him myself. Thing is, I'd have to throw away my badge after I did that."

He grinned at her. "You're my kind of gal."

They kept walking, looking around them as they lit out toward the rise of canyons dead ahead.

All the while Bess was thinking, *I'm going to find out why you got branded one day, Joe Noose. If we get through this, somehow I'm going to make you trust me enough to tell me . . .*

Noose himself had nothing to say for a while. Wishing the woman had not seen the mark of the brand on his chest or asked questions about it — there were some things a man kept to himself.

The cowboy remembered all too well how he got the brand. He remembered every day of his life. And was remembering now . . .

. . . It was always the same jumble of images he would never forget that flooded his skull, always his memory of that sizzling red-hot brand getting closer and closer . . . and other memories: four nooses dangling from the tree . . . four ropes tied to saddle pommels of the horses . . . the old man's severe hooked face and hard pitiless eyes without a trace of mercy . . . the horses' hooves pawing the dirt . . . the blazing Q brand coming ever nearer . . . the terrified faces of the men with the nooses around their necks, faces still familiar even as he had disremembered their names . . . the ropes connected to the nooses tightening . . . the two young boys crying . . .

the old man's shot-apart hand with no thumb or forefinger . . . that disfigured chicken claw of a hand clutching the scattergun and blasting it . . . the chorus of snapping necks . . . the fiery brand pressed against his naked chest, the white-hot agony and smell of his own burning flesh up his nose . . .

There had been a time Noose had tried to forget those events and put all that behind him but every time he looked at his chest he was freshly reminded. Just like the old man said he would be. Now Noose forced himself to remember because he knew the day he forgot, he was lost.

So it had become habit every day of his life that Joe Noose remembered the fateful day he was branded.

And the old man's words about being too young to hang . . .

257

CHAPTER 32

The gold pocket watch snapped shut with a metallic report that sounded louder than it was to the disgruntled ears of the man who had checked the timepiece five times in as many minutes. Frank Butler replaced the watch on its gold fob in the pocket of his black button-down vest beneath his duster.

What was taking that woman so long?

The lady marshal had left to answer nature's call a full half hour ago and still she hadn't returned. Butler looked around with a circumspect eye at the surly, antsy faces of his men sitting in the saddles of their horses with nothing to do but shove their thumbs farther up their behinds. They were all getting restless, their leader saw. Like himself, they were men of action and cooling their heels for no good reason didn't sit well with them, not with this kind of reward money at stake. They were like sharks, he and his boys. Butler once read somewhere that sharks swam or died because swimming was how they breathed, and while he had never seen a shark, he knew they were at the top of the food chain of nature's apex predator killers, just how he fancied his gang to be the most dangerous bounty killers in the West. Difference being, instead of swim or die with them, it was ride and shoot or die. And for the last half hour they had been doing none of either and it was getting tough to breathe.

Because the bitch was taking too damn long.

He would have sent some boys after the marshal's daughter to check on her by now, but she went off alone to relieve herself and Butler didn't want her surprised by his men walking up to her when she had her pants down around her ankles. That would not improve her disposition one bit and might get the unlucky gunmen shot. He was stuck with this vixen on this long ride because of her badge and he didn't want her to have any more of an attitude problem than she already had. But being a gentleman had its limits. They had a reward to get after and pretty soon he was going to fetch her himself whether she was taking a dump or not.

So where was she? He kept coming back to that. *What was keeping her?*

Butler's brain turned over the possibilities for her present absence. Might be that time of the month for her. Might be that the trail disagreed with her and her bowels . . . well, he didn't need to think about that.

There was one thing he could do.

Leave her behind.

Why not?

Just ride off with the gang and get on with their business hunting down Noose. Now Butler had an excuse to shake the troublesome marshal loose — it was her taking so long — if the marshal caught up later and gave them an earful.

"Mr. Butler, how long we going to have to wait for this woman? I say just get riding and leave her behind." Butler shot a glance to Sharpless, who had just spoken. From the looks on his shootists' faces and murmurs of agreement, the sentiment was a shared one. Daylight was wasting and with each passing minute their reward was farther from their hands. Butler himself was inclined to not further delay their departure until . . .

"Where the hell everybody figure that marshal got to?" Garrity wondered out loud.

"Maybe she run into Noose," Culhane joked.

That drew titters of amusement from

everyone in the gang except Frank Butler, who now wore a saturnine expression of considerable severity on his suddenly suspicious face. "Dismount. Everybody. Lock and load," the leader snapped abruptly as he swung out of his saddle and his boots hit the ground with a crash of spurs.

"We're going after her."

As the big cowboy and female lawman made their way down the canyon, step by steady step, she kept looking behind her up at the mountainside rearing above. There was movement behind them through the trees a few hundred yards above them. The sounds of boots and the *clanking* metal of guns were intermittent but audible and getting louder as the men who made those noises drew closer. The bounty killers were after them, all right. The entire gang coming on strong. They were making as much of an effort to keep quiet or conceal their presence as a steam train did highballing down the rails.

Noose and Bess came to a stop on the ridge and scanned their surroundings. Right now they had cover with the trees above them, and because of the canopy it was likely the Butler Gang didn't see them yet since no bullets had come their way. But both the man and the woman could see that advantage was about to end, because from this point forward it was open country for half a mile until a tree line at the forest base to the west . . . This wasn't going to work.

"They're coming," Bess tightly said. "I knew Butler was gonna know I been gone too long and figure it out. Was just a matter of time. He hasn't trusted me for a while now."

"Best keep moving, then." Noose helped her along the downward trail.

Bess threw a worried glance over her shoulder. "No. They're closing in. We're outnumbered. There's too many of them and they got more guns."

"We just have to —"

Noose looked down at his arm as Bess gripped it tightly, then looked up into her strong, honest eyes that stared back into his own with calm force. "We have to split up. You head west." She pointed. "That way. Plenty of cover that direction." Bess looked over her shoulder, lips compressed. "I'm going to go back and intercept Butler and his gang. I'll lead them in the other direction, get them off your trail. Point them east. Say I saw you head that way."

"What if they don't believe you?"

"That's my problem. I'm a U.S. Marshal and it's time I start acting like one."

"But —"

"No buts. I'm the law and I'm giving the orders around here."

"Fair enough."

She reached toward her right holster. "I'm gonna give you one of my guns so you're not unarmed."

He put his hand on hers as she touched her pistol and shook his head. "Bad idea. Butler is no fool and nothing gets by him. You can bet he'll notice one of your guns is missing and be asking questions."

"I'll say I dropped it."

Bess saw Noose give her a skeptical glance and she said, "Yeah, I wouldn't believe me, either."

Noose saw from her decisive expression there was no arguing with her. "Marshal."

She looked him a question.

"Thanks for everything you're doing for me." His face was holding back the emotion he felt. "You saved my life."

Bess returned a cocky smile. "Maybe you can do the same for me sometime."

"I always return a favor. Good luck."

With that, Noose turned and sprinted down the ravine into the rocks and brush, heading in the direction away from the sun into the rugged wilderness ahead. As he made tracks, he looked back twice over his shoulder.

The first time Bess was halfway back up the hill.

The second time she was gone.

Noose was by himself again.

But he didn't feel alone.

"Easy."

Marshal Bess Sugarland stepped out of the brush with her open palms spread away from the guns in her holsters.

Frank Butler glowered at her as he slowly thumbed the hammer of his Colt Dragoon he had pointed in her face out of cocking position. His black eyes never left her as he nudged his jaw, and the rest of the gang slowly lowered the guns they had aimed at the marshal.

Bess noticed Culhane and Lawson took the longest amount of time to take their guns off her, itching to kill her in the worst way and looking for any excuse.

"You have some explaining to do," Butler said suspiciously.

"I'm the marshal around here. I don't have to explain anything. Especially to you," Bess said, walking with a lady swagger into the midst of the bounty killers.

"What were you doing took you so long?" His eyes followed her. His voice was flat.

"Your job for you." Bess turned to face Butler, removing her canteen from its shoulder strap and unscrewing the cap.

The leader's impassive expression betrayed the tiniest twitch of confusion.

She took a swig of water. "I found Joe Noose."

Bess felt seven pairs of eyes tighten like a garrote on her. She had their attention now.

"Then what?" Butler whispered, taking a threatening step closer.

"I chased him." She splashed water on her face, cool and collected in composure. Her indifference riled Butler like she knew it would.

"Then?" He spoke through clenched teeth now.

"I lost him. He got away." Bess shouldered her canteen.

"Funny. We didn't hear no gunshots."

"Because there weren't any. I was trying to take him alive."

"You expect me to believe that?" the leader snarled. Bess shrugged, turning her back on the posse and began walking back the way she came. "Where you think you're going, Marshal?" his voice called after her.

She tossed her reply over her shoulder at him like discarded wastepaper. "After him. You boys coming?"

"Wait up."

Bess stopped but didn't turn around, placing her hands on her hips, looking down at her boots impatiently in a posture that said they better hurry it up because she had better things to do. It was all an act and Bess figured she was playing the part pretty well so far, except her stomach was queasy with tension and churned like bubbling molasses. She tapped her toe, acting even more impatient as she listened to the chorus of boots coming up behind her, until a big shadow fell over her face and she looked up to see Frank Butler step in front of her to block her way. Bess looked into his cold dead eyes staring back at her above his black handlebar mustache a foot from her face.

"Which way did he go?" Butler asked calmly.

"West," she replied less calmly.

He just grinned.

She blinked first.

Then Butler had his Colt Dragoon revolver out of his holster and huge barrel jammed up under her jaw so quick it choked her intake of breath.

He lost the grin.

The leader of the bounty killers spun Bess around and pinned her wrists behind her back with fearful strength using his free hand, while his other kept the gun to her chin. He looked to his gang.

"Take her guns. Tie her up. She's coming with us."

CHAPTER 33

The horse named Copper knew it would find him.

That in the end Copper's long journey would take it back to his friend was as much a positive certainty for this stallion as knowing the barn would be there when it came back would be for another horse.

The man was such a long way away the stallion could barely see him. A far-off tiny figure climbing down the hill was all that the horse could make out from where it stood but that was him, all right: Copper recognized the color of his clothes and his large body shape and something about the way his friend moved.

The steed's gut simply told him it was Joe Noose.

There had been another person with the man, a woman who had left and gone the other way, so now it was just his friend.

All the way across the rolling plain stood

the bronze stallion; a huge expanse of land lay between the spot its hooves stood on and the distant hill where the tiny figure of his friend came slowly and surely in his direction. Copper had been resting, exhausted from trotting at a vigorous clip during its search, picking up the pace in recent hours when it couldn't find his friend after looking everywhere and beginning to fret it never would. Just that morning, the horse had found the exact spot where he and his friend got separated after they tumbled when the man came out of the saddle and the horse fell in the river — but his friend was nowhere in sight. Since then, Copper had followed the many horse tracks nearby that had led it here. Now, laying eyes on his friend again, the horse experienced a unique and particularly equine joy, a bond and connection filling the stallion's heart with a fulfilling sense of purpose and belonging that felt like drinking water when it was very thirsty, its insides empty but now filled.

The horse considered walking toward his friend to close the gap between them and hasten their reunion, but the man was heading his way, getting closer though still far off and would be back in the saddle soon enough. Besides, for the horse there were other considerations — the cool spot of shade Copper was standing in felt nice on his coat after running under the hot sun all day and the tree that the horse stood beside had apples. The gorgeous bronze stallion was in the process of reaching its head up and biting into a sweet and juicy one that exploded with delicious flavor in its mouth when it noticed his friend had stopped walking and now just stood. Then he did something Copper couldn't understand:

His friend was walking again but had turned around and was going back in the other direction.

The way the girl went.

Bess felt the cold press of circular metal against the base of her chin. She felt the pressure of the muzzle increase and heard the *snick* of the hammer pulled back. She would have recognized Butler's smell even if he wasn't a foot from her face.

"We'll take those pistols, little lady," he said in a dead voice.

Bess's hands hovered, twitching, an inch from her father's twin Colt Peacemakers in their holsters on her belt but nobody was that fast — the cocked pistol against her neck was now on a hair trigger and the bullet would explode through her throat before she even touched, let alone drew, her guns.

Her stomach sank.

This was bad.

She'd been made.

"What do you think you're doing, Mr. Butler? I'm an acting U.S. Marshal."

"I already shot one marshal. Killin' two don't make no difference to me. Hell, two marshals would be a matched pair."

Bess's blood froze.

He'd admitted it.

"You shot my father. Not Noose . . ." Her voice came out of her tense throat as a dry rasp. Bess stared straight ahead, frozen in place, trying not to cry.

She saw his teeth glint in a cold chuckle.

"That's right, little girl." Butler loomed before her as he took a step closer, keeping his revolver jammed against her jawbone. The cold barrel against her skin suddenly felt colder to her, like ice against her flesh . . . it felt colder because there was no way this man would have admitted to the crime if he was going to let her live. He spoke again, slowly and calmly. "Now, I'm going to take your pistols. If you move to stop me, I'll blow your head clean off."

Bess nodded and kept her eyes on his face. There was the sound of a scrape of metal on leather and the weight on the left side of her belt lightened as she felt the bounty

271

killer remove the gun. Then she heard the rustle of leather as it was jammed in his belt. "You're gonna kill me anyway," Bess said, jaw set, looking forward. "You just admitted you killed the marshal to a sworn law enforcement officer. That reward's on your head now. If you think I'm gonna keep it quiet, then —"

"You ain't sayin' nothin' to nobody, sister." Her second pistol was pulled from her right holster and Bess was unarmed. "Tie her hands."

The last comment was to his men, and Culhane and Lawson quickly came over with a lariat and, grabbing Bess's arms so she couldn't move, lassoed the rope around her wrists and pulled it tight enough to cut off the circulation. Seconds later, they had the rope wound around her forearms and her arms tied off.

Frank Butler lowered his gun to waist level, keeping the long barrel pointed at the female marshal's midriff, and jerked his head to his gang.

With the captive in tow, they spent the next five minutes walking in silence back up the ravine. Bess could feel Butler right behind her and didn't need to look back to know his Colt Dragoon was aimed pointblank at her spine. That hammer was still cocked. As she walked, sometimes receiving a push from her captors, her arms tied in front of her, Bess looked left and right, trying to think of what to do but came up with nothing. She was screwed. Then before she knew it, they had reached the spot where the horses were tethered on the bleak trail.

"Put her on her horse," Butler ordered standing by his saddle. "She's coming with us."

The two bounty killers Culhane and Lawson shoved Bess across the grass to her grazing riderless dun-colored quarter horse. Both of the men were enjoying pushing her around and Bess flinched as one of the thugs, she couldn't see who, grabbed her denimed buttocks with his thick hands and hoisted her up by the behind while the other lifted her boot into a stirrup, heaving her unceremoniously into the saddle. The two pairs of dirty hands that helped her up on the horse groped her as they did. The young woman recoiled in disgust, tossing her hair out of her face. *How was she going to get out of this?* she wondered. The answer came fast: *she wasn't.* When Bess was settled in the saddle, her roped hands in her lap, Butler climbed onto his malevolent black stallion, rode over, and came up to her, stopping his horse alongside.

She held his malignant gaze, scared to death but trying not to show it.

"Reckon you won't be needin' this anymore," the bounty killer said. Reaching over with his leather-gloved hand, Butler plucked the seven-star silver marshal's badge from her shirt and tossed it in the dirt by the hoof of his horse.

Bess Sugarland's face suddenly colored. *"That was my father's badge,"* she screamed.

And spat in Frank Butler's face.

The mask of shock and surprise his face became as saliva dripped down his handlebar mustache was worth getting killed for, Bess thought recklessly. The leader was at a disadvantage for a few brief seconds but the sweet moment didn't last long.

A few of the gang whistled and hooted at their female prisoner's nerve in spitting on their leader, laughing even louder knowing what she would get in return. Butler flew into a rage and swung furiously in his saddle on the men who laughed, and they shut up fast as in the same movement he spun back on the woman on the horse beside him, pulling back his gloved fist, and punched her savagely in the face.

Bess held his gaze fiercely as the blow came.

When it did, it nearly broke her jaw.

Her head was sledgehammered sideways, blood flying from her lips and splattering her tossing hair. The force of his fist nearly knocked her clean out of the saddle, but she stayed on, blinding pain shooting up the side of her face. When she looked back, her vision swam and she could not see anything but his black-eyed stare locked psychotically with her own. His clenched fist remained raised, poised to strike again.

"Go to hell," an unblinking Bess hissed to his face.

Then Butler cracked a yellow-tooth grin, taking her measure. "I'll say hi for ya," he chuckled, nodding appreciatively.

Dropping her gaze, Bess broke the stare-down with Butler, digging deep to not cry, because she would have preferred the bullet she expected rather than have these scum see her weak like that. Butler knew this, she understood, because now she felt weak and debased, unarmed and captive. The lasso pinned her arms to her side, and her wrists were roped. Bess couldn't do anything but sit the horse. She was helpless, and when she finally gathered the grit to raise her gaze to meet Butler's again she saw the sadistic gleam of enjoyment in his eyes at bringing her low.

Then the clapping hands, chicken clucks, wolf whistles, and shouts of derision reached her ears on all sides as the gang of bounty killers mocked her. Bess grimaced in the saddle and avoided their gaze.

A piercing whistle from the leader shut the gang of vultures right up. "Daylight's wasting and we got a reward to catch, boys."

The rest of the gang mounted their horses.

Leather touched her hands and Bess Sugarland saw that Frank Butler had pressed her horse's reins into her fingers. He was leaning across over her saddle, his face an inch from hers and she felt his hot, animal breath but it was that voice of his that scared her as he whispered viciously in her ear.

"Spit on me again and I'll let my men take turns with you," Butler growled. He meant it, she could tell. With a violent sweep of his reins, the leader of the bounty killers swung his big black horse about and cantered off down the trailhead.

Bess, now a prisoner, was escorted on horseback by two of the other professional killers, Sharpless and Trumbull, as the gang rode off in single-file procession, relentlessly on the trail of their elusive prey, one Joe Noose.

CHAPTER 34

A half mile away, the bounty killers and their female captive rode along the trail. Butler and his men were keeping a sharp eye out for Noose, and their guns were out and fingers on the triggers.

At least they haven't shot me yet, she was thinking.

Up in front, Bess rode just behind the leader. She glared at the back of his broad-shouldered leather duster and the wide brim of his black hat, that hat turning with his head left and right in a steady movement as he surveyed their surroundings for their quarry, looking for sign.

The ropes painfully lashed around her wrists binding them together were tight enough to cut off blood circulation to her hands — it was getting difficult to keep the reins in her fingers. Balance in the saddle on the horse was tricky without the use of her arms, but she used her strong hips and long legs in the stirrups to stay mounted.

Bess was relieved that the rest of the gang was behind her and could see only the back of her head. Her swollen face throbbed uncomfortably with each stride of the horse and when she looked down she saw her shirt was soaked with blood dripping from her mouth. It shamed her modesty being in such a state among men like this, but she swallowed it because she had more important things to worry about . . . like her life.

Making a mental checklist as the posse doggedly rode on, Bess knew the first priority was staying alive — the second, because she was a sworn peace officer, was saving the innocent man Noose — the third was killing all these murdering bastards because, lawman or not, she was going to make sure not a single one of them got out of here alive. Bess meant to get her hands on some guns and when she did she would shoot all of them dead. Justice would be delivered with the barrel of a gun. These men deserved to die. She thirsted to kill them herself. If she got the chance.

First priority, she reminded herself, *stay alive.*

Hearing the impacts of the hooves crunching on the leaves in the dirt, it sounded to Bess like more than there were. Seven of these bounty killers remained but they sounded like fifty, like an army to her. It was because the bullets could start flying at any second, she knew. It was second nature to Bess Sugarland to anticipate problems. Her father had taught her that. The minute these shootists spotted Noose or he spotted them, everybody's guns would be drawn and fired indiscriminately. Bullets would be flying around her and she would be unarmed and directly in the line of fire. Already the young woman had figured out that when that happened she would throw herself out of the saddle, off the horse, and flatten on the ground, which would be the safest place. Then she remembered the horses' hooves. The animals would be rearing and running and if she was on the ground unable to move her upper body there was a good chance she would be trampled to death. Bess became lost in her thoughts as she tried to figure out what her next move would be then.

So when Butler spoke to her she was startled. "I know what you're thinking, sister," he said without looking back as he rode a few yards ahead. "You're wondering why we ain't killed you, wonderin' why we ain't done it yet. Yeah, you don't know why we ain't killed you yet, I'm bettin'."

He had read her thoughts.

That made her mad.

But she needed to keep her cool. Listen carefully. Figure out these killers. Get a step ahead of them. "Maybe I am," she said, just to keep the conversation going.

"I'll tell ya, then."

That's a tell, Bess thought. *Butler needs to show he's smarter than everybody else. He likes to hear himself talk.* The young woman suddenly realized she had found a weakness in the leader that she might be able to exploit if she had an opportunity. Bess wore a little smile as she let Butler continue.

"I'm figuring you make good bait. That's the reason. This Noose fella, he's a water-walker, a self-righteous, holier-than-thou, do-the-right-thing type of individual. Men like that just piss me off. Right this very hot second as far as he knows he has only his own ass to worry about. He's running for his life just now, and that's simple because all he figures he has to do is run hard and fast enough. But here's the thing, sister: my guess is you change that equation. I'd bet half the reward money that when Noose knows we got you, when he sees what we're gonna do to you, he won't be able to stop himself from coming to rescue you, walkin' straight into our guns, and that will be his worst mistake and his last one. He's a hero, and heroes die hard because there ain't no place for heroes in this world. That's for damn sure. That's right, little girl. You're gonna flush him out for us. Then it's all gonna be over and we'll get our money and we'll be rich."

But dead, Bess thought. *Good luck spending it.* "Sounds like you got it all figured out," she said.

Ahead, the back of Butler's big hat tilted up and down as he nodded. "Looks like you got some use after all. You gone from bein' a thorn in my side to my ace in the hole."

Wrong, Bess thought. *I'm going to be the finger on the trigger of the gun shooting the bullet with your name on it.*

If only he had a gun.

A weapon of any kind.

He should have taken the pistol Bess offered.

It had been a mistake not to. Had seemed a bad idea at the time for Bess to risk raising Butler's suspicion by giving up one of her revolvers, but now she didn't have any revolvers because Butler had gotten wise to her anyway. The way things had shaken out everything went south anyhow, so while it looked like the wrong thing to do then, if

Noose had taken the gun he'd be packing iron now . . . at least one of them would be. Lesson was *always have a pistol.* It's always the right choice, never the wrong choice to have one. In the future, if he found himself unarmed and somebody offered him a gun, Noose wouldn't refuse it for any reason no matter what. But until then he would have to improvise.

Noose peered through the bushes.

Three hundred yards away, down the embankment, the single-file procession of bounty killers made their way out of the tree line along the trail. The men all had their guns out and he saw the movements of their faces turning as they looked everywhere for him. Joe Noose made damn sure he kept his head down.

When he saw the woman on the horse riding with them his stomach lurched, seeing her hands were tied even before noticing her badge was gone. The marshal's daughter was their prisoner now.

Hell.

They'd taken her guns — her holsters were empty, he saw.

Bess hadn't looked scared before but she looked so now though her face was a stoic mask. This girl had guts, despite her young years, and the bounty hunter admired her plenty. When he saw natural character in a person he recognized it.

The horses kept moving, slinking in predatory procession, the gang passing below. Noose loved horses and knew even bad men rode good horses and it wasn't the horses that were wrong but the owners . . . but these steeds looked as foul as their riders, brutish and malignant, an aggressive surly gait and predation to their every step. It was as if the evil the bounty killers exuded had infected the horses they rode. While under normal circumstances Noose never shot a horse if he could avoid it, he would put these animals right down if the time came and he had the chance.

Bess Sugarland was a dead woman.

Even if Butler didn't know Bess knew Noose had been framed by the men responsible for the murder, there was no way the leader of the gang was going to let an officer of the law live to tell how she'd been taken prisoner, because he and his men would all swing from the gallows if she lived to tell the tale.

The horse with the marshal's daughter passed directly below him and Noose got the closest look at her he was going to get.

She'd been manhandled and punched in the face, judging by the bruise and swelling and blood on her mouth, but she was very tough. A normal woman would be a mess of tears and humiliation at that treatment and would look defeated but this girl did not. Noose could only guess why she was being taken along with them alive, but was glad they had spared her life. This gang was a piece of work.

None of the bounty killers looked in his direction, even as they looked almost everywhere else. His cover of branches and leaves was dense and he was in shadow. But Noose could see them all clear as day.

He had to get that girl out of there.

She didn't have much time left — every minute in that bad company was a threat to her life and limb.

But he had no guns.

He had no bullets.

Then he had an idea.

The large boulder on his left had been unstable when he took cover behind it a few moments before and it nearly tumbled down the hill. Luckily, he'd stopped it from rolling.

The gang rode from right to left below him and on the other side of the trail the embankment steepened, overgrown with thick bushes and undergrowth. It was too steep for horses but a person could get down it and be lost to sight a few yards in. Noose saw how he could create the perfect distraction, and if Bess had the brain he figured she did, the marshal's daughter could use the confusion to escape.

He hoped she had a good head on her shoulders.

Noose shoved the rock.

The crashing of a heavy object tumbling through the bushes above them, rolling down the embankment, made all the bounty killers look up and aim their guns at once.

Bess's head swung around at the gang and saw nobody was looking at her.

All the men's eyes were locked on the approaching boulder that rolled over and over down the hill toward them. Culhane and Lawson, too quick on the trigger, blasted their guns uselessly up into the woods. To the credit of the rest, their reflexes were fast and most of the gang didn't fire a shot or waste a bullet. All of them saw it was a falling rock even before it glanced off a thick tree trunk that sent it tumbling harmlessly out of their path.

"It's nothing," growled Butler.

The guns were lowered.

Thumbed-back hammers were slowly released.

You could hear a chorus of exhales.

Butler rotated his head to look fiercely back at his men. His eyes widened in fury.

Bess's saddle was empty.

She was long gone.

CHAPTER 35

Four long miles away from where Joe Noose was, the two Jackson Hole lawmen riding in his direction heard the shots.

Marshal Mackenzie reined his horse on the narrow trail in the valley above Hoback and put up his gloved hand for Deputy Swallows to halt. The peace officers turned their heads toward the mountainous rise ahead and adopted an intensely listening attitude.

A string of distant *cracks* emanated from somewhere in the towering pine forest blanketing the rugged barrier range of the Hoback Junction where the Snake River forked . . . where exactly the lawmen couldn't be sure, but the sound of gunfire was unmistakable and plenty of shots were being exchanged. The echoes of the guns reverberated in the amplification of the walls of the forested canyons a few miles ahead.

Finally, it stopped.

The reports dispersed in the light wind.

Mackenzie and Swallows swung their glances to each other, both thinking the same thing: *maybe this thing is over and the U.S. Marshal's killer has been shot dead.*

No way to tell.

They had to keep going, see firsthand.

At least they knew they were headed in the right direction.

The lawmen spurred their horses and rode on.

"Something ain't right about this," said Mackenzie.

"Damn right it ain't," retorted Swallows.

"I heard tell about that gang of bounty hunters. Them boys that passed through and is chasing this reward," the marshal said. "You were out running an errand when they stopped by."

"What did you hear?" the deputy inquired.

"None of it good," his boss replied, and left it at that.

"That so?"

"Let's just say there ain't no dead or alive about those boys. They always bring the men in dead."

"Ain't against the law."

"Even when they don't have to kill 'em, they do. It's like they take pleasure in it. Frank Butler and his boys like shooting

288

people, they say. You missed that gang when they rode through Jackson a couple days back. Like a black cloud it was."

"I'll take your word for it, sir."

"Those bounty hunters brought to mind a kettle of vultures."

"Buzzards they sound like, for sure."

"Their leader, Butler. That man had killer's eyes. Dead." Mackenzie shook his head.

"The bounty hunter profession ain't a nice line of work," Swallows replied. "That's why you and me, we do this. But somebody got to do that."

"I don't like them. But like's got nothing to do with it. In this job, we have to deal with all types." The marshal thumbed his chin, thinking for a minute. "Now, as I recollect it, when Butler and his boys stopped by our office they found out about that fugitive Jim Henry Barrow, the Victor bank robber there's the reward on. They said they were going after the bounty on him. Joe Noose had come through earlier, asked us the same questions about Barrow, then went after him. You were there." The deputy nodded as the marshal kept talking. "Noose, he said he meant to bring Barrow in alive. Anyhow, I told them Butler boys Noose had a head start on them on that reward. As I remember, they took off like their asses were on fire."

"What are you getting at, sir?"

"Hell if I know. Reckon we'll soon find out."

Both lawmen laughed a little. The conversation lagged for a while and neither man spoke for a few minutes as they rode over the grassy plain. A cloud passed over the sun in the lowering skies and a shadow fell across the Teton Pass mountain range miles west to their right. The deputy lapsed into a thoughtful silence, then finally shook his head *no* to himself. The marshal, who had been rolling a cigarette in his saddle and was now in the process of licking the paper, looked over at his man.

"Joe Noose, he don't fit the type to kill Marshal Sugarland," Swallows said. "Why would he do it?"

"Folks kill people." Mackenzie shrugged, striking a match. "Ain't always a why. Wish there was. It would simplify things and make our job a lot easier." He puffed.

"There's got to be a why."

"The marshal and he had some kind of disagreement we don't know about, at least not yet." Mackenzie shrugged.

"I heard lots of stories about Noose," Swallows added. "Colorful individual. He was a lawman out in Cody. Ran cattle in New Mexico."

"He don't wear a badge no more. Heard about Noose, too. He's been in jail. Killed a man."

"I never heard that."

"Justifiable homicide was the charge. Five-year sentence. They suspended it. He was let out because the local law needed him for something, disremember what. It was dangerous work and he's a dangerous man, so they say, and he had the skill set required."

"You sure that was Noose?"

"Pretty sure. The name is memorable."

"I don't see him killing Sugarland, Marshal. Something ain't right about this."

"Listen, Swallows. Nate Sugarland's own daughter called in to get the reward authorized for Noose and she was the deputy. I say 'was' because with her father dead she's the acting marshal right now. I know that girl and you do, too, and she's got a level head. Bess must have seen Noose do it or why would she have telegraphed us? Stands to reason she's a witness."

"Mebbe."

"Maybe what?"

"Well, mebbe she is. Or mebbe one of Butler's boys had a gun to her head. Or otherwise put her up to it someways, somehow."

"A thing is what it looks like. Most of the time, in my experience, exactly what it looks like. Regardless, this is why we're riding over there to intercept them and get to the bottom of this."

"Hold up." Both lawmen slowed their horses to a trot at the obstruction they had come to.

A wide stretch of the mighty Snake River lay before them, a powerful surging flow of flat rapids moving slowly through a wending ravine in the valley floor.

There was a sheep bridge across it.

A narrow, weathered, rickety wooden structure wide enough for only one horse to cross at a time.

It stretched over a two-hundred-and-twenty-foot width of muddy blue-brown water serpentining through the valley.

"I hate this bridge," the marshal said.

"I hate it, too," the deputy agreed.

"Why those heathens didn't build the damn thing wide enough for two horses to cross side by side, I'll never know," said Mackenzie. "Well, let's get across. I'll go first if it makes you feel better."

That settled, spurring their horses, the two lawmen trotted down the declination toward the shoreline and moments later rode their horses in a single-file procession across the old bridge spanning the Snake.

CHAPTER 36

Her boots kicked up the dirt.

Bess Sugarland had seen her chance and seized it when seconds before she had jumped out of the saddle off the horse. Her trammeled hands were bound in front of her so her departure wasn't graceful by any means: she landed on the slope like a sack of potatoes but the sound of impact when her shoulder slammed to the ground of the muddy embankment was muffled by the loud din of the falling boulder so none of the gang heard her running feet escape down the hill.

Now Bess barreled like a mad steer through the undergrowth — half running, half sliding, half falling, and getting up again in her rushed descent down the hill, not looking back.

No bullets came her way.

That was all she needed to worry about.

She was shielded from view by the thick

trees and branches and when the shots finally came they missed by a mile. Bess knew these boys could shoot. The gang could not see her or where she went from their present position, or they would have hit what they aimed at.

Even so, Bess Sugarland thought the best idea was to keep running and that's exactly what she did.

That falling rock was no damn accident — Butler knew better.

It was Noose.

He'd known that taking the woman hostage would flush out their man sooner or later but Noose had outsmarted him and been a step ahead. Now Butler had lost the girl, a live witness to the frame-up, and if she talked to anybody the jig was up.

She had to be silenced.

The leader of the bounty killers reined his rearing black horse around with one hand, his cocked Colt Dragoon clenched in the other gloved fist, his keen observant eyes cutting back and forth scanning the slope above his gang. All he could see were thick rows of conifers, bushy branches, walls of dense green — that slippery bastard Noose could be thirty yards away and Butler might still not see him. If he was out there, he was being quiet as a ghost.

Too quiet, in fact. No shots had come from above, and Noose would have a clear shot at Butler and his men, which meant only one thing: Noose was out of bullets and defenseless.

That was the good news.

The bad news was Butler was going to have to split his gang up. They couldn't let that marshal's daughter get away, and she had a head of steam on now, probably already a quarter mile away in woods it would be easy to hide out in.

And with Noose so close he and some of his boys had to chase him down, because without the man's corpse slumped over a saddle there wouldn't be no reward anyhow.

"Culhane! Lawson! Get after that woman!" Butler roared. "If you see her, shoot her! Blow her damn head off if you can! I want her dead! Dead, you hear me?"

With terse, obedient nods, the two bounty killers followed orders and quickly dismounted, tying the reins of their horses to the trees. Drawing out their Winchester and Sharps rifles, the thugs jumped down the slope below the trailhead and hurried after the female marshal in the direction they saw her depart. Soon the shootists were lost to view in the dense woods.

The leader swung his gaze to Sharpless, Garrity, Trumbull, and Wingo. "The rest of you, come with me! That son of a bitch we're after can't be far! Time is money! Let's finish this business!"

Jagging his spurs into his stallion's flanks, Butler charged the frothing beast directly up the hill into the slanted tangle of trees. The pounding hooves of the horse's muscle-bound legs cut into the dirt as it drove its hulking body relentlessly upward, climbing with ferocious lunges of speed, the steed's eyes as insane as those of its master. Birds exploded from the trees in frightened flight at the clamor of the dangerous horse and rider.

In Butler's furious wake, Sharpless, Garrity, Wingo, and Trumbull drew their rifles and pistols and galloped in single-file formation after their leader, ready to shoot anything that moved . . . even, it might look to the casual observer, each other.

She'd gotten away!

That beautiful sight had made Noose's heart leap with hope and his pulse skipped a beat with excitement.

The marshal's daughter, smart as he'd counted on, used the distraction of the falling rock to jump out of her saddle — she was off her horse and away down the slope in mere seconds, it seemed.

They gang was splitting up. *Good.* Below, Noose saw the chaos and confusion of spinning horses and heard Butler yelling orders — then two of the bounty killers were dismounted and racing down the hill after the woman and the leader and his other four men were riding up the hill in his general direction.

And that was not good.

So Noose started running.

As he heard the thunder of the approaching hooves and creaking of saddle leather, the cowboy saw glimpses of the riders through the leaves.

They had a lot of guns out.

He didn't have any.

Bad odds.

Staying low, avoiding the tree branches so as not to make noise or movement, Joe Noose sprinted across the muddy dirt, keeping his boots squarely in the undergrowth. He wanted to avoid leaving sign they could track. He could hear the bounty killers getting closer but they would not know where he was exactly. And up here with him, they were down to five. That was a whole lot better than twelve, as yesterday had started.

The gang was at a disadvantage splitting

up with their numbers reduced. If Butler didn't know that, he should. Divide and conquer was Noose's plan. The cowboy pushed on through the woods, seeing nothing ahead but more trees and patches of sky through the treetops.

What Noose needed to do was take down one of those riders and steal his horse, getting the man's guns — then he'd have a fighting chance to shoot it out with Butler and the other bastards. But to do that, Noose couldn't be out front — he'd have to get behind them somehow . . . or *above* them.

He switched his gaze to the pine tree twenty feet to his right.

The nearest branch was just low enough.

They sounded like they were no more than a hundred yards behind her on the other side of the thick tree trunk Bess stood pressed flat against, not moving a muscle.

Sounded like three of seven men, maybe two, she couldn't tell — but only a few of the gang were after her. The rest would be after Joe Noose, so she whispered a hushed prayer for him.

Holding her breath, not making a sound, the young woman just kept her ears open and listened. The fat tree trunk she knew

299

shielded her from view. The unseen bounty killers mumbled curses and spat on the ground, making no effort to be quiet as they lumbered like oxen through the underbrush. Muffled voices sounded through the bushes.

"— *You see her?* —" Culhane. Crap. She knew his voice.

"— *Bitch* —" Lawson. Of course.

"— *Wait a minute. Think I heard her* —"

The two bounty killers who most wanted her hide were the ones Butler had sent after her and that meant Butler wanted her dead, not recaptured.

For a long, scary moment, Bess tensed up and clenched her eyes shut as the boot falls of the professional killers stopped and it got very quiet while they strained their ears trying to hear some sound of her.

"— *I don't hear squat* —"

"— *Which way?* —"

"*That way.*"

Patience wasn't these lowlifes' long suit, and seconds later Bess heard them on the move again.

The footsteps were moving away from her, deeper into the forest down the declination below. When the clumsy noises they made became distant, Bess chanced a glance from around the edge of the tree trunk and saw the flash in the nick of time before the heavy-caliber round blew off a fist-sized chunk of bark and wood that showered her face with splinters as the shot missed her nose by an inch. She cried out and then they knew exactly where she was.

The woman took off.

Bullets flew past her ears.

Bess didn't dare look back.

She just watched where she was putting her feet as the rutted ground dropped and rose, rose and dropped, side-skidding her boots down the muddy slope — a twisted or broken ankle at this moment would end her. Gunshots rang out behind — muffled *cracks* in the forest — and slugs sang through the leaves and branches, rebounding off rocks and tree trunks to her right and left.

Either they were bad shots or she was faster or they were slower than she thought.

Right now Bess was alive and her adrenaline was pumping so she ran for her life away from the bounty killers chasing her down. And she had a little more motivation than they did: her own skin.

With her hands tied in front of her, the rope lashed around her wrists threw her off balance on the uneven ground.

Jumping over a boulder, she scampered down a ridge.

CHAPTER 37

Marshal Mackenzie and Deputy Swallows had just ridden up the mountain trailhead into a densely forested glen and decided to rest their horses a moment, when no sooner had they swung out of the saddle than the two strangers showed up.

The Jackson lawmen noticed them first. Saw both individuals were very out of breath, panting heavily. The men had clearly been running. Two big fellows in long dusters and no hats, carrying Winchester and Sharps rifles and, judging from their perspiring winded faces, busy chasing something or being chased by something right up to the moment they saw the two lawmen. Then they stopped dead in their tracks, regarding the interlopers with flat eyes and after a beat started to come across the glen in a casual stride toward the peace officers. Cool customers indeed, the marshal judged, going from running like the devil was on their tail to walking like they were just passing the time of day without a care in the world.

His deputy was reading his thoughts. "Huntin'?" Swallows said out of the side of his mouth.

"Hunting somethin'," Mackenzie replied out the other side of his.

One of the approaching men, who had a beard and a scar across his face, raised his hand in greeting.

"Howdy," the other called across the grass, a long and thin man with features like a battle hatchet.

"Howdy back," said the marshal.

His deputy made do with a nod.

Seeing as the strangers were coming to them and despite their big guns and aggressive appearance that indicated they meant harm, Mackenzie and Swallows went back to tying off their horses' reins on the tree and refreshing their mounts with water from a canteen. Mackenzie was laconic in all things, slow in his movements from age; Swallows moved slow for other reasons having more to do with lethal cool — but both men moved very quick and drew very fast when the occasion demanded it and their metal badges were in plain view on their hats and the lawmen's Winchester and Henry repeater rifles were in easy reach on their horses' saddles as were the Colt Single Action Army revolvers in their gun belts. If these men heading toward them were in the market for some trouble, the Jackson Hole U.S. Marshal's office would give them all the business they could handle.

The armed men kept on coming, easy as you please, taking their sweet time in the approach. The marshal guessed this was a deliberate attempt to act casual, given how dodgy an entrance they'd made moments before.

Never taking his muddy brown eyes off the two blurry figures expanding in his field of vision, Mackenzie took a swig of his canteen and splashed it on his hot face. His eyesight was bad at distance and his hard stare that they probably took for hostility was just the old man hoping his vision would clear enough to see who he was dealing with. Didn't matter in the end — his reliable deputy had perfect twenty-twenty vision and the old man didn't need to move his head to know Swallows had just loaded his long-range Henry rifle because he heard the familiar *snick* of the hammer being cocked.

Mackenzie's attention was trained on those two strangers who had made their presence known and, even though he could discern only their blurry shapes, several thoughts traveled through his mind.

What are these men doing out here in the middle of nowhere? Had to be one of two things. *They're being chased by or chasing something on four legs or two.*

And whatever they want, what is it?

As the bounty killer called Lawson was halfway across the field toward the lawmen he had identified by the gleam of sunlight glinting off the metal of the marshal star on the hat badge, he suddenly recognized the old one and nudged Culhane, walking beside him. "Look. That's that marshal from Jackson we handed over Bonny Kate to."

The other gunman lifted his hand to his brow to block the sunlight and made visual confirmation. "Good call. That's him, all right. Other one must be the deputy. Wasn't there when we were. Won't know us. We got nothing to worry about. Marshal won't remember seeing us, neither."

"It was four days ago."

"Could be two seconds ago. Won't know your face. Trust me."

The bounty killers were a good two hundred yards from the peace officers who they had a pressing question to ask of, too far away for their conversation to be overheard, but they kept their voices down anyway so as not to take any chances. They were professionals and it was their job not to do anything stupid.

"That old-timer's been looking straight at us this whole time," Lawson said tightly. "Must recognize us."

"He don't recognize us." With a smile, Culhane shook his head and didn't drop his stride.

"He's looking right at us."

"Don't know our faces."

"Excuse me, friend, I have seen that look on many a lawdog's face before and that look is, *I recognize you, boy.* That look is, *I know your face.*"

"Nope, what that look is, indeed, is, *I'm staring in your direction and squinting because I can't see nothing.* That old man over there can't see the nose in front of his own face."

"You don't know that. I say you're wrong."

Culhane cocked his head to Lawson, giving him a narrow glance. "Think back, friend. You need to be more observant like I always tell ya, Long Gone. Remember back at the marshal's office? Were you paying attention?" The other shootist nodded. "The old man had to keep putting on and taking off his thick glasses every time he looked up from his desk. Took 'em off to look down at the papers on his desk, put 'em on when he looked up. Them glasses were for *distance.* You and me was standing right over him at his desk two feet from his face when we signed on that reward receipt and all our faces was to him was a big old blur."

"You sound mighty confident about that."

"I notice things. You should get into the habit."

Lawson returned the side-eye. "You're so cocky, put your money where your mouth is. A third of my share of the Noose bounty says that this marshal remembers us right away when we ask him our question. So, he don't recognize us, I pay you, let's see, with five of us down, that's up to fourteen thousand dollars and change apiece for each now. Let's call it five thousand dollars you pay me, if the marshal knows us, when we collect the reward." Lawson leaned back at his waist and peered down his nose at Culhane.

Who merely replied, "So if he recognizes our faces or remembers meeting us I pay you five thousand bucks."

Lawson nodded and Culhane shook his head.

"I never take a bet I don't want to win."

"Have you officers seen a lost woman out

here all by her lonesome somewhere the last few miles?" the larger blur said, asking the question it seemed they had come over to ask.

Mackenzie was three feet from the speaker and couldn't make out his features with his piss-poor eyesight. The marshal kept his gaze squarely fixed at the upper part of the blur, figuring that's where the man's eyes were, so the guy he was talking to would feel intimidated thinking Mackenzie was looking at him fearlessly in the eye like any U.S. Marshal should. His distance glasses were in the case in his saddle and the marshal considered walking over and getting them, but that would mean he would have to show weakness by breaking the staredown with the out-of-focus stranger. Couldn't do that. You never wanted to be the one to blink first. Never wanted to be the one who broke a staredown, even though he couldn't say for sure if this man was even looking at him. The proud old lawman was image-conscious as part of the job and that age vanity was getting worse with the advancing years. He figured, wrongly, that folks didn't know he was half-blind if he simply stared in their faces when he talked to them. "Lost woman, you say," Mackenzie responded gravely after a suitable pause.

"Our sister," the second blur, who the old lawman could see in the corner of his eye without having to turn his head, replied a bit too quickly. "She got lost in the woods and we gots to find her."

"We thought maybe you good officers might have seen her along the trail while you were riding," the bigger blur said. "We're mighty glad we run into you. She'll be, too, if you can point us in her direction. If you happened to have seen her, that is."

Marshal Jack Mackenzie's eyes were bad but his nose was good . . . he'd smelled these men before. Wasn't sure where but he recognized something about their odor that sent warning signals through him. *Where had he met them?*

So he asked them.

They both said they had never met. Said it at the exact same time, like it was a planned response. The marshal's hunting dog instincts tingled and he'd get back to that in a minute with them. "The girl you say is gone missing who you're after, what did she look like?"

"Five feet high. Comes up to my shoulder. Bright brown hair. Hot as a pistol."

"Yeah, she sure is."

Mackenzie eyeballed the men, his aspect laconic and mock observant. "Hell, boys.

That fits the description of Bess Sugarland. Maybe you know her. U.S. Marshal's daughter. She's a deputy."

"Never heard of her."

"No?"

"Nope."

"And she's a marshal now. Her pop, Nate Sugarland, got murdered two days ago up in Hoback. You boys heard about that?"

"We're not from around here."

"Strange, you seem damn familiar."

"We got those kind of faces."

"I mean you smell familiar. I got a nose like a bloodhound. Never been one to remember a face. But I always remember a man's smell and my nose says we've met before. Yup, I know you boys."

"Like I say, we're just passing through."

"Chasing some runaway tail."

Mackenzie scowled. "*Tail* is a funny word to use about your sister, mister."

The bigger blur jumped in. "Our sister, she don't know the woods, scared of animals and such. Want to find her before she gets eaten by a bear. Well, we'll keep looking."

"Good luck."

The tense, awkward encounter ended as the bounty killers headed off toward the woods.

Marshal Mackenzie went to his saddlebags, took out his thick spectacles and put them on, turning to look with crystal vision in the direction of the departing pair.

"Mister." Mackenzie didn't say it as a question.

The men stopped, backs to the lawmen. Frozen.

"Can you boys look this way a minute?"

Lawson and Culhane slowly turned with blank, dead expressions.

Mackenzie saw both their faces clear as day with his glasses on.

The bounty killers saw the marshal had his glasses on now. His face had that look lawmen got, the look they had been talking about before, the look that told Culhane and Lawson they had been made. The shootists' jaws clenched. This could get messy. The way this day was going, real messy. Butler wasn't going to like it.

"I remember where I know you boys from," Mackenzie muttered quietly.

The marshal hooked his fingers in his belt and looked the gunmen square in their faces, switching his unblinking gaze between two pairs of jumpy unpredictable eyes. His big hands were nearer to his guns than theirs were to their own. "You boys were with Frank Butler and rode with that bounty posse done brought in Bonny Kate Valance three days ago. You were in my office in Jackson. I definitely remember you. All you guys made quite an impression. Probably got both your signatures on that reward receipt on my desk and could find your names if I looked. Last I recall you and your pals were riding out to Hoback to try to track down that reward on the fugitive Jim Henry Barrow. Riding in the direction of Hoback when I last saw you. Puts you right about here. And here you be."

"Yeah, that was us. Disremembered." Culhane turned up his palms in a vague gesture of surrender that brought both hands an inch closer to the smoke wagons slung in his holsters.

Lawson didn't do or say anything but was thinking about it.

"So you *do* know about the marshal being shot." Mackenzie didn't say it as a question.

With cold empty eyes and steel nerves, Culhane and Lawson watched Mackenzie and Swallows. "Don't know nothing about no marshal getting shot . . . *Marshal.*" The flat tone of Culhane's reply made the implication sound like a threat.

The deputy kept his hands on his rifle, and the marshal gripped his big knuckles on his belt, widening his liver-spotted old hands on the strap ever closer to his holstered pair of Colt SAA .45 revolvers. Mackenzie's jowls jiggled in a toothy chummy grin but his eyes held no warmth. "Why sure you do, boys. Butler and his gang called in the reward yesterday morning and are chasing down his killer and you're in the gang like you just said."

"I don't know what you're talking about."

"And I disbelieve you, son."

"I don't know what you're talking about because we split up with Butler two days ago."

"That so?"

"Me and Long Gone here both parted ways with the man."

"Why was that?"

"Had our money. Bonny Kate was a big payday. We're taking us a vacation. Fishing and such."

"With your sister. The one who got lost and you're looking for."

"Just so. No law against it."

"A sister who fits the description of Bess Sugarland, the dead marshal's daughter. Deputy Bess Sugarland, who called in the reward Butler is chasing down."

"Don't know nothing about that. We don't ride with Butler no more."

"When was the last time you saw Frank Butler?"

"Two days ago. At the bend of the Snake by Hoback Junction. That's where we went our separate ways."

"I'm supposed to believe that?"

"Believe what you want, Marshal. You want to charge us with something, be my guest. Don't see how anything in this game of twenty questions you've been playing the last few minutes has anything to do with any crime other than killing a marshal but you said that Butler is already hunting down Joe Noose for the reward so your problems are over."

"I never said his name was Joe Noose."

A shadow passed over the sun and the forest grew dark as the air suddenly crackled with tension as did the bodies of the four men facing one another in the woods. It got very quiet. All eyes were locked. Seconds passed and nobody spoke.

"Yes, you did," said Culhane softly.

"No, I did not."

"You said 'Noose.' I clearly remember. Didn't he say 'Noose,' Long Gone?"

"You said 'Noose.' Just now you did."

"You both need better ears or better lies because the whole last five minutes we've been talking I never once said his name was Noose. Now, keep those hands away from those gun belts and before I tell you boys to raise your hands and place you under arrest, I want to know —"

Culhane didn't blink as he interrupted. "You told us at your office. After we delivered Bonny Kate. After Mr. Butler asked about that reward on whoever his name was, you clearly said Joe Noose is a bounty hunter done already gone after it. That's what you said."

A moment passed, then Mackenzie raised a hand from his belt to scratch his head. "That is what I said, isn't it?"

"Yes, sir, it is."

"Still. It don't add up." The marshal shook his head slowly side to side, wearing a hooded expression and shuttered gaze. "Something ain't right."

Culhane clapped his hands together in loud report and boomed cheerfully, "Lot of things ain't right in these here United States of America, Marshal. That's a fact. Now, if you'll excuse us, we're mighty worried about our sister and want to catch up with her before a bear eats her or she gets snakebit. So . . ."

"Be on your way." Mackenzie waved them off dismissively.

The bounty killers headed into the trees.

They were gone from view a minute later.

■ ■ ■ ■

Fifteen minutes later, Culhane and Lawson
had returned to Frank Butler, telling him
Jackson Hole marshals were in the area
sniffing around their business and what was
he going to do about it.

That same fifteen minutes later Marshal
Jack Mackenzie was still kicking himself for
not thinking quick enough when he was
questioning the men — yes, it was plausible
those men heard him mention Joe Noose's
name but that would have been a full day
before Marshal Sugarland's murder and the
reward placed on Noose . . . *If these bounty
hunters had parted ways with Frank Butler's
gang when and where they claimed and Butler
and the rest of his men rode south to Hoback
before the marshal's demise even took place,
there's no way those sons of bitches could
have known about the reward on Noose
because they weren't there!*
And Mackenzie had let these sons of
bitches just walk away.
They had been lying through their teeth.
The question was *why?*
Why also were they chasing after a girl

who had to be Bess?

What the hell is going on here?

Chapter 38

Bess ran for her life, dashing around the large rock to her left and looking back over her shoulder.

She didn't see the two men ahead until she had bumped right into them.

Bess nearly cried out — had already pulled her clenched fists back to pummel the two men with punches and hit them with her fiercest blows, half figuring since they were going to shoot her anyway she might as well go out swinging.

But then she saw who they were.

And caught herself just in time.

Two familiar, friendly, and utterly unexpected faces looked back at her, dumbstruck.

It was the Jackson Hole lawmen Marshal Jack Mackenzie and his good-looking young deputy Nolan Swallows. She couldn't believe her luck, them showing up like this. Whether them riding like the cavalry to the rescue was by accident or design the woman didn't know nor care — that they were here was what mattered. The lawmen were both as clearly startled to see her as she was them — both her counterparts wore blank expressions of slack-mouthed shock. The peace officers were standing by their two horses, leading them up the narrow trail when Bess had come scrambling ass over teakettle around the big rock and crashed headlong right into Mackenzie.

It took the female lawman an instant to realize why the men were looking at her with such alarm: she understood her appearance must look shocking — bloody, bruised, her clothes tattered and her wrists bound with rope.

About to faint, Bess was too dazed to think of anything else to do but grin hello and then her legs gave out.

"It's all right, Bess, we got you." Mackenzie caught her. He was already pulling off his jacket and wrapping it around Bess's shoulders. The dismayed old man was visibly shook up with horror at the distressed sight of her.

Bess leaned against his barrel keg chest in exhausted and grateful relief. "Th-thank God you're here. Thank God. Thank God. It's so good to see you men. I thought y-you

— I thought you were *them.*" It sounded to Bess like she was babbling, her voice separated from herself.

Mackenzie hugged her tightly, covering her shoulders with his huge bear arms and rocking her. "What bastards done this to you?"

"They're coming." She gasped. "W-watch out. Be careful."

The marshal drew his knife from his belt and cut the rope binding the young woman's wrists and arms. Bess nodded thanks and rubbed her wrists to get the circulation going.

Hauling his Winchester repeater rifle out of his saddle holster, Deputy Swallows had already levered it several times, jacking several rounds into the breech, keeping a sharp lookout on the dense tree line rising up the steep ridge on all sides, scanning the area for any sign of movement. The young peace officer was listening so intensely it looked comically serious on his Johnny Appleseed freckled boyish face but looks were deceiving — Swallows was a deadly shot who wouldn't hesitate to pull the trigger. If any man popped his head out at this precise second, Swallows would shoot first and ask questions later — one bullet from the deputy anywhere up to a hundred yards and the man on the receiving end would be dead before he hit the ground. The deputy listened to the trees, his gun and his head moving left to right in perfect coordination. His nose went where his muzzle went. But other than a little wind in the leaves it was quiet, almost too quiet — the only sound was the hyperventilation of Bess's forced respiration and the rustle of clothing on her body against Mackenzie's.

Bess couldn't seem to use her words. Her mouth worked like she wanted to say something, but nothing but sputtering breaths escaped her lips.

"Was it the man who shot your father, Joe Noose?" the marshal asked gently, doing the talking for everybody, it seemed.

Adamantly and repeatedly, Bess shook her head *no.* Then the words came and once she started talking she couldn't stop. "No! No! Joe Noose didn't hurt me. Never laid a hand on me. And he didn't shoot my daddy, either. That was a big damn lie told by Frank Butler to get the reward."

Mackenzie and Swallows exchanged curious glances and looked completely confused. "But — I don't understand . . . you telegraphed from Hoback —"

"Forget all that." Bess shook her head and waved her hands dismissively, fixing her fellow lawmen in a steady penetrating gaze that held their attention. She continued, her voice calmer, "This is what happened, what really happened: Joe Noose was framed by this gang of bounty killers run by a man named Frank Butler. He's as bad as they come, fellas. Butler shot my father in cold blood just so he could frame Noose to get a reward put on his head that his gang could hunt Noose down and collect. This thing, it's all about money."

"You telegraphed us yourself about the reward —" Swallows was still confused, half his attention focused on guarding the perimeter with his rifle.

"I know I called in to get the reward authorized, but it was because they tricked me. My dad had been shot and I was upset and didn't know what to do and these killers used that advantage and railroaded me. These bounty killers, these are the same ones took me hostage and roughed me up. Same ones I just escaped from. And they're close by. The leader, Frank Butler, I mentioned is a no-account bloodthirsty murderer."

"I met him and you're right," Mackenzie agreed.

"Then you know he's a very dangerous individual. His posse are bad but Butler's the worst, and his gang do what he tells them. Noose killed a few of the gang. Five so far. Joe Noose is tough as hell but there's still seven of them to his one. We need to help him."

"Did this gang know you were a U.S. Marshal?"

"They knew."

The old marshal's face flushed with rage. "This won't stand."

"How many of these killers you say there is?" Swallows brooded.

"Counting Butler? Seven," Bess replied.

"And three of us," the Jackson marshal fretted.

"Four," she corrected. "Including Noose."

"Well, I don't know this Noose fellow's whereabouts and looking around this here group I count three. Up against seven. We're way outnumbered."

"So how do you think Noose feels right now?"

"If I was him I'd be shaking in my boots but he ain't my immediate concern, Bess. You are. The U.S. Marshals Service lost a good man yesterday. Ain't gonna lose his daughter, too. And my first order of business is getting you the hell out of here and back to Jackson directly. We're getting you to safety, then we're going to round up and deputize a posse and come back up here directly and get these killers and make 'em pay for their deeds. It won't take long, neither. We'll organize a hunting party and be back here in a few hours."

The woman's eyes were moist. "Noose may have minutes, not hours."

"Like I said, Bess —"

"Marshal Mackenzie — Jack . . . we got to help Joe Noose. It's seven-to-one odds and they have guns and bullets and he's unarmed. He's tough but nobody's tough enough to face those kind of odds."

"Bess, your father was a good friend of mine and —"

"I know but —"

"You're the marshal's daughter, Bess, Saving your life is the Marshals Service's priority."

"I can handle myself."

"Look at the state you're in, girl."

Bess hardened suddenly with controlled rage but kept her temper even though her voice was steel. "When my dad was gunned down, as his deputy I became the acting marshal of Hoback, Jack, you know that, and I still am. This crime happened in *my* jurisdiction and I intend to save this man with or without you. If you ain't gonna help out, give me a gun and ammo and get out of my way. I'm gonna kill that son of a bitch Frank Butler myself. He murdered my father, your friend, a U.S. Marshal, and now he's trying to kill an innocent man he framed to collect a fat reward he shot my dad to get. If that ain't evil, I don't know what is. This man must die. Today. I mean to pull the trigger."

Mackenzie watched the fearless and dangerous expression in Bess's determined face. She looked suddenly ten times tougher than he remembered. *What the hell happened to her?* he wondered. He didn't want to know the answer.

Bess wasn't done. "And I will not let Joe Noose die. Not on my watch. Not when there's a chance I can do something about it. That *we* can do something about it. Do those badges you're wearing mean something or not? We're the damn law. You boys gonna help me, or aren't you?"

Mackenzie and Swallows exchanged nodding glances. There was no arguing with that, or with her.

Without blinking, Bess stared straight into their faces.

Mackenzie fixed her in a narrow stare. "Just like your old man. Stubborn and muleheaded. No talking to him, either." He looked at Swallows and shrugged. Then he looked back at Bess. "Okay then, Marshal, we got a job to do so let's get to it. You want to take on these curs we'll put 'em down like the dogs they are."

"Thank you." Now, suddenly, Bess looked unsure of herself. "So what's our first move?"

"You asking us? I thought this was your show."

"I've had this job two days, Jack. You've had it twenty years. You've been in actual gunfights and captured real gangs of outlaws. You tell me what we're supposed to do."

"Fair enough." He looked slyly at his deputy. "You thinking the same thing I am?"

Swallows nodded laconically. The men seemed to Bess to have a shorthand. "Yeah. Reckon that's one thing we got in our favor."

"What?" Bess said eagerly, looking like a kid again.

Marshal Mackenzie cocked his rifle and looked up into the woods. "We have the element of surprise. They know about you but not about me and him. If we play our cards right, we can bushwhack them."

"They saw where I went."

"That's right. Where *you* went," Swallows pointed out.

Mackenzie nodded. "These boys don't

know you have backup. They don't know more marshals were coming their way, and they damn sure don't know we're already here loaded and locked down. They figure they're chasing one poor defenseless woman all by her lonesome."

Bess nodded, shrugging her agreement.

Mackenzie's eyes turned flinty. "So to keep the element of surprise, the best thing for us to do is not dissuade them of that notion. The smart move is dangerous for you, Bess, and it's gonna require you stickin' your neck out."

"I'll do what you tell me, Jack." She had no fear.

"They think you're still on the run. That's what we want 'em to keep thinking. The tricky and dangerous part is you got to get near them and let them spot you. Then they'll chase you and come out in the open and expose themselves to our line of fire . . . that's when me and Nolan surprise them and hit from behind from either side and ambush the crap out of them. Those bounty killers won't see us coming. But it's going to require you putting yourself in harm's way just until we get a clear shot at these boys."

"Let's do it." If Bess was frightened she wasn't letting on. The trio collected their guns. Bess walked to Mackenzie's horse and studied the array of heavy-caliber firearms packed in his saddle, shooting him a questioning glance.

The Jackson marshal returned a curt nod that granted her permission to take whatever guns she wanted. Bess selected two Colt SAA revolvers, checked the loads, holstered them, and rummaged through the ammo bags to stock her bullet belt.

"Where was the last you saw them?" Deputy Swallows asked as he led the horses off the trail to a quiet spot.

Bess pointed up the hill. "Five hundred yards that way. On foot. They couldn't be far off." Her face screwed up in worry and she gnawed her lip. Switching her gaze to the watchful faces of her fellow lawmen, she came out with it: "The thing is, they split into two groups. One group, two at least, came after me. But the other group was chasing Noose, and Frank Butler led them."

"What are you worried about?"

"Well. We don't know where those other men are. What if . . . ?

"We'll keep our eyes peeled. Two groups means less men to face. Divide and conquer is our play."

The three lawmen grouped together, did final checks on their guns, and were ready.

Mackenzie said a few words before they went up into the forest after the bounty killers: "Shoot to kill. Put 'em down so they stay down. There's too many to try and take prisoner anyhow. These men all deserve to be shot dead for what they done to Nate and to Bess here. And be careful."

The marshal and deputy mounted their horses and saddled up.

Bess inserted the last cartridge into her cylinder and spun the revolver shut, shoving it into her holster. "Remember one thing," she added, looking over her shoulder as she started climbing back up the hill.

"What's that?" The men were right behind her.

"Nobody kills Frank Butler but me."

CHAPTER 39

Joe Noose was halfway up the tree when Butler and the four others rode past below. Noose was hunkering on a heavy branch that easily supported his considerable weight of solid muscle and was right above them twenty feet up when the marauders suddenly stopped.

The top of Frank Butler's black Stetson was twenty feet straight down right below his boots and if Noose just dropped from the branch he'd come down spurs first on the son of a bitch's head and snap his neck like a twig. Noose coiled and got ready to spring, adjusting his position slightly because what he intended to do was land on Butler's back, knock him from his horse, grab his revolver, and use the leader as a body shield as in four shots he took out the other four shootists, using the element of surprise, shooting Butler in the skull with the fifth shot if the leader's body hadn't already been riddled with his men's bullets trying to shoot past him at Noose. Up in the tree, Noose saw the whole thing play out in his mind in a space of five seconds, knew exactly what he was going to do in advance and the way it was all going to shake out until something happened he just didn't expect.

"Mr. Butler! Marshals are here! Mr. Butler! The law is here!" two of the jackass bounty killers were yelling from the trail down the hill. Hearing that, Frank Butler snapped his head in their direction, spurred his horse, and charged down the hill followed by his four men, and Noose missed a once-in-a-lifetime chance to kill his enemies in one fell swoop.

Cursing his foul turn of luck, the cowboy crouched in the tree and watched bitterly as the seven distant figures of the Butler Gang briefly exchanged a few words out of earshot, then swiftly rode off the trail back toward the ravine.

Noose's only satisfaction was Frank Butler looked mad as hell.

The two Jackson Hole lawmen rode in single file up the rough trailhead and stopped their horses in a small grove. Taking point, the female marshal was fifty yards ahead of them, on foot, both Colt SAA revolvers drawn. Big trees surrounded them on all sides and it was very quiet.

The deputy looked around, saw the marshal was doing the same, as the two met each other's gaze.

Mackenzie's head disappeared in a red galaxy of spraying blood, brains, skull, and flesh before Swallows even heard the shot — one moment the deputy was looking in his boss's eyes and the next the face was gone, the trees behind the headless body visible through a waterfall of bright oxygenated blood on the decapitated marshal's body. Swallows winced, grimacing as his own face was splattered with splinters of bone and warm, salty arterial spray. He blinked in shock. Mackenzie's messy headless upper torso sat for a second upright in the saddle shivering, then the startled horse took off and the corpse flipped out of the stirrups and landed in a heap on the ground as pumping blood gusted in a geyser from the ragged neck stump.

A Colt Dragoon is an ugly weapon.

The single gunshot reverberated through the tall branches of the trees. Birds took flight and scattered in all points of the compass.

Swallows's eyes briefly met Bess's as Mackenzie's Appaloosa crashed into her in its urgency to escape, knocking her clean off her feet and spattering her with the marshal's blood flying off the saddle as she landed on her stomach and her guns flew out of her hands.

As the shell-shocked deputy swung his head left and right in a confused desperate gaze at the trees for the source of the shots, at the same time socking the Winchester to his shoulder, Swallows was thinking he hadn't heard the first shot before he saw the bullet kill Mackenzie and wondered if he would hear the shots about to kill him.

That thought was carried out the back of his skull as the next round drilled him between the eyes, instantly extinguishing his life as five more bullets slammed into his chest in rapid succession.

As it turned out, he never did hear the gunshots.

Frank Butler swung out of his saddle on his big black stallion and his muddy boots and spurs hit the dirt. He was already reholstering his smoking pistol because the badman knew there were no lawmen with the men he just killed. Just the girl.

The bounty killer leader stepped out of the trees and walked emotionlessly over to the dead marshal and deputy gruesomely sprawled on the slope below the tall canopy of the shadowy green conifers festooned with their blood.

Two more Wyoming lawmen whose deaths Butler intended to falsely blame Joe Noose for. With any luck, the story should stick.

As the leader trudged through the clearing toward where Bess was crawling away on the ground, he threw a speculative glance to his gang, thinking if his men were all were dead, too, it would mean a bigger reward for himself.

Business was booming, he had to say.

When Butler was coming toward her, Bess was covered with blood, crawling on her belly for the gun, but it was too far away, and then she heard the *click* of a hammer being pulled back. Terrified, lying on her stomach facing in the other direction, she put up her shaking hands behind her head. "Don't shoot."

He didn't. Yet.

"Stand up," Butler said.

Bess rose.

"Turn around," he said.

She turned to face the bounty killer leader, shaking and in shock, her hands raised high to show she was unarmed.

"Changed my mind." Butler cracked a mordant evil sadistic grin. "Sit down."

He shot Bess in the left leg, which collapsed under her as she crumpled in the dirt, screaming and sobbing and holding her blood-spurting upper leg.

"You can train any dog, even a bitch," sneered the blackhearted bastard. Butler gestured for his men to ride out of the trees. "Let's see her try to run away now. Put her on a horse. Then let's find that son of a whore Joe Noose and finish this thing before this bitch bleeds to death and ain't no use no more to us as bait."

Bess was too weak and traumatized and racked with pain to resist as she shut her eyes so she didn't have to see anything anymore. She felt the rough hands pick her up and submitted to being loaded onto a saddle where with her eyes closed everything was black as a tomb and all she heard were the hooves as she was taken away with the bounty killers as they rode off.

They hadn't even bothered with a tourniquet for her leg.

Noose heard the gunfire and thought, *What in hell?*

He counted the shots.

Eight.

The distant, muffled reports came from above to his right in what he guessed was a northwestern direction — too far away to have been directed toward him.

Then who?

Those were the bounty killer gang's guns that he had heard — Noose recognized the make and caliber of Butler's pistol at least — *but who were they shooting at?*

He was on foot now.

It was slow going down the steep embankment of the gorge, the slope plummeting at a ninety-degree angle, the fifty-foot-high pine trees jutting like clustered steeples at a canted angle to the grade.

His boots skidded down the muddy terrain, the traction slippery and treacherous — he had to use his hands to catch himself as he descended the yawning gorge.

The bounty hunter regretted not having a horse but was guessing by now he would have parted ways with it anyway regardless — no way that a horse could have made it down this slope.

What was all that shooting about?

Fear juddered in his gut as his mind went first to the possibility that Butler and his gang had executed the woman marshal. It had worried Noose for some time that that would happen. Then he more or less dismissed that possibility because it sounded like one pistol had fired the shots he had just heard and they wouldn't use all those rounds on one simple girl. Didn't think they would, anyway.

Perhaps she shot some of them . . . shot Butler, even.

In that case the outcome was the same and she was dead. The female peace officer was heavily outgunned and would have been felled by the other bounty killer's bullets directly had she opened fire on them. The fact that she might have reduced their number and improved his odds of survival was cold comfort if the marshal's daughter had lost her life in the process.

Still it sounded like one gun, not an exchange of gunfire.

Down he sidestepped along the ridge at a swift rate of descent, the angled trunks of the big pine trees sweeping past. The scent of soil and sap filled his nostrils.

If it wasn't the woman then it had to be someone else. A gunfight breaking out in the gang of bounty killers was a definite possibility. Likely Butler had plugged one of his own men. The tensions had been flaring among the thugs for some time now and these were not coolheaded types.

The feeling of being completely unarmed

was not a good one. He had nothing but his two hands.

Noose's strong body hurt all over as he descended the steep grade, his clothes wet with mud and blood and sweat and stuck to his chest and legs. He felt like an animal. All around him was titanic forest, and the view below was looking more treacherous and the gorge grew steeper and the jagged granite boulders far below became visible through the tree line as he approached. The cowboy couldn't see too far ahead and could be heading for a straight drop to instant death on the rocks for all he knew. But the only way out was down.

The law.

Of course.

The marshals those two bounty killers back there had yelled to Butler about had showed up.

The U.S. Marshal's office in Jackson Hole would have sent a few armed officers to intercept the fugitive blamed for the Hoback marshal's murder and they knew which way he was coming. The telegraph requesting the authorization for the reward would have told them that.

And that's when Noose slipped.

His boots went right out from under him.

Then he was tumbling.

Over and over he rolled as the ground gave way and he somersaulted down the steep declination. His vision went upside down and sideways as trees and rocks and branches smashed past his face. His hands went everywhere, clutching vainly for purchase on the muddy, rocky, moss-covered walls of the ravine. Head over heels he toppled and flipped, victim to the pull of gravity, as down the hill Noose fell. Rocks and stone and buried trunks of trees sledgehammered his torso and extremities and the impacts against his wounds sent screaming agony through his wounded body. Fresh bruises tattooed his skin with each successive impact. Blood filled his eyes. Noose was still rolling over and over down the sheer embankment and just when he thought the fall would never end, he hit hard flat ground and lay still.

The bounty hunter had come to rest at the top of a ridge. He blinked and saw red, so he wiped the blood out of his eyes with the back of a big dirty hand, spitting crimson saliva onto the ground.

The whinnying of the horse snapped him to attention.

Not good.

The sound of the horse's vociferations and *clack* of its hooves were very close by.

Slowly raising his head, expecting to see the bounty killers and get a bullet between the eyes, Noose looked in the direction of the sound of the horse.

He saw just one Appaloosa.

It stood alone.

Saddle splashed with blood.

The solitary horse was frozen in place, lathered with sweat, staring him straight in the eye.

Strapped to the saddle was a cleaned and oiled Winchester rifle and a spare Colt .45 pistol along with two bandolier belts loaded with ammunition.

"Good horse," Noose whispered reassuringly.

He saw the U.S. Marshal brand on the saddle that was drenched with gore, the seven-star sigil jutting like scar tissue in all the blood, and Noose right away knew what those gunshots had been: the Jackson marshal had met up with the bounty killers and they'd shot him to pieces.

The horse had fled. Probably a wise decision. Definitely a fortuitous one as far as Joe Noose was concerned.

Staggering unsteadily to his feet, using a boulder for leverage, Noose stood and took a few tentative steps toward the nervous horse. He didn't want it to shy and flee.

Anything but. Holding out his hands, making a gentle *tsk* sound with his lips, his gaze confident and friendly, for Noose was good with horses, the cowboy approached.

The stallion's eyes widened apprehensively and it jerked its head nervously once or twice, but the horse didn't run, and in a moment Noose had it by the reins. He patted its head and quickly made a friend.

"Good boy, good boy," he said, grinning.

The Appaloosa responded to his sure touch, apparently almost as happy to see him as he was to see it.

What pleased the cowboy even more were the marshal's guns and ammo in the saddlebags. Looked like a hundred rounds or more.

Noose was rearmed.

Fully loaded.

And back in the fight.

Looking up into the sweeping, forest-carpeted canyon above, his keen blue eyes cutting across the spectacular vista, Noose saw no immediate sign of the posse. Didn't mean they weren't there, though.

He quickly drew the Winchester from the saddle holster, levered it, and slammed a full load of slugs from the bandoliers into the breech. Cocked it. Then he did the same with the Colt .45. Both guns were in excel-

341

lent condition.

He couldn't say the same for himself but he felt a lot better armed again.

No bullets came his way from the tree line above or below him.

Those shots had been five minutes ago, maybe less.

The horse had bolted right after it so violently became riderless and it couldn't have gone far on this rugged trail, so the bounty killers must be close at hand, not far behind.

As he clutched the reins, Noose saw what had frozen the horse. The trail it had come down was clearly visible upward through the trees — no going back that way because that would be straight into the guns of the gang — but the trail had bisected at the edge of the ridge — the horse was afraid to go any farther. Around a copse of rearing conifer trees a few yards away, Noose spotted what the horse clearly hadn't: a narrow rut down the side of the ridge that could easily be ridden. Where it spilled out was anybody's guess, but that was the way out.

"Easy, boy," Noose said gently.

He hitched a boot into the grisly stirrup and swung up into the saddle, the blood-soaked leather *squishing* squeamishly under his butt. It was a nasty, disagreeable sensation sitting on a dead man's horse in a saddle wet with the dead man's blood but Noose got his boots in the stirrup.

With easy command, he led the stallion out onto the trail and they trotted into the trees. His guns were close at hand and he kept a sharp lookout.

This had been the bloodiest day he could remember.

And it wasn't over yet.

He reined the horse around and started riding it back up the hill because that's where the bounty killers were and that's where Bess was.

He had a job to do, bad men to kill, and a good woman to save.

Joe Noose just hoped he wasn't too late.

CHAPTER 40

Frank Butler reached and grabbed Bess Sugarland by the scruff of her shirt and with a fierce jerk yanked her clean out of the saddle, dumping her in an untidy heap in the dirt.

She screamed in raw agony as her leg with the bullet in it twisted underneath her, and her lungs didn't hold back.

Her wrists were roped and she couldn't rise or sit so just thrashed about on the ground in pain.

Like a trapped, cornered animal in the dirt, Bess looked up at Butler towering ferociously over her, matching her own feral gaze in raw intensity. The six other bounty killers had ridden their stallions around in a circle closing her in, and now were dismounting. Their boots and spurs struck the soil noisily and they quickly moved to form an oval within the circle of horses, walling Bess in and preventing her escape. The young woman's head snapped this way and that as she cut her gaze desperately back and forth upward at the grim faces of the bad men.

"I didn't want to kill you. Not at first. Killing two U.S. Marshals is crossing the line even for me, especially a father and daughter." Frank Butler's eyes were dead as he stood over her, looking down pitilessly. "Knew I should've right at the start. Knew I'd have to in the end. Tried to cut you slack. But you had to push your luck. You had to push me. Fact is, sister, you been a giant pain in my ass this whole trail. It's just . . . Truth is . . . You are too much trouble." Butler scowled fiercely and the ends of his facial hair turned down with the edges of his thin lips, making him look feral. "You shoulda stayed back in that town and planted your daddy and then there wouldn't have been none of this trouble."

He shouldn't have said that.

Bess's eyes darkened with bottomless hatred. She screwed her mouth up and spat up at Butler's face but missed by a yard.

She shouldn't have done that.

"That's it," the leader snarled, his frozen grin a tetanus rictus below his black handlebar mustache.

Frank Butler lost his grin at the precise

moment he took a step toward Bess and began reaching for his gun.

At that exact second, not far off, Joe Noose got himself squarely situated in the saddle, ready to go in with guns blazing.

Snapping the shotgun closed in his left hand with a clean jerk of his wrist, he cocked back the hammer of the Colt .45 in his right hand with his thumb. The reins hung loose. A cocked and loaded Winchester and another pair of Remington revolvers were easily in reach in his saddlebags.

His powerful legs were tightly gripped on the stallion's flanks because he was going to ride in hard without using the reins because he needed both hands to shoot with.

The sun was at his back so it would be in their eyes.

Noose's lethal and deadly gaze was fixed on the circle of men and horses two hundred yards distant just beyond the trees below — he could see Bess on the ground and knew what the dirty miserable sons of bitches were planning to do to her. Unlucky for them, the fool bounty killers wouldn't see him coming because their backs were turned to face the woman they planned to execute and had all their horses positioned blocking their view of their surroundings, so Joe

Noose's ambush was going to be their worst surprise.

This human garbage has been sucking my air far too long.

It's time to kill them all.

Nobody left standing.

None of them gets out of here alive.

The dead marshal's Appaloosa stallion Noose sat astride was an ornery, cussed beast who chomped at the bit, ready for action, its snorting breath huffing from its nostrils, front hoof pawing the dirt like a bull ready to charge, just waiting on Noose's go. This was a warhorse, a lawman's mount, a steed who had been trained to run into a fight and was meaner than a snake.

Noose leaned down to whisper in the horse's ear something he believed the animal already knew: "Listen to me, old horse, those men out there murdered your owner and that's his blood on this saddle, so you and me, we're going to make 'em pay with their lives. The next blood on this saddle will be theirs. I need you mean, boy, mean, you hear? You ready?" Noose could have sworn he heard the cantankerous old warhorse bellow in rage as it scraped the ground with its hoof. He figured the stallion probably saw the marshal get shot and had its own score to settle.

All Joe Noose needed to do was tap the heel of his boot to the stirrup and his disagreeable stallion took off like an artillery shell fired from a mortar, reaching a full gallop in seconds, head down, tearing up the tundra in a barreling charge at the circle of the other weary horses.

"On your knees, bitch."

Bess knelt, beat and cowed, head hung low.

Butler spun the cylinder of his Colt Dragoon with a rattlesnake *whirr* and put the barrel against the back of the woman marshal's head.

He took his sweet time cocking back the hammer.

"Last words?" Butler said.

On her knees, as Bess feels the cold muzzle of Butler's Colt Dragoon pressed against the back of her skull and hears the hammer cocked back, she closes her eyes and knowing they will be her last words, whispers softly, "I'm sorry, Daddy. I did my best . . ."

. . . She thinks she hears her father answer . . .

. . . An answer to her secret prayers for her daddy to rescue her like he always did when she was a little girl, because now she is all alone and so very scared, on her knees, about

to be shot in the head and put down like a horse, a disgusting way to die, and here, now, Bess Sugarland doesn't feel brave at all, not like a marshal or even a grown woman but like a little girl wanting her daddy, hoping against hope for him to come rescue her, and she thinks she hears her father answer her prayers, listening to his horse's hooves galloping to her rescue as she waits for the bullet to enter her skull and end her, the beat of hooves growing louder, yes, definitely she hears those hooves, and Bess smiles because her prayers have been answered and her daddy is riding in to save her, then suddenly she knows it is not her daddy who is rescuing her, it is . . .

Bess's eyes popped open —

— just in time for her to get blood in her eyes from the exploding left gun hand of Frank Butler blown off from thumb to middle finger as the Colt Dragoon shot out of his hand showered sparks from the bullet that just hit the metal as it spun uselessly through the air like a fireworks pinwheel. Butler's eyes bulged in horror as he clutched the ruins of his left hand and glove and staggered back, turning in circles, screaming his lungs out in a hideous high-pitched porcine squeal that turned into a string of blasphemous profanity —

— on her knees, Bess's eyes were wide as a child staring up in shock and awe at her actual rescuer: the formidable heroic figure of the towering cowboy on a gigantic horse galloping toward her with guns blazing like great lightning bolts, bodies falling before him, backlit by the sun into a blinding vision of a true hero, not her father but Joe Noose —

— and the instant she saw Noose, Bess transformed from a little girl to a grown woman blinking blood out of her eyes as she caught Butler's bloody revolver as it spun through the air before it hit the ground, got her hand around the stock and finger through the trigger guard and was up on her good leg and all the way back to U.S. Marshal — except now Bess wasn't planning on making any arrests and the only law she cared about was the Law of the Gun as she fanned and fired and shot Garrity smack between the eyes —

— Bess was surprised he had as many brains as flew out the back of his head —

— Noose straight-armed the shotgun and the pistol out in front of him, waiting until the other horses cleared — murderously mad as he was at the gang, he had no truck with their horses and although he wouldn't lose sleep if one of his bullets dropped

Butler's evil nag, he wanted to avoid any unnecessary horse casualties. He braced himself in the saddle, his own hips matching the Appaloosa's hurtling stride, and took aim down his gunsights, waiting for the wall of stallions they bore down on to clear —

— as soon as the other horses heard the oncoming hooves of Noose's beast and sensed the fury in its ferocious approach, part those steeds did — the stallions bolted for cover like a curtain pulling apart on the circle of men who realized what was happening a second too late: they were all exposed to Noose's line of fire and he did not hesitate —

— pulling the first trigger of his scattergun, he blasted Lawson square in the chest with a full load of 12-gauge buckshot and blew him out of his boots, his body like a limp rag doll flying fifteen feet back to where he hit the ground dead —

— Butler was the first to react, simultaneously swiveling at the waist and drawing his second revolver with his intact right hand, quick-drawing and firing a string of shots as he ducked right. His evasive action threw his aim, and six bullets were wasted. By then Butler had tossed the first gun and, fumbling out a second from the saddle of his horse, his eyes wild and terror filled as he looked up at Joe Noose sitting high in the saddle on the Appaloosa stallion as it rode right into the center of the startled bounty killers —

— *"Get down!"* Noose yelled at the top of his lungs down to an armed Bess, who was hopping on one leg out of the way despite both hands being tied, and tumbled to earth —

— the dead marshal's horse reared and Noose stayed in the saddle, turning the beast on its hindquarters so that its front legs jackhammered out and kicked Wingo in the skull with a wet *crack* that spun his eyes like white marbles rolling up in their sockets and sent him staggering to his knees. In a string of split-second perceptions, Noose saw as his horse reared again that Wingo just had whatever brains he used to own kicked out and was incoherent and no threat, so the cowboy whirled in the saddle, straightening his scattergun arm and aiming in the direction that he last saw Butler, but the leader was already taking cover behind his nasty horse. Having a sixth sense where the next bullets were coming from, Noose swung around in the saddle and took aim with his Colt at Sharpless and Trumbull right as the ducking men lunged with their irons and began shooting. Everything became explosions of gunfire and Noose felt a bullet slam into his saddle as another creased his ear with a burning sting, but he kept blasting, swiveling the barrel of the pistol in his fist to the man on the left as he leveled the second barrel of the shotgun to the man on the right and unloaded the second cartridge —

— Trumbull's right leg was blown out from under him into bloody fragments as he was flipped right onto his face, screaming like an animal. All in the space of a few fateful seconds under heavy fire, Noose's brain ticked off Trumbull like it did Wingo as no longer an active threat, and Noose shot the last bullet in his pistol into the gun smoke behind where Sharpless was returning fire — Noose heard the flesh impact and the man started hollering, dropping his gun and clutching his wounded arm and pain-dancing in circles —

— the air was already thick with a hovering haze of gun smoke and targeting was tough in the close quarters of the gunfight's tight proximity theater of combat. It was point and shoot or simply shoot. Silhouettes of men ducked and darted and muzzle flashes erupted in all directions. Huge shapes of horses bolted to and fro and Noose's Appaloosa continued to rear. Noose realized it was a big target and that he and his stallion were in the eye of the hurricane and surrounded by armed men loading up and firing back on all sides —

— perhaps forty-five seconds had elapsed since Noose had loosed his first cartridge and in that brief span of time there had been a lot of blood and things were moving in slow motion now they were all in the thick of it —

— revolving on his horse, Noose's eyes swung back and forth as he tossed the empty shotgun and snatched the Winchester repeater rifle from his saddle holster —

— *Bess!* —

— A quick glance down showed the woman crawling away, trying to untie the rope on her wrists with her teeth and still clutching Butler's pistol and inching on all fours toward Wingo, shivering and staring into space on his knees, his face a mask of red from the kick he took to the head. Bess got the rope off her wrists, closing in on the bounty killer. She meant to take his pistols, Noose figured, and the first thing she would do is put him out of his misery with the first bullet —

— *Butler.* That question was answered by a heavy-caliber round screaming past Noose's face from behind — it would have blown the back of his head off had his horse not been moving so much in the smoke. The cowboy jammed the empty revolver in his saddlebag and took up the Winchester with both hands, already levering off several booming rounds as he sighted down the barrel at the figure in black behind the big black horse behind him. The bastard was using his own horse as a body shield like he knew somehow Noose didn't like to shoot horses and would hesitate, and although Noose hated that bastard's mean horse, he was right. Butler ducked down and fired beneath the stomach of the stallion up at Noose like a Comanche. They traded fire but that mean ebony horse was already on the move and Butler with it, changing position —

— a fleeing quarter horse rushing past in the melee cleared a clean view of Culhane, who had his pistol clutched in both hands, taking potshots at Noose in plain view. The bounty killer was screaming in fury like it would make his shots hit harder but all that hollering did was pinpoint his position. Culhane's shoulder suddenly exploded in a ragged red crater of an exit wound that didn't come from Noose's gun. The cowboy switched his gaze to the right and saw Bess on her knees beside the stuporous Wingo with his smoking pistol in her hands and an all-business expression on her angry face, and just as Noose realized Bess had shot Culhane and saved his hide, Bess turned the pistol on Wingo and shot him in the shoulder even though she was aiming at his chest —

— needing to get to ground because he was too clear a target astride the horse, Noose swung out of the saddle, clenching his Winchester and Colt .45 and landed on his boots in a crouch —

— when the scream of rage behind Bess jerked Noose's gaze up he saw Culhane swing an ax at her back but he was already too close to her and Noose couldn't risk his bullet hitting Bess, so he fanned and fired once from the hip, blowing a hole through the bounty killer's arm that spun him to the right in a broken stagger, Culhane coming full around with the hatchet in the other hand now, swinging it with raw rage at the woman's head as she looked back, still too close for Noose to get a safe shot at the man so murderously intent on killing her and instead Noose fanned and fired a second time and took off Culhane's left elbow, the ax flying harmlessly from his limp grasp and by that time Bess had rolled on her back, clenching her stolen pistol in a sure two-hand grip and shot Culhane fatally in the chest, blowing him clean off his feet, his chest trailing geysers of blood as he landed in the dust and lay still, dead as dead gets —

— there was a lot of screaming coming from a lot of badly shot men who had just been schooled in the fearsome tradecraft of the shootist by Joe Noose. His ambush had been successful. The Butler Gang had been pounded and taken a beating. It was time to clear out while he and Bess still could. Mackenzie's roughneck stallion stood a few yards to his right, still as a post, not even flinching as the bullets flew past it so that rugged old fighting horse was either tough or deaf, but on that nag's blood-splattered saddle was how they were getting out of here. The cowboy whiplashed his gaze back between Bess and the horse, gauging distance and calculating next moves with instinctual animal precision — his decision came fast: she was too far away and it would waste time gathering her up and getting her back on the Appaloosa — the horse was closer, get it, then get her and get out of here before the shock of the surprise ambush wore off on the bounty killers, who were professionals, after all, and the men got a mind to start shooting straight —

— Noose's boots propelled him up off the

ground like an uncoiled spring and both big hands grabbed the saddle, pulling himself into the stirrups already swinging his far leg over and grabbing the reins, sitting erect, barely spurring the horse because it was off like a shot, now in furious motion cantering right past Bess on the ground, that stallion so happy to be in action it wasn't going to stop for her. Bess's eyes were wide with wild and desperate hope as Noose approached in a thunder of hooves, her hand reaching out for him and Noose leaned hard out of the saddle to his left, leaning the horse, catching her arm in his big fist and not letting go as the Appaloosa charged past the woman, the velocity of its gallop and iron grip of the man plucking the woman like a feather off the ground, her agile hips doing the rest as Bess dropped into the saddle behind Noose and threw her arms around his chest to hang on for dear life as he spurred the warhorse hard now, driving it forward at full gallop, escaping across the field and down a grassy incline ever farther from the carnage of the bounty killer ambush left in their wake.

By the time the shots did come the guns were out of range. Soon the shots were fewer, quieter, barely audible above all the screaming in the distance.

It was sweet music to Noose's and Bess's ears.

And they were away.

CHAPTER 41

It was a rout.

No other word for it. No fancy bow to put on things nor rosy way to look at it. Noose's ambush had been a massacre and a bloodbath with the bounty killers on the losing end, plain and simple.

Frank Butler sat on a rock, racked with pain as he methodically wrapped a cloth around his blasted-apart left hand, binding his remaining fingers together. His pain threshold was high and made higher by the swigs of sour mash whiskey he took from the bottle beside him, which numbed the pain a little. His thumb and forefinger were gone forever and he'd never be able to shoot a pistol again with his left hand, but with practice should be able to manage handling a rifle. The leader was still in shock and the seething intensity of his bloodthirsty rage at the bastard who wounded him and the rest of his men, those he hadn't wiped out, washed the pain away.

Fifteen minutes ago he watched that slippery son of a whore and the bitch marshal ride away intact and his reward along with them. This whole last two days counted for naught but lost men and fingers, and likely the loss of the Butler Gang's lives if those two made it to Jackson, because if they told their tale, he and his men would be swinging at the end of ropes.

Butler had to stop them from getting there. He had to get after them. But he couldn't do it himself and one look around told him that was going to be his problem . . .

His men were sprawled, moaning and wailing and rolling on the ground, filled with bullets and bleeding everywhere. Everyone had been hit, at least once.

Butler rose unsteadily to his feet and recovered his balance. The leader needed to be standing upright on both boots. Standing on the bloody field in the center of the carnage, Frank Butler looked around with a grim, saturnine expression at what was left of his gang, and took inventory:

Culhane was dead.

So was Lawson.

And Garrity.

All three of their bullet-scored, lifeless

bodies were sprawled near the horses.

Trumbull was hit in the leg. He sat on the ground in misery. Was in the process of binding a tourniquet around his upper leg below the thigh and looked like he would recover. Butler knew Trumbull was a steady reliable type and he could definitely still ride a horse.

The horse-kicked Wingo was on his feet fifty yards away, wandering in dizzy circles with a glazed, vacant look in his eyes. Blood gushed down the side of his head. The bullet wound in his shoulder wasn't doing him any good but Butler didn't think the young gunman felt much of anything because his brains had been scrambled like a plate of eggs. Could he ride and shoot? was the question. The leader figured he'd shove him into a saddle and see what he could get out of him.

All the horses were still within the perimeter. None had run off, that was one good thing. Although Butler wouldn't need three of those nags now, he could scavenge the rifles, pistols, and ammo.

"Get up, boys," Butler barked.

His men looked up at him like animals licking their wounds, with pain and incredulity in their eyes.

"What the hell are you talking about, Mr.

Butler?" Will Sharpless whined, nursing his ragged arm.

"Up on your feet. Everybody. Mount up. Our reward's getting away."

"Screw you, Butler. We're shot to pieces," Trumbull snarled.

"You're still breathin', ain'tcha?" Butler swung in intimidating circles in a half stagger around his surviving shootists. "Mount up! We gotta get after that son of a bitch! Our reward money is getting away!" The leader was out of his mind with agony and sheer raging obsessive fury. His eyes were crazed and the three remaining men were scared of him. It showed in their faces. None of them moved. Butler held up his bandaged bloody stump of his left hand, displaying it. "I got shot, too! Noose shot my damn hand off! You don't hear me complaining! That's why I got me two hands for, 'cause the other one I'm gonna shoot him dead with! Now, on your horses, boys! I ain't gonna tell you again!"

The wounded possemen exchanged miserable glances, and Sharpless was the one to speak up. "It's over."

"What did you say?" Butler hissed.

"It's over, Mr. Butler," the ill-at-ease Sharpless said quietly. "We're done. We're all shot up. We picked the wrong man to frame and he kicked our asses but good. And that reward is gone, Mr. Butler. That's a fact."

"Time to face reality," Trumbull seconded. "We got to get us to a hospital."

"Time to face reality. Okay, then." Frank Butler's face was as pale as a ghost and his eyes were bloodshot and radiated a mad stare. Lightning fast, he drew his Colt Dragoon with his right hand and shot once into the ground an inch from Trumbull's leg. Dirt jumped and with a cry of alarm the bounty killer had leapt to his feet and was hobbling on his unwounded leg.

"I am reality," Butler snarled through a curled pallid lip below his black handlebar mustache. "Face me." As he said it, he cocked back the hammer of his revolver in his right hand and stepped sideways to get the last three of the gang in his killing range. His straightened his gun arm and switched the aim of the barrel back and forth, slowly back and forth, back and forth.

Wingo was incoherent but Sharpless and Trumbull froze, neither of them daring to go for their guns because even if they could reach their weapons both at the same time, this was Frank Butler, his hammer was cocked, and he'd gun all of them down before they got a shot off. They could all see their leader had gone over the edge and

lost his mind, and they knew he was dangerous enough when he was thinking straight
but was as unpredictable as a rabid dog
when he wasn't.

Standoff.

Butler spoke calmly through gritted teeth.
"Get up, mount up, or I'll shoot you myself.
Go get that reward for myself. Got a full
load in this smoke wagon. Six .44-40s. Bullet for each of ya. Best if it's just me going
after the reward not to leave any witnesses.
I'd be doing you boys a favor putting you
all down, y'see. Because it ain't just about
losing that reward money. Nossir. It's about
losing everything. *Everything.* Noose and
that marshal, they make it to Jackson Hole
and tell their story, tell what they know
about us, it's the end of the trail for this
gang. Every U.S. Marshal in the country
will be on our tail and we'll all be hunted
down and hanged. Nowhere to run the law
won't run us to ground. It's all or nothing,
boys. Get Noose or get *the* noose. So what'll
it be?"

The gang exchanged glances. Saw he was
right.

In great pain, with excruciating slowness,
Trumbull and Sharpless retrieved the fallen
guns from the ground and staggered to the
saddles of their horses. Butler holstered his

pistol and used his right hand to haul himself up into the saddle of his black stallion, wrapping the reins around his left forearm and drawing his Colt again. He watched, eyes glittering with malevolent impatience, as Sharpless, the only one who hadn't received a serious injury, helped Wingo and Trumbull into the saddles. The horse-kicked Wingo didn't look like he knew where he was.

In less than five minutes, what was left of the Butler Gang still looked no less like a pile of raw meat but they were mounted up and they were armed, and when their psychotic leader screamed *"Yee-ahh!"* the four bounty killers galloped fiercely off with the frightening force and terrible purpose of a last charge into hell.

CHAPTER 42

As she leaned against his back, her arms around his shoulders holding on, her hands gripped his chest because it was the biggest part of him to cling on to, and without meaning to, her fingers involuntarily touched the scar. Next thing she knew, Bess found herself gently tracing the mark of the branding iron with her fingertips in idle curiosity.

Noose looked straight ahead, gripping the reins, as he steered the stallion down the treacherous ridge with calm control. Now and then his gaze cut left and right, keeping a lookout for the marauders.

If he minded or even noticed that she was touching his branding weal, he didn't show it.

"How did you get that, Joe?" Bess asked softly, looking over his left shoulder, her face by his cheek. She couldn't help herself. Bess always spoke her mind.

"It's a long story."

"It's a long ride."

"You ain't gonna let up, are you?" Noose sort of smiled and shook his head to himself.

"I want to know," she pressed. "It ain't every day you see a man branded like a steer."

"No, ma'am, it ain't. And I reckon that was the whole idea. It was a long time ago."

"How long?" she asked, and the horse found its footing and trotted down the ravine.

"I was thirteen."

Appalled, Bess stiffened her grip on his upper body in sudden stupefaction, gaping in horror. "What — *who* would — *brand* a little boy like an . . . an — ?"

"It was better than the alternative."

"Which was?"

"Hanged."

He felt her listening.

"You want the story, okay, I'll tell you." Over the next fifteen minutes, Noose spoke more words than he had said all day as the tale spilled from his lips in his low, laconic drawl. He told it softly, voice grim and reflective as he shared his past, and when he was finished, Bess Sugarland felt she knew everything there was to know about Joe Noose. She understood him now.

"First thing you got to understand is I never had no parents, none that I knew," Noose began. "From the age of five I was on my own up in Montana, living hand to mouth, no schooling. Never knew right from wrong, nobody ever taught me, and I did a lot of bad things as a kid because I didn't know no better. Fighting for food, a place to sleep, stealing clothes off folks' backs, rustling horses, it was all just surviving to me. I fetched up in every kind of place. A blur to me now. Shot my first man when I was eight. It was near Billings. I was big for my age and looked older but he was bigger and mean. And drunk as hell. He was passed out in a dark alley behind a stable. I was scoping the corral out to steal one of the horses when I saw the drunk and had a mind to steal his wallet and gun and the bottle of whiskey in his hand. Got the gun out of his holster and the wallet from his coat, but then he woke up and went for my throat. I'd stolen me a big old Remington Peacemaker from him and I drew down and plugged him easy as breathing. Didn't feel bad after. It was him or me. Didn't feel nothing. 'Cept hungry most of the time," Noose said in a voice not proud.

"Must have been rough being one boy alone in the world," Bess commiserated.

"No family. No one there for you."

The cowboy shrugged. "Didn't need anybody. Could take care of myself. I hurt a lot of folks. Used my fists against anybody who got in my way or had something I wanted, which is how I thought the world was. I had no sense of things. No sense at all. Come to find out, people saw me as a dangerous man and the wrong type of men respect that. In turn I fell in with a bad crowd, a bunch of rustlers and robbers, and we spent one summer in Montana raising all kinds of hell, sticking up stagecoaches, stealing cattle, robbing whores, and a bunch of people died. Some by my gun. Some by theirs. We were dirty miserable low-down sons of bitches, that's a fact, Bess. I did a lot of things I ain't proud of now but didn't know what shame was then. Like I said, I didn't know good from evil nor right from wrong, just didn't think that way. Didn't think at all, truth be told. I was just thirteen.

"Well, come that fall we happen upon this big spread with fields of steer far as the eye can see and we get us a mind to steal a few. We scope the place out. There's this big ranch house in the middle of plenty of grazing land, nobody and nothing around we could spot. So we set to it, my four so-called friends and I. Guess they must have seen us

370

coming, suppose word had spread about our gang, because out of nowhere this old rancher and his two sons about my age, they started firing from behind some trees near the fence and shot our horses out from under us. We was so busy falling we never had time to get to our guns, and the old man and his boys had us disarmed and hog-tied before we plumb knew what hit us.

"The old man, he had a face like a crow, and I didn't know much back then but one look at that face I knew pity was not in his nature and he would show us no mercy.

"His boys and him, they tossed ropes over the branch of this big tree, and that's when I saw the coal fire and irons they'd been branding steers with just before we showed up. Old fella made his boys tie the nooses. Five ropes. Five nooses. One for each of us. He was telling his boys what to do, telling 'em it's time they took part in a hanging, 'cause they were going to be men soon enough and needed to have the guts to dispense rough justice when it was called for. Got to tell you, Bess, these boys of his weren't happy about it, taking part in the executions of five men. They didn't want to be in no hanging party but the old man, he made 'em do it. Them boys was shaking when they tugged the rope around my pal

Chester's neck and stood him up, then put the next noose around Richie's neck, tightened that, then Ike had a rope around his neck, and Leroy, too. There was my four friends standing side by side about to be hanged from that branch and all I could wonder was why I wasn't standing there with 'em with a noose around my own neck. Thought maybe they run out of rope. The old man's sons, they was shaking real hard knowing they were going to have to do this thing and kill some men because their father was standing there with his big scattergun in one hand and a horsewhip in the other. He cracked it hard against his youngest son's behind when he took too long tying the other end of the hanging ropes to the saddles of the horses under the tree. All the while watching this, I'm thinking that if this is what a father does, then I'm glad I never had me one. Me, I'm lying on the ground, not going anywhere 'cause I'm hog-tied arms and legs behind my back, just waiting for my turn to get a noose around my neck. Sure enough, the oldest son starts for me with the noose and I'm figuring this is it.

" 'Not him,' the old man says. 'This one's underage. Not a man yet. Only a boy. How old are you, son?' he asks me, walking up to me in his big black boots, and I'm looking up at him against the sky and I say I'm thirteen or thereabouts.

"The old man seemed a hundred feet tall looking down on me like the wrath of God. He had the hardest eyes I'd ever seen and by a trick of the light his eyes was glowing in the light of the coal fire with little flames and sparks dancing in 'em. I remember the thumb and forefinger of his right hand had been shot off, leaving only half a hand and that didn't make him look any friendlier.

" 'You got parents?' he asks me not like a question but more like my folks, they didn't raise me right for me to end up in this situation. I say *no.* He asks, don't I know it's wrong to steal? and, hell, I don't know what to say 'cause I don't know what wrong is or right, neither, and the old man suddenly realizes this about me. 'You don't know right from wrong, good from bad, do you, boy?' Saw clean through me with those burning eyes of his. 'Poor soul. My sons have me to teach them right from wrong but you never had nobody to show you good from bad, and that puts you at a powerful disadvantage.'

"I asked if he was going to hang me and he told me to watch.

"Then he blasted that scattergun at the ground by the horses' hooves and they took off like their asses were on fire. Those ropes tied to the saddles jerked those nooses so hard my friends flew right off the ground when their necks cracked and Ike's head tore clean off. They died bad and they died ugly.

"The old man's sons took the sight of violent death harder than me. They felt bad watching men die but I felt nothing. It was what it was, nothing more nor less. But I saw a change in their faces when they watched my friends die. The old man's sons got harder and tougher right before my eyes. The rancher's lesson did what he intended it to do to his boys and I saw he took pleasure in that. Now he turned his attention to me. I didn't cry. Didn't beg. Didn't show that old man nothing. Wouldn't give him the satisfaction. I just asked him if he was gonna hang me next.

"Old man walks up. Looks down. His words are, 'You're too young for me to hang 'cause you ain't a man yet and it's wrong to kill a boy. You're still a boy but you ain't ever gonna be a man 'less you learn right from wrong, son. A man with no conscience is an animal, no better than cattle, and cattle get branded.'

"Directly the old man gets his boys to hold me down and tear my shirt off. Then he takes a red-hot monogrammed branding iron from the fire and walks back and holds it by my face, that *Q* brand smoking and glowing in front of my eyes. And now I feel something, fear and plenty of it. Because I know what's coming next."

Riding in the saddle behind him, Bess winced as Noose continued.

"He pressed that hot brand hard against my chest and held it there and pressed harder and burned me to where I could smell my own skin sizzling like charbroil. That damn searing brand felt like it was roasting its way right through my whole body, setting my damn heart on fire. It hurt worse than anything I have known before or since. I screamed, all right. You bet I did as the old man pressed down on the handle of the brand and put his mark permanent in my flesh with it. Finally he took the iron off and threw a bucket of water over me and left the brand etched in my chest for all time."

"Dear God," whispered Bess.

"Afterward, he crouches down beside me. I can't move, just half alive. And the old man says to me, 'Every day you look down at your chest for the rest of your life you'll see that brand and you'll remember there's a right or wrong. Fitting it's my brand because if you live long enough to grow to manhood you'll think back that it was me done taught you good from bad on this very day.' "

Bess shook her head, not sure what to say, so she just asked what happened after that.

He shrugged. "They threw me on my horse and sent me on my way."

"I'd have killed him. Did you ever go back and settle the score? Did that horrible old bastard ever get what was coming to him?"

Noose shook his head. "Never saw him again. Don't even know his name. But I'm grateful to him. From that day forward I have thought about right and wrong. And have tried to do what's right."

"Grateful? You were a boy and he *tortured* you."

"I know that rancher tortured me. I realize he was brutal. But even though it don't make sense, I owe that old man."

"For *what*?"

"For making me who I am. For setting me on the right path. For giving me what some folks call a conscience, I reckon. Making me think about good and bad, right and wrong, hell, just considering the consequences of my actions. I know it sounds stupid, but mean and bad and brutal as that old man was he was right: every day of my life I look upon that brand on my chest and am reminded there's a right and wrong choice to be made that day. The boy he branded was an animal that might just as well have walked on four legs and if he hadn't used that hot iron on me I would never have got up off four legs, stood on two, and become a man. In his way, that stranger was the closest thing I ever had to a father."

"That's one way to look at it, I reckon." Bess sighed, remembering. "I was lucky that I had a father who loved and cared for me and never once laid a hand on me. His way was to live by example. And because of who he was and how he was with me I always knew right from wrong, or think I do anyway. Sometimes it's tough to tell what's the right thing to do."

"You said a mouthful, Marshal. Know what I wish?"

"An army of U.S. Marshals are gonna show up any minute?"

"That, too." Noose chuckled. "But I wish that old man had taken the trouble to explain exactly what is right and what is wrong because ever since then I have been trying to sort that out, just like you said. But maybe that's the answer right there," reflected the cowboy. "Each of us got to figure out our own personal right or wrong and act accordingly."

CHAPTER 43

Frank Butler swung out of the saddle and grabbed his long-range Sharps rifle from his saddle holster, dropping into position by the boulder at the edge of the cliff he already knew would be essential to steady his arm.

Squinting his eyes, he peered over the rock down the steep hill at the distant figures of the horse and its two riders shrinking into the green open valley. Noose and the marshal's daughter were already a quarter mile away. Their lead would only widen, because a quick glance down the two-hundred-foot-steep, ninety-degree declination showed the bounty killer leader there was no way he and his gang could make a direct pursuit without breaking half of their horses' legs and likely their own fool necks as well. Plus his men had been badly shot up and were likely to screw up anyway.

No, he and his men had to double back at

least a half a mile to catch the lower trail to the valley floor. That would set them back fifteen to twenty minutes and in that time his quarry would be one or two miles ahead and in spitting distance of Jackson Hole. Only the Snake River stood between them. Butler knew Noose was making for the bridge and if he made it across it was a straight shot to town and over for Butler in more ways than one.

Even if the bitch lawdog bled to death — he knew she'd been badly hit — Noose had quite the tale to tell to whoever was manning the U.S. Marshal's office.

All this ratcheted through Frank Butler's mind in a matter of seconds and only one possible solution presented itself: he had to drop the fleeing people with his rifle from here in this exact spot and precise position.

Socking the long-range rifle to his shoulder, he flipped up the circular sight and crooked his elbow against the boulder he crouched behind. He jammed a .52 caliber cartridge into the breech and jacked the bolt. The problem with these long-range Sharps was you could fire only one bullet at a time before reloading, but that did not vex him for Butler knew he would probably get only one shot at them anyhow.

One shot and then they would be out of range.

Butler peered down the sight and steadied his aim.

Down the crosshairs, he sighted the tiny horse and riders. Five hundred yards away at least and getting farther every second. His professional and methodical shootist's mind performed his mechanical and logistical calculations like a machine, mental wheels turning. They were too far. It was an impossible shot. Ten seconds to make this shot, at most.

The breeze on his cheek told him from experience the wind was coming in from the southeast at twenty-three miles per hour.

Butler aimed for the horse because it was the biggest target plus if he could dismount the riders and put them on foot, then he and his boys could catch up.

His rifle barrel tracked the horse, then looking down the gunsight Butler shifted his aim two inches up and an inch to the right, the barrel moving with infinitesimal smoothness and precision, estimating the position of where the horse would be in a couple seconds from now when it was lost from view.

The deadly killer made his final split-second adjustments for the shot trajectory, calculating for windage, elevation, and bullet drop and, decision made, his finger tightened on the trigger.

It was going to be a tough shot.

When the top of the horse's head blew off, Noose and Bess flew out of the saddle and were flung headlong over the neck of the falling steed as it somersaulted over itself.

The cowboy compensated for the impact as he flew through the air and spun a few degrees so he landed on his good shoulder, but when he hit the grass it knocked the wind right out of him.

The lady marshal's piercing scream of agony snapped Noose alert and he was already on his feet, his boots pounding the dirt in her direction, but not before the lifeless horse came to rest on top of the wailing Bess, its entire dead weight crushing down on her leg with the bullet in it. Her face was flushed in pain and helpless agony as she pawed at the ground and punched and tugged at the saddle but she was pinned fast. Seconds later, Noose was at her side and sized up the situation. He had to do what had to be done and do it quick — there was no time for gentleness and he hoped that this woman was as tough as she acted because there was only one way to do this — a quick glance up at the ridge where the shot had come from showed the distant bounty killers were already on the move.

"This is going to hurt," was all Noose said.

"What are you waiting for?" she screamed at him, which he took for a *Yes, she was ready* as he crouched down, gripped one huge hand under each of her broad shoulders, dug the spurred heels of his boots into the tundra, and gave Bess one mighty yank to pull her leg out from under the saddle. When the bone snapped it made a muffled *crack* and Bess screamed her damn head off but Noose kept pulling and her wounded leg slid free from under the horse. She almost passed out and her eyes rolled up as he set her down and took a quick look at her leg.

Bess wasn't walking anywhere. If she didn't get some medical attention she wasn't walking ever again. The leg was not only shot, the bone was broken. Blood soaked the entire left trouser leg. He had to get her out of here. The bounty killers were coming on fast. They were out of sight behind the trees but the cowboy didn't have to see them to know they were taking the low trail to the valley floor.

Noose was going to have to carry Bess out of here.

No way he was going to leave her behind.

He had to make it to the bridge.

Somehow get across.

If he could just cross over the river before they did, if he just had a minute, even, less than a minute after he and Bess got across, he could end this thing in their favor.

One rifle would be all he could take because his hands were going to be otherwise occupied, so he grabbed the Winchester rifle and a fistful of cartridges from the saddlebag on the dead horse and stowed them. Noose didn't bother to take any more rounds for the Colt in his holster because he needed a rifle at the bridge, not a pistol, and the revolver had a full load anyway.

Taking a deep breath, the big cowboy ignored all the pain shooting through his own body as he reached down and picked the female marshal up. Noose threw Bess over his shoulder, heaving her onto his back, and bore up under her weight, adjusting her limp body so his right arm cradled her shoulders and his left arm cradled her hips, with his own shoulders and the back of his neck bearing most of her weight. Deciding he had as solid a grip on the woman as he was going to get, and knowing every second counted, he started walking.

Joe Noose made off across the valley, carrying Bess Sugarland draped over his big shoulders. He put one foot after the other, trudging forward step by exhausted step. His gaze hung on the crest of the hill far ahead across the expanse of grass where he could just make out the embankment that dropped into the Snake River and just about see the ramparts of the sheep bridge that crossed the water.

That structure was more than a mile away.

He was never going to make it, not with a full-grown woman on his back, not with a bullet hole in him and couple ribs broken, not a chance.

It didn't matter what his chances were.

He was going to try.

The brand on his chest suddenly felt very warm, and again he was reminded a man always has a choice between right and wrong.

The right choice was keeping this good woman alive and that's what he meant to do with his last ounce of strength to his very last breath.

He took another step.

Kept walking.

The bridge seemed a little closer.

But so were the bounty killers — he could hear their distant galloping hooves in the lower part of the trail to his rear and soon they would reach the valley floor and would run him down.

The hell with them, Noose figured.

He wasn't dead yet.

Wasn't giving up.

Just hoping his shaky legs wouldn't, either.

Bess wasn't moving, her lithe body hot and soft and draped around his massive shoulders. Her small breasts were pressed against his upper back and in their firmness the cowboy could feel she was still breathing. He felt her sweet breath against his right cheek where her head slumped sideways, her face down, left ear toward his.

As he trudged relentlessly forward toward the inaccessible bridge to safety he knew they would never reach, life felt suddenly precious to Joe Noose, who knew in a few minutes he was going to die.

If these moments were to be his last, *do some good, be a man — give this strong and brave woman some hope and carry her as far as you can.*

Trudging determinedly across the valley, Noose turned his head toward Bess's face. He brushed his lips by her ear and spoke to her purposefully. "I will let no harm befall you. I will keep you safe. Nobody's gonna hurt you, not while I'm around. You're going to be okay. You're going to be okay,

Marshal," he repeated. "You're going to be okay, Bess Sugarland." And as he repeated it he realized he was making a promise and a vow and keeping a promise is right and breaking a vow is wrong and the brand on his chest began to burn like the red-hot metal was pressed there again like a forge and it owned a power that began to course through Joe Noose and a renewed strength filled his huge legs that stomped ever forward.

". . . We gotta get to the bridge, that's all. When we get to the bridge that's where I end them. You're wondering how, well, I'll tell ya." Bess was half-conscious and not doing any talking, her head slumped on his shoulder, so he held up both ends of the conversation, hoping she could hear him. "The bridge, y'see, it's very narrow, maybe eight feet wide, so only one horse at a time can cross. That's good for us but bad for a gang of men, because they have to ride single file across that bridge high over that fast river. One man with a rifle can pick 'em off from the shoreline. On that bridge they're exposed and trapped, wide out in the open, and if I shoot fast and true enough, they won't know what hit 'em. They can't turn their horses on that bridge so can't turn back and can't run except to jump off the bridge and I can pick 'em off in the river like fish in a barrel. Most likely what'll happen when I start unloading on them is those horses they're riding will panic and rear, cause the others to panic front and back, and not one of those dirty miserable sons of bitches will be able to draw a gun let alone get a shot off. I just got to get us to the bridge, then get us across it and find me some cover on the other side with a good vantage on the bridge, yeah, that's all I gotta do."

Noose didn't know if Bess was listening, but he kept talking because he needed to.

". . . Then I just got to aim carefully so I don't hit the horses. I never shoot a horse. Hate any man who shoots a horse. Hate it when any horse gets shot. It ain't their fault. Ain't the horse that's bad, it's the man riding it."

The cowboy kept on walking under his heavy load, beyond endurance, pushing forward long past any hope of reaching his destination. He forged on in raw stubborn perseverance. One foot in front of the other, one step at a time, but so many steps to go . . . too many.

". . . That's my plan. Savvy it's a good one?"

She didn't answer. He didn't know if Bess

was listening.

All Noose knew was it was a good plan.

And all he was thinking as he staggered across the uneven ground and thick grass on legs so weary they barely held him up, all he thought as he held the limp woman on his shoulders no matter how bad it hurt his busted ribs, was that bridge was just too damn far.

He could see it now up ahead, the rickety wooden span of the bridge with its rope railings and supports that looked hammered together with spare wood. It was a mile away if it was an inch. On foot, carrying the weight of an unconscious woman, it would take him an hour to get there. Another ten minutes to get across.

The thundering hooves of Frank Butler and the vicious dregs of his gang of murderers grew louder behind him. He wanted to look back but couldn't turn with Bess on his back, not and keep walking. He didn't need to look back — his ears told him the horses were on the valley floor and galloping in his direction. Noose didn't hear any gunshots, which was strange because he gauged their distance close enough for him to be an easy target. But he knew why. Butler wasn't going to shoot him in the back, not make it easy for Noose like that, nor Bess, either. Frank Butler wanted them to see it coming: he would be looking them straight in the eyeballs when he pulled the trigger that ended them so the last thing on earth they saw was his face.

In every problem there is an opportunity. That meant Noose had a few minutes more before they caught up.

But it didn't matter.

He had run out of time.

It was then his legs gave out under him and he dropped to his knees on the grass.

Bess hung over his shoulders like a sack of cornmeal, her blood all over him.

Joe Noose hung his head.

Set the woman gently down on the grass.

He couldn't feel the brand in his chest anymore, just a numbness around the scar.

The battery of hooves behind him was louder but had slowed their pace it sounded like, as the killers took their time, savoring the end of the hunt and about to pleasure themselves in the good, bad kill.

The horse came suddenly out of nowhere, at full gallop, to his right.

Noose saw the steed in the corner of his eye at first — the golden bronze of its mane and withers agleam like armor on the stallion. The cowboy swung his head to look straight into the face of his old friend Copper, saddle still soaked from the river the horse was being washed away down the last time they saw each other. Man and horse locked eyes and then Noose grinned savagely because that horse whose life he once saved was now returning the favor and rushing to the rescue at a juggernaut gallop across the valley. Noose had never seen a horse move so damn fast. It was less than a hundred yards away, now fifty. Bess was on her hands and knees, her opening eyes watching the approaching mustang in a hushed awe. Damn, the horse was smart. Copper slowed his clip for just a few seconds as it reached Noose and Bess, and the cowboy was ready for him, already hoisting the injured woman up onto the saddle as the stallion broke back into a full gallop just as Noose heaved himself into the saddle behind Bess and jammed his boots into the stirrups.

And then they were off.

Instantly, Copper pulled away and ahead from the Butler Gang's horses.

Giving the reins a quick tug, Noose steered Copper toward the bridge but the horse seemed to know that's where they were going. The cowboy gave the stallion a little spur and the horse near doubled its hurtling gallop with great reaching strides of front and back pairs of legs. Horse and rider understood each other intuitively. Bess was securely straddling the saddle, and Noose had one hand on her as he held the reins while his other hand unslung the Winchester rifle from its strap and he spun it around his hand, cocking the lever as he did.

Throwing a steely glance over his shoulder, Noose saw the hard-riding bounty killers falling back, horses unable to keep up with Copper — it was as if the abused, browbeaten other horses were unnerved by the transformative rebirth of their old stablemate and just plain rattled by it. By now the bullets had started flying. Noose saw the flashing muzzles and heard *cracks* of gunshots of the gang's weapons. He was getting away and nobody was worried about shooting him in the back now. He smiled. But the bullets went wild because Butler and his boys were having trouble aiming with any accuracy at full gallop, shooting at a moving target.

The Winchester was clenched unfired in Noose's hand — he was saving his bullets for when they would count — right across the bridge on the opposite shore.

Copper charged tirelessly, blindingly fast

like a bolt of bronze lightning across the cleft of the valley where it met the Snake River, and now the bridge was in clear view, less than a quarter mile ahead. Noose could smell the river in the air now, a muddy and fresh wet scent that filled his nostrils and lungs like pure oxygen. Bess's hair was whipping in the wind, as the ride seemed to be reviving her. The pounding drumbeat of the stallion's hooves drowned out the fading sounds of the posse who were falling ever farther behind as Copper put more and more distance between them. When Noose looked back one last time, he saw the gang was a half mile behind and losing more ground every second.

The bronze horse and two riders galloped across the narrow trail over the grassy uneven ground, the walls of the rugged Wyoming canyons rising up on either side. Overhead, the lead sky was cloudless and the light unforgiving and metallic.

He knew it was there just beyond his view, then suddenly he saw it: dead ahead, the trail ended in the wooden boards of the narrow structure that stretched across the Snake River, railed in by two ropes on either side stretched taut with the weight of the scaffolding. The bridge was in poor shape, weather and ramshackle construction contributing to its visible disrepair. And it was small. Only wide enough for one horse to cross . . . and that's what Joe Noose was counting on.

If they could just make it to the other side, and it didn't look like anything could stop them now, the evil Frank Butler and his gang of cutthroats were dead men.

If ever men deserved killing it was these villains.

Joe Noose didn't need his brand to itch to know it was the right thing to do.

Right then the sound of Copper's hooves on dirt became the sound of hooves on wood as the horse took the bridge and began the crossing of the Snake.

CHAPTER 44

"Yee-ahhh!"

Joe Noose held fast to the saddle, one arm around Bess crumpled in front of him, shielding her with his body as with the other he gripped the horse's reins. The animal was straining as it charged forward at a full gallop.

The bounty killers were not far behind.

Before him, Noose's view of the bridge jounced and vibrated with the beat of the horse's hooves.

The injured Bess was in bad shape and he could feel the weakness in her body beneath his bicep but he held her fast. Her gumption was draining with her strength. The wound had to be tended to in a proper hospital.

She was going to live.

He was going to make sure of it.

But that meant he couldn't die, either.

Noose gritted down his teeth as he heard

the hooves of his stallion impact the wooden boards and the narrow expanse of bridge-work rushed past below him as on either side far below down past the rope railings, the great Snake River coursed wide and fast.

A bullet whistled past his head.

The gang of bounty killers were coming, hot on his heels, a few hundred yards back up the trail in a noxious cloud of rampaging hooves and kicked-up dust the cowboy saw as he swung his head to look over his shoulder, then swung it back again to steer his galloping horse on the narrow bridge. Noose was halfway across now, Bess slumped against his arm, and with luck they would make it.

As long as the horse didn't get shot.

Or slip.

The other side of the riverbank drew ever closer.

Pow! Pow!

The insectile *whine* of a round buzzed past his head and there was a puff of dirt on the bank ahead as it impacted in the ground.

The end of the bridge rushed up in his field of view, then his fast horse was cantering over soft earth and they had crossed the river.

Noose had to move fast.

Even as the cowboy swung out of the

saddle of the slowing horse, he could hear the hooves of the gang slowing as they approached the bridge on the opposite bank. As Noose's boots hit the ground he was already half hauling the bronze stallion down a small ridge. While he sprinted, holding Bess in the saddle and leading Copper, Noose was gripping his Winchester tight. Finding safe cover below the edge of the hill, he tied the animal off on a tree and made sure that the woman was safely situated in the saddle. Levering the repeater rifle, Noose scampered back up the hill, poking his head over the edge and staying low as he got a clear view of the bridge and the gang of marauders preparing to cross it.

Raising his Winchester to his eye, Joe Noose rested the barrel comfortably and securely on the ridge of grassy dirt, squinted down the crosshairs of the gunsight, and knew this was going to be a turkey shoot.

Four bounty killers were about to have a very bad day.

The posse of four horses had slowed to a crawl as the Butler Gang had to proceed across the constricted rickety wooden bridge in single-file formation. Butler was in the lead but his big yet weary black stallion didn't like the bridge one bit . . . despite the bloodthirsty leader kicking it in the sides with his spurs — a brutality to the animal that fueled Noose's fury — the horse took the bridge one tentative step at a time. The mean stallion didn't like the height or the unsteady footing of the old boards its hooves cautiously trod upon and, though it obeyed its master, took its time and advanced slowly. Behind Butler, the other three horses and wounded riders couldn't go any faster because they were behind his stallion and couldn't pass it.

Noose was calm and in no hurry.

His patient finger rested taut on the trigger.

Waiting for all the horses to get on the bridge.

He had clear and easy shots now at the gang but needed to pick the exact right moment.

Noose didn't want to hit any horses if he could avoid it . . . none of this was their fault.

On Copper's saddle a few yards away, Bess Sugarland looked groggily up and saw the lone figure of Joe Noose with his Winchester fixed to his shoulder as he took position on the hill, and she could hear the approaching hooves of the gang's horses on the bridge even though she could not yet see them.

The woman feared the worst.

"Noose . . ." she gasped.

He couldn't hear her. As his finger tightened on the trigger the loud *crack* drowned out all other sound.

The last bounty killer bringing up the rear, Wingo, flew out of the saddle, a fist-sized hole in his chest.

Noose recocked the lever of the Winchester in less than a second and by the time the surprised bounty killers had their guns raised he'd put a second round in Trumbull's upper body. Screaming in pain, blood gushing from his ruined shoulder, Trumbull shot blindly, shooting at flies.

By now, the three last bounty killers had all realized the grave mistake they had made riding horses single file on a very narrow bridge because those same horses had started to panic and rear. Sharpless and Trumbull tried to manage them from the saddles but their stallions couldn't turn in the confines of the structure — there was no retreat and they couldn't go forward, either, because the lead horse, Butler's, had frozen. The faces of the gang were masks of pure terror as they realized they were trapped, sitting ducks.

Frank Butler alone had pinpointed the location of Noose's firing position and was trading fire at him straight-armed with his Colt Dragoon, but the cowboy was safely bunkered behind the crest of the opposite hill and his enemy's bullets struck uselessly in the dirt. Behind Butler, Sharpless and Trumbull were trying to get the hell off the bridge but Wingo's stallion prevented their retreat as it staggered and stumbled with the dead body of its rider caught in the stirrups — the only way was forward and Butler was still blocking them. The two men yelled for their leader to clear the way but Butler's stallion was rearing and pawing the air with its hooves even as its master viciously kicked it in the flanks with his spurs, drawing gushes of blood.

Two more of Noose's shots busted loose. The first bullet hit Sharpless between the eyes and the back of his head, exploded in a splattering crater of skull and brains. In all the violence and pandemonium Noose's second shot sadly slammed into the side of the dead man's horse, killing it as dead as its owner. Sharpless's corpse slumped in the saddle as his stallion's lifeless legs collapsed on the shaking bridge amidst the turmoil and the two of them tumbled against the rope, snapping it like a whiplash, toppling the dead horse and rider over the side. Both fell fifty feet off the sheep bridge down into the surging flow of the Snake River, a splashing impact that shot a volcanic geyser of water skyward as man and horse sank below the sweeping rapids now coloring a spreading red shade.

Noose was going to get them all.

He knew it.

The last stand on the bridge was going to be the end of all of these murderous sons of bitches and the cowboy shot clean and true, again and again. Cocking, firing, recocking and firing, Noose cranked the lever of the Winchester and pulled the trigger over and over, empty shells slewing from the breech, his steely eyes peering down the barrel of the repeater rifle smoking and hot in his hands, as blood exploded on the bounty killers on the bridge.

Trumbull took a round in the arm and dropped his gun as his hand went limp, his stallion jerking sideways, eyes widened and mouth frothing, its hooves slipping on the boards and losing purchase by the snapped rope and gap where Sharpless's horse had just tumbled through. The front legs of the horse slid off the blood-slick platform and its back legs followed a moment later. Then the wounded bounty killer and his pawing horse plunged from the bridge and were plummeting upside down through dead air toward the big river.

Noose swung the muzzle of the Winchester. Taking quick and deadly aim, Noose blew Trumbull's head clean off and the killer was dead before he hit the rapids. The rushing sheet of the surface of the Snake River was now turning a florid crimson.

From her bleary vantage point in the saddle, the weakened Bess smiled as she saw Noose had the bounty killers boxed in and was taking them out one by one. She couldn't shoot herself, not in her wounded state, although she wished she could. The man's deadly skill with a rifle was a fearsome thing to behold and it took her breath away.

A loud ricochet flashed near Noose's head as one of Butler's bullets zinged off a rock and showered his face with stone fragments, and Noose knew he needed to finish this.

Centering his rifle and levering the handle, he shot Frank Butler in his left side, the impact of the slug turning the leader's shirt a swash of red as it catapulted the screaming man clean off the saddle, dumping him in a heap onto the floor of the bridge. Butler's own furious horse's kicking rear hooves trampled the wooden boards and its stomping front hooves nearly crushed the leader's legs as he rolled out of the way but Noose put a stop to that for two reasons:

First, Joe Noose was going to be the one to kill Frank Butler not his damn horse . . .

Second, there was something Noose had wanted to do all day . . .

Taking careful aim, he perfectly lined up his Winchester repeater crosshairs on the evil black stallion's thrashing head and shot it right between the eyes, killing the horse dead.

It fell sideways, a jet of blood shooting from its skull, and collapsed on the bridge.

Empty smoking .52 casings flew from the breech of the Winchester and landed in the grass.

Looking down his repeater rifle, Noose quickly tracked the barrel back and forth, left and right along the edge of the bridge but couldn't see any sign of Frank Butler. The leader hadn't run across the bridge because the cowboy would have spotted him and shot him, and he hadn't fallen off the structure because Noose would have seen the splash if he had hit the river. A flash of black cloth suddenly appeared and vanished right over the edge of the ropes. Butler was staying below the railing, out of sight. Noose cursed. He couldn't get a clear shot at Butler on the bridge because the slippery bastard was crawling on his belly and staying down out of his line of fire, making a desperate escape once Noose had shot his horse between the eyes.

Pulling the trigger a few times, the cowboy fired at him anyway but his shots went wild, punching out chunks of wooden bridge platform and by the time the smoke had cleared, Noose saw just the back of Frank Butler's duster departing the bridge at a flat-out run, safely disappearing behind the hill on this side of the river.

Noose cursed that one got away but he had nearly killed them all.

The butcher's bill was almost paid in full.

There was just one left.

The baddest of them all.

He had saved the worst for last.

CHAPTER 45

Copper was looking at him with big moist eyes as Noose untied the reins and pressed them in Bess's bloodless hands. She looked at him half-conscious and confused. "Take this horse and get to Jackson," he said firmly.

"N-Noose, I — I . . ." she whispered, incoherent.

The cowboy gently brushed a lock of the woman's sweaty hair from her eyes. "Just ride Copper straight east. He'll find the town. Get to a hospital. You're gonna make it just fine."

Woozy, Bess sort of nodded. Her pallid lips tried to form words but he touched his big finger to them to hush her. "Go," he said. "The rest is mine."

Gripping the bronze horse's muzzle, the cowboy nodded to it, and somehow they understood each other.

Before the woman could argue, he

smacked the stallion on the hindquarters and off it went at a full gallop in the direction of Jackson.

The cowboy watched Bess and Copper disappear safely in the distance until they were out of sight, then swung his steely gaze to the jagged honeycomb of canyons on his side of the river.

Joe Noose drew his Colt Peacemaker, cocked back the hammer, and walked into the granite canyon range where Butler was, and would be expecting him.

He didn't want to keep his enemy waiting.

Weather changed in Wyoming fast.

Under the baking relentless heat of the sun, the bounty hunter walked through the bleached and barren high rock formations. His pistol was drawn, his eyes constantly on the move.

He recognized the raspy voice that viciously rang through the rocks. *"Just you and me now, Noose!"*

The cowboy fell into a crouch, listening to his enemy's voice, directionless in the labyrinth of canyon.

"I plugged that hot filly deputy and she's probably dead already, 'n if she ain't she soon will be! I know she knows it was me shot the marshal and you figured she was going to tell

the law, get you cleared! But she ain't gonna make it and you know that. There's no witnesses now, Noose! So what are ya gonna do now? Now that there's nobody gonna get in the way of my big fat reward when I put one in your brain pan and bring in your body slung over a saddle!"

Noose was blinded with murderous rage. He yelled above and around him, turning his head as he shouted, *"I'm comin' for you, Butler! I killed all your men, you dirty miserable sonofabitch, and now I'm gonna kill you!"*

Butler's disembodied voice echoed directionless around the rocks. *"I owe you a thanks for killing my gang, Noose, 'cause now I got nobody I have to split the reward with! I keep all the money! More for me! I couldn't have planned it better myself!"*

"The only reward is on your head!"

Ka-boom!

Ptang!

A shot rang out close by and the slug ricocheted off the edge of the granite wall.

Ptang! Pang! Ptow!

Noose ducked in alarm as the bullet rebounded in a deadly zigzag around the close confines of the canyon. The ricochet could have killed him.

He saw a blur of movement across the chasm as Butler's black-coated figure moved into a better position.

Drawing a quick and deadly bead, Noose fired twice.

Ptang!

Pkow!

Pang Pang Ptang Pkaow!

The shot boomed and the ricochets of the two bullets were scary in their violence as they caromed around the ravine.

A chuckle.

"Damn, boy!" Butler shouted with mirth from somewhere nearby. *"If the shots don't kill ya the ricks will, bouncing off the canyon like that."*

Noose moved out and got into a closer position in the maze of the canyon, moving nearer to the sound of his enemy's voice. *"Just keep talking, Butler!"*

The cowboy lifted his revolver and checked the cylinder to see he had three bullets left.

As if by telepathy, the bad bounty hunter chided him. *"So by my count you're down to three rounds!"*

Noose cursed. Lied. *"I got two pistols full!"*

"Don't talk! Shoot!"

The dark wraithlike shape leapt out from behind a ravine wall twenty yards away and opened fire with two revolvers and Noose shot back, then jumped back against the rock just in time.

Blam! Blam!

Ptow! Pang! Pang! Pkow!

The terrifying, deafening rebounding bullets showered Noose with rock chips as they careened again and again off the canyon enclosure, whistling past his nose, too close for comfort.

It was as if people were shooting at him from all sides.

When the slugs died, he chanced a glance around the edge of the gully.

Butler was gone.

On the move.

Noose moved, too.

The cowboy squinted, checking his load.

Down to two bullets . . .

"You're good, Noose, I'll give you that! You made me work for my money this day! But nobody beats me, boy! I'm the toughest son of a bitch ever walked the West!"

The canyon was quiet.

Noose moved like a ghost, his boots crumbling gravel.

Pebbles fell.

His eyes scanned the deep ruts in the gorge, where piercing sunlight failed to pry, scanning for any movement.

None.

A lizard scattered and Noose nearly shot it.

Catching his breath, slowing his respiration.

The sun high and hot overhead.

A cloud passed over the sun erasing all shadow.

The cloud moved on.

And then he saw the shadow.

Down in the crevice.

Sucking wind, Noose hugged the granite wall like a reptile. Bringing up his pistol near his face, he cocked back the hammer as quietly as he could and lined up the notches on the sight to the man-shaped shadow hiding behind the canyon wall fifty feet below.

"C'mon . . ."

His finger tightened on the trigger.

The flap of the duster appeared around the edge of the rock.

Noose fired.

The duster jumped and he fired again, his last round.

Just as a gust of wind blew the empty duster on the stick.

It was a trick.

Noose turned the corner of the canyon base and there Butler was five feet away.

Both men drew down at the same time

pulling the trigger at the exact same instant, pointing their guns at each other's chests out of pure reflex but Noose knew he was out of bullets.

Butler fanned and fired.

His aim was thrown off by his flinching at the *click* of the empty chamber of Noose's gun.

Noose stood his ground.

The shot went wild.

Joe Noose and Frank Butler faced off at six feet in the narrow space between the rock crags, frozen where they stood listening to the last deadly ricocheting bullet rebounding off the granite walls past their faces.

Ptang!

Ptow!

They didn't blink.

Ptang!

Eyes locked.

Guns empty.

Somehow knowing the ricochet roulette of the zigzagging round against the walls of the chasm would kill one or the other of them in the next few seconds.

The suspended moment went on forever as time stood still.

Ptow!

Ptang!

A drop of sweat poured down Butler's forehead like a drip of clear blood.

Noose wasn't sweating.

Not a drop.

Ptang!

Butler blew him a kiss good-bye.

Thud!

A red dime-sized hole appeared between Frank Butler's eyes as his brains flew out the back of his skull in a messy crimson mist. The ricocheting bullet had ended its journey, shooting him square in the head, killing him instantly.

His black eyes rolled up in their sockets, revealing the whites.

The bad bounty killer tipped like a felled tree in the dirt. Dust settled on his sprawled akimbo, skeletal corpse.

"Reckon you got your reward, Butler." Noose smiled, adjusting his hat.

EPILOGUE

Two days later, three men in a horse-drawn wagon with four coffins in back rode into Hoback.

One of the men was much larger than the others and heavily bandaged, wearing freshly cleaned and pressed cowboy clothes on his broad frame. The other two were undertakers and were dressed in black with felt top hats. The coffins in the transom were empty. The wounded man appeared weary and wan but worked tirelessly side by side with the two morticians as they carefully retrieved the body of Nate Sugarland from the small house behind the U.S. Marshal's office and placed it in one of the wider coffins that had been prepared for his body. Then the three men went into the saloon, carried out the body of the bartender, and he too was placed in a waiting coffin. The men's business finished, they climbed into the wagon and rode off down the trail west, for they had more stops to make that day.

It was nearly sundown before the three men carried the sad remains of Jack Mackenzie and Nolan Swallows down from the ridge above the fork of the Snake. In turn, those bodies were placed in the other two coffins.

The older of the morticians asked the big man who had showed them to the locations of the dead lawmen about the whereabouts of the bodies of the gang of gunmen that killed them so they could be buried, too.

The big man said he disremembered.

In truth, they didn't deserve a proper burial.

Joe Noose figured he'd leave those corpses for the buzzards.

It was June.

A month had passed and Joe Noose stood in the open doorway of the U.S. Marshal's office smelling the fragrant summer air in one of the first days of what promised to be a long, hot summer. Outside the sturdy wooden structure, the streets of Jackson Hole were bustling with wagons and pedestrians. The cowboy had been feeling a lot better the last couple weeks now the bullet wound was healing and the bandages were already off his ribs. Today, he felt healthy, and for the first time in a long while, pretty damn good.

"You're taking the money," Bess's voice barked from inside the office.

They'd been through this before.

"You already paid me," he replied with a small smile. It was the same conversation they'd been having every day for a month.

"You been paid the reward for Barrow," she said. "I checked with the bank again today. You ain't picked up the reward for my father's killers you got coming to you. Now, why is that?"

"I'm letting the money earn interest."

"Sure you are."

Noose grinned. He could come right out and tell Bess why he wasn't taking that reward money but he guessed she already knew and just enjoyed arguing with him, which was fine with Joe Noose because he just liked the sound of Bess Sugarland's voice when she got a high color on.

Truth was, no way in hell would he take a red cent of that blood money of a reward that that only existed because her father had been murdered to get it. Noose still felt responsible for Nate Sugarland's death because if he hadn't messed with Frank Butler in the first place, then, well, he'd been through that over and over in his head. Who knows how things would have gone? Point was Noose felt that money belonged

415

to Bess, that she deserved it and could put it to good use. But it was a tricky subject to broach. So Noose ducked the issue, hoping the woman would forget about it in time. So far she hadn't.

There Bess was behind the U.S. Marshal's desk — she was now by law the acting marshal of Jackson Hole until the Wyoming U.S. Marshals Service's headquarters in Cody replaced her. Noose didn't think that was going to happen anytime soon. With the murders of Marshal Jack Mackenzie and his deputy Nolan Swallows, Marshal Bess Sugarland of neighboring Hoback automatically assumed the mantle of interim acting marshal of Jackson Hole. Bess could have passed on the job because of her injury but she didn't, just like Noose knew she wouldn't. Her responsible nature and sense of duty saw her at work the day after she'd gotten out of the hospital.

Jackson Hole had an independent-minded and influential female citizenry who ran businesses and held office and they loved Bess Sugarland. The minute she had come to town, being one of the two heroes who killed the evil gang of outlaws who had murdered three local lawmen in the space of three days, Bess had been a celebrity. Never mind she nearly died from the severe bullet wound in her leg and was still limping around in a leg brace and on a crutch, never mind it was Noose that had done most of the heroics, the point was she was a woman — a hero woman marshal to the women in town. Bess was an inspiration to the powerful female constituency of Jackson, and Noose's best guess was that this group of women were going to use all of their considerable persuasion to remain damn sure she stayed U.S. Marshal of Jackson Hole.

Whether Bess liked it or not.

Noose figured she would eventually.

Personally, the cowboy thought she'd make a damn good marshal of the growing town. He'd seen Bess in action, seen her under fire, knew what she was made of, and understood her sense of duty, justice, and morality were unbreakable and incorruptible. Noose admired Bess right down to the ground, and was behind her a hundred percent.

Bess had telegraphed the state U.S. Marshals' headquarters in Cody telling them about the death of the two local lawmen and they'd ordered her to remain in place as marshal until they could replace her. They had an old Cody marshal they'd send to relieve her as soon as they could get hold of him, but the old-timer was supposedly chasing some gang out in the remote part of the gigantic 70 percent unpopulated least populated state in the union.

Noose had told Bess not to hold her breath, and said he would help out getting on top of the outstanding warrants and paperwork the previous now deceased marshals had been involved with.

To her credit, Bess looked like she knew what she was doing sitting straight upright behind the desk, seven-star silver badge pinned to her bosom on the clean leather vest over her denim shirt. Her auburn hair was pulled straight back, her appearance clean-cut, officious, and authoritative. The bruises and scratches on her face still showed, but she was one of those tomboy outdoors girls who a few scuffs looked good on. The spanking-new twin Remington Peacemakers slung in holsters, gifts from the town, did not look too big for her, cannons though they were. "What are you looking at?" Bess said with a tone of displeasure, cocking an eyebrow up at Noose across the room. She'd sensed him watching her.

"Just thinking you look the part, Marshal."

"Thank you. We're not done about this money thing."

"I reckon I guessed as much."

"We're gonna talk about this." Bess got up from her desk, using the barrel of a Winchester as a support for leverage, then, with her leg brace and using the gun as a cane, hobbled stiff-legged to the door and leaned against the frame across from Noose, looking him square in the eye. "Now's as good a time as any."

The big cowboy looked at the woman marshal, sighed, lowered his eyes, looked out at the street, then looked back at her again. He shook his head. "I just want the money for Barrow that I earned. The rest of the reward money is yours. It was your father who died for it, and he would have wanted you to have it, almost like he left you something. It's the right thing to do."

Bess got uncomfortable and bristled. "I resent the implication that my dad got murdered to leave me money and that somehow that justifies anything or means I should have the reward because it was all he left me." Her eyes were moist.

Noose, confounded by this difficult woman when he was trying to be nice, spoke plain. "Your father left you more than that. He raised you right, gave you his guts and sense of justice. That's something money can't buy. If you don't want the money, give it to the town of Jackson. Do some good with it. But I ain't taking it, Bess, and that's it."

A female voice piped up in a husky whiskey cadence from the cell. "How much money we talking about?"

"What's money to you, Bonny Kate?" Bess threw a sharp glance to the fiery redheaded troublemaker behind bars. "You got a date with the hangman in three days."

"Then what difference does it make whether you tell me or not? Who am I gonna tell, swinging from the end of a rope?"

"It's none of your business is what it is, outlaw."

"I gotta use the crapper."

"There's a bucket in your cell," Bess shot back.

"I need to use the outhouse," the prisoner complained.

The marshal socked the stock of the repeater rifle under her armpit and lurched fiercely over to the bars. "Miss Valance, you know damn well you can't leave that cell without an escort and you see perfectly plain I'm in no shape to provide you one. Use the bucket."

Bonny Kate's twinkling eyes slid contemplatively to Joe Noose still leaning against the door frame, all six foot three of him, his arms crossed on his big chest as he returned her look idly. "Why can't your friend give me an escort to the commode?"

Marshal Bess switched her gaze to Noose, back to Bonny Kate, then back to Noose. He shrugged. She shook her head. "I don't think it's a good idea for you to be leaving this cell, Miss Valance."

Noose watched the exchange, observing with interest the two women. Bess limped to the front door, and his pale-eyed gaze that missed nothing saw her uncharacteristic nervousness with this woman prisoner, so Noose inquired about it. It was all about letting Bonny Kate out of her cell long enough to use the outhouse under escort but Bess seemed unduly worried about it. Bess came right out and said, out of earshot to Bonny Kate, that she did not trust this woman and everything about her was wrong.

"Hell, woman," he said. "The latrine is right outside the window over there. You can stand with a rifle and keep a bead on it the whole time she's using it." Noose grinned when he said he was feeling better and could handle her so Bess gudgingly let Bonny Kate out of jail. The female marshal keyed open the lock and spread wide the cell door. Then she leaned back against the edge of the desk and rotated the Winchester repeater rifle out from under her armpit into her hands, business end squarely trained on Bonny Kate. Noose reached over and took the prisoner by a strong hand, towering over her as he guided her out the front door to the outhouse, the barrel of Bess's gun tracking her midriff the whole way. The lady outlaw was hot to the touch and a sweet heat of a perfume radiated off her when his hand closed on her bare bicep. Noticing all the looks and glances, Bess, with a conflicted mixture of misgiving and jealousy on her face, watched them go outside; then she grabbed her rifle and took up position by the window. It afforded a clear view and clean shot at the outhouse, and she waited at the window until their uneventful return.

Some unspoken challenge passed between them, the marshal saw, but the cowboy returned the condemned outlaw safely to her cell. Bess, seeing Noose could handle Bonny Kate Valance, got an idea. She had been reviewing Swallows's orders to deliver the outlaw to Idaho for her date with the gallows. Bess was the only law in the area, but she was in no shape to escort the outlaw, even armed. She decided to ask Noose if he would accept the job if she deputized him.

Bess limped back to the doorway Noose stood against laconically, his arms crossed, and addressed him deferentially. "Listen, Joe. I'm in a bit of a fix. The Victor office telegraphed again. They can't get any lawmen over the pass to take this hussy to the gallows. It's two days from there to here and back again and her hanging is set for three days from now and they won't change it. They need us to do it. The U.S. Marshals' headquarters in Cody ordered the Jackson Hole marshal's office to take her. Mackenzie and Swallows were all set to go before they got shot but the orders still stand, and right now I'm the marshal so . . ."

With a friendly, regretful sigh, Noose shook his head. "We both know you ain't going anywhere with that leg, even in a saddle and definitely not over that pass."

"I know that, Joe. Thing is, I don't got nobody here in town I can trust with that job." Bess pursed her lips and fixed Noose in a level stare. "But you."

"Take Bonny Kate over the Teton Pass to her hanging in Idaho. That's the job," he said.

Bess nodded.

The cowboy shrugged. "Reckon I can manage that."

"The job pays three hundred dollars."

"Deal." Noose spit in his palm and held out his hand. Bess spat in her palm and they shook on it.

The marshal smiled tightly, less pleased than she might have been. "I'll deputize you for the job. It's there and back over the pass. Need to get the prisoner to the gallows by Thursday. Get her to Idaho, hand her off to the hangman, turn around, ride home. Drinks will be on me."

"Consider it done."

"Thanks."

"After Butler and his boys, this'll be a vacation."

"I wouldn't be so sure. You be careful, Joe. That bitch is a piece of work with an ugly reputation. And she's got nothing to lose."

"Bess, with me she's got two choices: she can go the easy way or the hard way but either way Noose is getting her to the noose."

Bess stared at him flatly. "That supposed to be some kind of joke?"

"Just a plain and simple fact."

"Well, I'm betting she'll pick the hard way and you should, too."

"I'm twice as big as she is."

"Bet the other ten men she killed said the same thing."

"I hear you." Noose nodded to Bess and

both turned their gaze across the room of the U.S. Marshal's office to the corner cell where Bonny Kate lay curled on the mattress, snoozing away. He said, "It's too late to start now. We should leave in the morning when the sun is up."

"Sounds like a plan." Bess smiled and went to a shelf, taking out a five-star metal deputy badge and tossing it over to Noose, who caught it. "Raise your right hand."

On the mattress on the dusty wooden floor of her jail cell, Bonny Kate Valance had one eye half-open. She was only pretending to be asleep. The eavesdropping woman outlaw had heard every word that had just been uttered.

With a taut cunning little smile, her eye slowly shut.

Dawn broke and the morning air had a cold snap.

Marshal Bess Sugarland stood at the window of the U.S. Marshal's office, cradling her loaded rifle. The sun was in her face while she looked far across the plain where Joe Noose rode with Bonny Kate Valance out of Jackson Hole toward the mountains. He had begun his journey escorting the condemned outlaw over the Teton Pass to her date with the hangman in

Idaho. Bess watched the two figures on the horses getting smaller and smaller in the distance and the sight filled her with unease that she would never see her friend again.

Bess had the window open so she could get an unobstructed shot if necessary. While Noose had Bonny Kate in the outhouse yesterday, Bess had stood in this same spot right by the window with her loaded Winchester ready to drop the woman with one shot. This morning, standing at the same window with the same rifle in hand, the female marshal saw the woman and man were now far enough away that they were out of range of her weapon and she was seized by a sense of powerlessness.

Because now Noose was outside her immediate protection, alone with an infamous female outlaw — a bad-to-the-bone woman Bess's gut told her was capable of anything. The lady marshal couldn't shake a free-floating dread that Joe Noose wasn't going to make it out of this one. It was irrational, she told herself: Bess had seen firsthand how well her friend could take care of himself. Joe Noose was the toughest man she had ever met — he had handled Frank Butler and his gang of marauders and could handle one woman. So what if she was a notorious outlaw with nothing to lose?

Then suddenly it came to her in a flash.
Those bounty killers had been men.
This outlaw was a woman.
And hell hath no fury.

ABOUT THE AUTHOR

Eric Red is a Los Angeles-based novelist, screenwriter, and film director. His films include *The Hitcher, Near Dark, Cohen And Tate, Body Parts,* and *The Last Outlaw.* He has written seven novels, including *Don't Stand So Close, It Waits Below, White Knuckle, The Guns of Santa Sangre,* and *The Wolves of El Diablo.* Red divides his time between California and Wyoming with his wife and two dogs. Find out more about Eric Red and his books and films on his official website EricRed.com, on Facebook at OfficialEricRed, and on Twitter @ericred.

The employees of Thorndike Press hope you have enjoyed this Large Print book. All our Thorndike, Wheeler, and Kennebec Large Print titles are designed for easy reading, and all our books are made to last. Other Thorndike Press Large Print books are available at your library, through selected bookstores, or directly from us.

For information about titles, please call:
    (800) 223-1244

or visit our website at:
    gale.com/thorndike

To share your comments, please write:
    Publisher
    Thorndike Press
    10 Water St., Suite 310
    Waterville, ME 04901

CPSIA information can be obtained
at www.ICGtesting.com
Printed in the USA
FFHW021703270319
51284517-56774FF